SANKARAN

IS AGAIN ON THE

COCONUT TREE

<u>Other titles by the Author</u>
Phansigar
Bigfoot – A tale told twice

SANKARAN

IS AGAIN ON THE
COCONUT TREE

Jo Nambiar

PARTRIDGE

To order additional copies of this book, contact
Partridge India
000 800 10062 62
orders.india@partridgepublishing.com

www.partridgepublishing.com/india

This work is dedicated to every individual
Who having slid back to square one
Found the chutzpah
To undertake
To climb again

Thanks to

Bridgette, for your invaluable encouragement
Sabrina Bernadine, for the support and the coaxing
Adhvith and Aaryaman, for the time we
could have otherwise spent together

CONTENTS

SANKARAN AND THE WORLD ORDER

Author's Note

Initially this work was intended for the Malayalee reader. A glimpse at Kerala through their own Sankaran's eyes. If you are a Malayalee, you don't need any introduction to him. But for over a year I mulled over publishing this book only for Malayalees.

Later, since having written the book in English, I felt it would serve a more useful purpose. That of demystifying the Malayalee. Where exactly are you from? Malay? Malaysia? Maldives? Malta? Mali? Mayville? Maligaon? Of course, when asked, it's difficult to say an absolute "No". You probably will find Malayalees in all these places.

"You really think so?"

Yes, I'm sure. But that's another story. To begin with, to justify the title of this book, let me tell you something of the Malayalee's obsession with the coconut tree. And this can be best illustrated by what one of the earliest traders (I don't remember if he was an Arab or a Phoenician) that landed on our coast, wrote in a letter to his family back home.

He wrote, that the common people (of Kerala) lived in large spacious houses, the roofs of which were designed out of layers of woven coconut leaves, that made it watertight while also insulating the interiors from the summer heat. This roof rested on a sturdy framework of coconut rachis or mid-rib wood tied together, with coir, which is rope made from coconut fibre. The roof, thus rested on pillars of coconut trunks. He further wrote that the walls of these houses were of beautifully inter-twined coconut-cadjan walls reinforced with coconut-shell wall panels. That the people slept on woven coconut-coir mats, hammocks and charpoys and used coconut fibre, coconut-shells and coconut husk for fuel. He went on and on about coconut-shell bowls, spoons and ladles, of coconut-shell toys, coconut-shell jewel boxes, from boats to baskets to jewellery and weapons. That the inhabitants in this region used coconut oil for cooking and made toddy, nectar, milk and vinegar from the coconut tree. That the natives of this land made 152 delicious dishes, 44 varieties of sweets and several medications from this fruit in combination with other foods. He went on to extol the coconut furniture, handicrafts, the hand-held fans, brooms, brushes, umbrellas, writing material, fabrics and body-armour, all made from the coconut tree.

The poor trader received a reply some months later at another port where he had docked. The letter from his home begged, "Please! Have you gone nuts? Come home and you will feel better." That was the degree of disbelief elsewhere in the world to the fact that one tree could provide so many human necessities.

The coconut palm is cultivated for its many culinary and non-culinary uses, apart from a decorative avenue tree. Virtually every part of the coconut palm can be used in some manner of significant economic value. Coconuts' versatility is sometimes noted in its naming. In Sanskrit, it is *kalpa vriksha*, "the tree which provides all the necessities of life." In the Malay language, it is *pokok seribu guna*, meaning, "the tree of a thousand uses." In the Philippines, the coconut is commonly called the "tree of life."

You can definitely get your three basic needs from the tree. Food, clothing and shelter. And, if you wish, a drink to celebrate the fact too. The other uses when listed are so varied that it seemed to me that an entire human civilization might have spawned and thrived only because of the coconut palm. I once tried to make a list of the uses the various parts of the tree could be put to and failed. There was always one more use being discovered. From its leaves to its roots, its various uses and applications, listed initially by me to be about 123, rose to 145 then to 166 and kept growing till at one point I stopped counting. If the vanished Easter Island people had cultivated coconut they wouldn't have been left stone faced. Literally.

The coconut was possibly the biblical story's "forbidden fruit" in Genesis. Who in Kerala remembers God after a few rounds of coconut toddy or *charayam*? The talking snake must have known that.

The Malayalee constitute Muslims, Hindus, Christians of every denomination, Buddhists, Jews, Jains, atheists, rationalists, occultists and sorcerers all living in relative peace with each other. The sportsman, the army service man and the godman might be found in the same family. The state enjoys the distinction of being 100% literate together with the highest consumption of alcohol in the country and ninety varieties of fish as bar nibbles. Shows 100% literacy is not a guarantee for education and common sense. As languorous as a *mundu* might look, the Malayalee is a busy man.

The other peculiarity the non-Malayalee could get flummoxed by is our names. It is less common today, but at one time it was a practice to carry our addresses with our names. Take for example the famous athlete and Olympian P.T. Usha from Payyoli, Kozhikode. Her ancestry, lineage or family's ancestral home can be traced from her name. Pilavullakandi (slope with jackfruit tree) Thekkeparambil (southern compound) Usha. Address with landmarks included. The other confusing suffix to many a male name is "an". Krishna in the rest of the world becomes Krishnan in Kerala. But even though he is named Mr. Krishnan, we would verbally call out to him as "Krishna!".

Similarly, Sankaran becomes "Sankara!" and Yohanan, a biblical name, becomes "Yohana!" The Malayalee takes pride in this style of name-calling.

Malayalam is the language spoken by a Malayalee. The word "Malayalam" is also unique in that it is a *palindrome*. It spells the same both ways. "Wow!" you say? Well, you just said a palindrome. "I did, did I?" you ask? That's also a palindrome, a multiple word one! *Don't nod*. Because that act would be a two worded palindrome. Sankaran was at a crowded bar one evening sipping some Old Monk with nothing to munch. "No lemon, no melon," he complained palindromically. His belly ached "Red rum, sir, is murder," he remarked palindromically. "Dammit I'm Mad!" Aha, another one!

Despite many other impediments to depicting this culture in English that I experienced, good sense and courage prevailed. Anyway, why the hesitation, Jo? After all who doesn't know a Malayalee? Who has never come looking for the Malayalee? Ask Nebuchadnezzar, King Solomon, Kublai Khan and Julius Caesar. Ask the Sumerians, the Greeks, the Romans and the Pharaohs of Egypt. Ask the Chinese, the Persians, the Phoenicians and the Moors. Everyone knew and knows the Malayalee for over 8000 years. The Egyptians stole the folded-up *mundu* our sarong-like white lower garment and shamelessly depicted it in their hieroglyphic picture-writing like it was their own. Julius Caesar was killed in one. Maybe two. He draped a second *mundu* over his shoulder and called it a toga. I've yet to take a close look at the Turin Shroud. You just never know!

Anyway, in recent years, ask any man, woman or child in any one of the Arab states who the Malayalees are. They know who we are, but they still get it wrong! They only know of Malabaris! *Shukran*, dear Arab brother, for further confusion.

The people who had the greatest difficulty finding the Malayalee for his pepper and spices were the so-called civilized races of white Europe. We were all happily partying while they were living out their dark ages. Finally, the white man felt enough was enough and began travelling out of the darkness of Europe. When you come out of the Dark Ages the first thing you wish to do, naturally, is to spice up your life. The need for pepper suddenly became more important than salvation.

But now he faced a dilemma. The recently enlightened white man discovered that all the ancient texts containing knowledge of seafaring and navigation had been burnt in a pile along with their oracle, their druid, their soothsayer, witch and sorcerer. It's a wonder how the Dark Ages remained so dark with so many fires burning.

Now with only a pope to guide them, they were left with no choice but to request their monarchs for help. Whatever means they finally chose to determine the direction they should sail in order to procure pepper, the entrails pointed to a specific coast of a specific peninsula on the planet. Yet, until a few hundred years ago, however much they sailed, their sextant and their compasses pointed in every direction but to the Malayalee. You can still find these silly western compasses in use. The needle points to an N instead of an M.

So they sailed about for a few hundred years guided by the wrong alphabet and landed in North Africa, North America, North Carolina, North Jamaica. North Ireland etc. Everywhere else but to the Malayalee.

"What took you so long?" an exasperated Sankaran was left asking the Portuguese, the Dutch, the French and the English when he finally discovered them. They weren't exactly the best line-up of buyers. Very few carried gold. Most carried scurvy.

One of them, a sailor named Cristoforo Colombo, even had the gall to announce to the world that he had named a whole new race of people half way around the globe from India, "Indians". Here's a snippet of conversation between Cristoforo Colombo and a native chief from a ship-log that was lost at sea and discovered recently.

Santa Maria   Date : 25ᵗʰ May, In the year of our Lord, 1492
Time: Evening, an hour before supper
Logged by: Private Secretary to Cristoforo Colombo

Captain Cristoforo Colombo combed his wind swept hair down till it was neatly in place and politely addressed the native chief.

"Dear savages, I come in peace on behalf of King Ferdinand and Queen Isabella. Are you Malayalees?"

"No," Chief Threshold To Big Extinction replied. "Do these feathers make me look like I'm doing Kathakali?"

"Do you have pepper and spices?"

"No. We import them under Section 16, Clause 2, Annexure 44 of the Special Spice Act of the kingdom of the Samoothiri from the Malabar. There's a ship that comes from Malabar precisely every third moon."

"You mean you know where these Malayalees live?'

"Oh my giddy aunt!" exclaimed Chief Threshold To Big Extinction. "Which planet do you people come from? Don't you numb-skulls know who a Malayalee is?"

"How can we find this land? The land of the Malayalees?" asked Captain Colombo. "Tell us, how many moons away is it?"

Chief Threshold To Big Extinction burped, looking extremely bored. "Judging by where you've landed, tell me, how many moons can you count, pal?"

"We come in peace for trade in pepper and spices," explained Captain Colombo. "If you could just show us the way to get to the Indians, particularly these Malayalees, we have with us gifts. See these nice red Genoese hats, cloaks, coloured beads..."

"Whatever," Chief Threshold To Big Extinction yawned and turned to his daughter. "Pocahontas, The Naughty One! Would you be so kind as to look for our dear friend Climbing and Sliding Wolf and bring him to me at once? I'm feeling stressed. These foreigners are giving me gas. Only Climbing and Sliding Wolf can explain the direction to the land of the Malayalees."

"Yes, Daddy," Pocahontas, The Naughty One replied. "That's only if he will listen to me and understand what I ask of him. He's always tanked up with fire-water, singing and revelling on the top of our tallest totem pole."

Chief Threshold To Big Extinction shook his feathered head. "Oh no! Not the freshly painted one! Who gave him fire-water to drink?"

Pocahontas, the naughty one shrugged as innocently as she could. "That very totem-pole daddy. The freshly painted one. He's imagining it to be some palm tree and pining to go home. He doesn't seem to be able to wait until the ship from Kozhikode or Kochi arrives in the next moon."

"Holy mackerel! Get him here somehow, Naughty One," begged Chief Threshold To Big Extinction. "I don't seem to get through to these Over-Dressed Numb-Skulls of the Blue Sea."

"Holy mackerel!" Yelled Chief Threshold To Big Extinction again when Pocahontas arrived dragging Climbing and Sliding Wolf by the arm. "Look at what you've done. Why did you climb on to that pole? Can't you tell between Pocahontas and a freshly painted totem pole, Climbing and Sliding Wolf? You're completely coated in red. Is this the way you present yourself just when we have guests?"

"I just need to go home! The ship left me here three moons ago so that I could learn your language. Now that Pocahontas the Naughty One had taught me your language can I leave with the Over-Dressed Numb-skulls of the Blue Sea, Chief Threshold To Big Extinction?"

"No. By Geronimo! Not with that lot," screamed Chief Threshold To Big Extinction. "Unless you want to get lost forever, Climbing and Sliding Wolf."

"Stop calling me Wolf. I am an envoy of the Samoothiri. My name is Sankaran!"

"That's my Pocahontas, the Naughty One who named you that, Climbing and Sliding Wolf. She must have her reasons. I trust her judgement of men."

"That's right, daddy!" Pocahontas squirmed in delight. "Climbing and Sliding Wolf must remain with us a few more nights, eh days, I mean moons, till the ship from Kozhikode or Kochi arrives. He needs to get back to Malabar. After all he is an INDIAN."

"Aha!" twenty sailors of King Ferdinand and Queen Isabella exclaimed aloud in unison at the only word they understood since weighing anchor. "The red one is an Indian? Aha, so that's what they all are." They held hands and did a jig around the deck of the Santa Maria in triumph.

"Imagine that! Their mischievous chief," Cristoforo Colombo giggled, preening his long hair with his fingers. "Keeping us guessing like that. Naughty boy! Save the hats and the beads, boys. I think we've found the Indians. How many moons, ha! ha! What a joke to fall for? Naughty chiefy! Naughty! Naughty! Now about turn, boys! We'll need to make another trip, fitted with vats and stuff to carry away pepper and spices on our next voyage to India. How does my hair look against the wind?"

So, having written this book in English seemed a waste if I couldn't get more readers to read about my people, the Malayalees, whose diaspora now rivals Hepatitis B. Check your DNA. Somewhere locked among the two biopolymer strands coiled around each other to form a double helix, there is definitely a coconut fibre. Trust me, the Malayalee has been everywhere.

The chapters in the book are arranged in chronological order so that events from Kerala's history which I have chosen to tell you about are historically sequential too.

But in publishing worldwide and offering all-and-sundry readership of this book, I do have some unresolved problems. For example, I have recently had access to a declassified document of the government of the United States of America, a section of the transcription of the air-to-ground voice transmission from the Apollo-11 mission, dated July 20-21, 1969. Odd as it may appear, even though this document has emerged from a US government office, the contents may only be understood by a Malayalee. I have therefore relegated it to the end of this book with due apologies to non-Malayalees. But, I can also now understand why it remained classified especially throughout the Cold War period and for so many years since. Apart from that last chapter, titled "1969", dear Reader, Sankaran awaits to take you on a trip through Kerala like no other.

THE IMMORTALS

I need to reflect. Should I commence my story by telling you about Ashwatthama? Or do I begin by telling you about the ridiculous happenstance at the Dubai International Airport?

There is this undead one, Ashwatthama. An immortal of sorts. What in our part of the world they refer to as a *Chiranjivi*. He has been living in the central regions of India these last 5118 years since he was cursed by Lord Krishna, following the Kurukshetra war. Try Googling him up sometime. Listen to eyewitness accounts on Youtube of those who have seen him in recent times. They will describe a tall, emaciated, foul smelling recluse, whose body festers with wounds and sores, attracts swarms of flies and is invaded by flesh eating maggots. He lives among garbage. You'll find out. He exists, even in our times.

But so does Sankaran. Contentedly reclining upon a sofa in the plush comfort of the departure lounge of one of the most splendid civil aircraft facilities on the planet. And arguably the busiest. The UAE government has spared no effort in making a traveler's transit unmatched in all history. Even the USA and China vie for the unique distinction that Dubai holds: that of the most international passengers travelling through its airport annually.

Sankaran was on his way home in his new Ray-Ban glasses. With the Onam festival around the corner, he had to get to Kerala in South India. Back to his wife Ammu and children Bindu and Kunjumon. He hoped to land a day before the Onam eve. He had transferred a tidy sum of money into his wife's bank account back home in Kerala so that she could do some preliminary shopping for the festival. He had also transferred a larger sum of money from his earnings of twelve years in Dubai through a local money launderer, the *kuzhal panam* or *hawala* operator, to be spent on completing the home he was discreetly building for his family, thereby avoiding revealing too much on his income-tax returns forms.

But with Ashwatthama things were very different. As you come to know more about him, you will feel a sense of pity and abhorrence. He was cursed by Lord Krishna for launching the forbidden weapon, the *Brahmashirsha astra*, towards the end of the war, followed by some more vile and cruel deeds for which he could not be forgiven. A convicted war criminal. Nobody ever let him into their homes since. Society shunned him. No village or town in the entire sub-continent gave him any shelter. In recent times even Mother Theresa refused to take him in. So Ashwatthama still roams through the steadily shrinking forests of his country somewhere between Gujarat, Madhya Pradesh and Uttar Pradesh, living off garbage, a Nephilim shorn of all his powers. An occasional glimpse of him in the night by truck drivers, in their headlights, have led to terrible accidents on the highways of these states.

Before I tell you of the "ridiculous happenstance" that occurred here, I would have you know that Dubai International Airport, where Sankaran sat, developed into a world class facility under the rule of His Highness Sheikh Mohammed Bin Rashid Al Maktoum. A brilliant and energetic individual, gifted with wisdom, foresight and tolerance. A man who learnt to dream early in life and convert those dazzling dreams into reality for the benefit of his subjects as well as for the rest of the world. There are few who can match the varied accomplishments of this man on our planet. He is responsible for the growth of Dubai into a global city. He is a masterly businessman with the heart of an artist, the brain of an economist and the multi-tasking hands of a superman. A Nobel prize is long overdue to him. The West envies him while the East is in awe of him. And Sankaran loved him.

So sitting on His Highness Sheikh Mohammed Bin Rashid Al Maktoum's plush sofa at the Dubai airport, with the Onam festival due in a couple of days, Sankaran closed his eyes to reflect: On his last visit home to Kerala more than two years ago, he had invested in a piece of land and 40 coconut saplings, strictly adhering to the custom of planting the seedlings just before the South-West Monsoons. In Kerala, which is on the western coast of India, the South-West Monsoon is severe and one has to be particularly efficient at planting coconut. Each sapling has to be meticulously placed in fertile soil, free of white-ants, mixed with powdered cow-dung, salt and fish-waste. The soil must drain adequately but must have sufficient water-holding capacity. One had to ensure the existence of a water table within three meters as well as confirming there was no rock or hard substratum within two meters of the surface. Tricky business, but all this was done usually in the beginning of the South-West monsoon. If irrigation facilities had been available on his land, Sankaran would have had Ammu take up planting at least a month before the onset of the monsoon, well before Sankaran himself arrived from Dubai, so that the seedlings became well established before the heavy rains. Nevertheless, Ammu and Bindu had taken good care of them and Kunjumon had recently sent him excellent Whatsapp images of the now flourishing coconut grove, with its new tawny laterite stone wall protecting the compound, broadcasting to his neighbours Sankaran's new prosperity in the Middle East, a region popularly referred to as the *Gelf.*

"When is Sankaran returning from the *Gelf*?" was the persistent question of the old Nair landlord for whom Sankaran had toiled in his youth, before a chance visa brought forth the opportunity many

Malayalees like him await their entire lives: A job in the *Gelf*! Sankaran was his tenant, whose family occupied a small house on the edge of the Nair household's rambling compound. The landlord, a pesky, old and retired railways employee refused to acknowledge Sankaran's new status. He abhorred the sight of Sankaran arriving in a cab every two years to meet his wife dressed in her perpetual nighty and watching the children bustling out of the house to wheel large suitcases filled with newly acquired lucre down the dirt-drive. Followed finally by the outrageous sight of a spruced-up Sankaran in jeans and Ray-Ban sunglasses, who would have definitely overpaid the servile cab-driver in a flourish of currency notes. He hated even more receiving gifts of syrupy dates, Chinese electronic knick-knacks that barely lasted and t-shirts he wouldn't be seen alive in.

"Let him rest for a day with his family and his spoils," The landlord would then mutter to his wife. "He'll be back in orbit, back in his up-wound *lungi*. You watch how I make him climb and harvest all our coconuts for free before Onam. Since working in the *Gelf* he is too proud to ask for wages. So be it!"

"When will he ever retire from his job in *Abu-Dubai*, I wonder?" the landlady would mutter aloud.

"It's Abu Dhabi! Dhabi! Dhaaabi! How many times have I corrected you? That fellow cares for his freedom more than his family! The *Gelf* has spoiled our boys. It was quite different during my generation when Malayalees worked in Borneo and Singapore. They came back home to their families with money and dignity."

Unlike Sankaran, the freedom of leaving and returning to this sub-continent was not an option for Ashwatthama. He could not afford to be seen by mortal men. His abnormal height, ragged clothing, hideous face and scarred forehead were a dead give-away. He was not just a prisoner of time. He was reduced to hiding from humanity, marooned in the solitude of forests, ravines and caves or in the land-fills of a city's waste dump by the circumstances of Lord Krishna's curse. It had vanquished him to an eon of suffering, destitution, disease and dejection minus all human company. If you read-up the Mahabharata, you will find that Lord Krishna had a hand in many other divine misdemeanors, particularly towards immortals, apart from Ashwatthama.

Take the case of King Maha Bali Virochana, fondly call Maveli by his people, another immortal of sorts, for instance. Grandson of the great Prahlada. The man was doing a better job than Sheikh Mohammed in his time. He was a benevolent king of Kerala and Kerala was a land of plenty. There was no poverty. Like the UAE it traded with the rest of the world. Merchant and seafarers consisting of Egyptians, Phoenicians, Persians, Greeks, Babylonians, Roman, Jews, Arabs, Chinese - all dropped anchor here and sat on plush cushions at King Maha Bali's seaports at Kochi, Kozhikode, Muziris, Pattanam, Mappila Bay and Thalassery. The weary merchants did not have to deal with sandstorms, heat and traffic. There was no red-tape, passport confiscation or the exploitation of workers from poor countries - especially laborers and maids. King Maha Bali made it easy to find a sponsor, organize a bank account, obtain a chariot driving license and most of all somewhere to live. Your essential work and residence permits and schooling for your brats was a one-window accomplishment. No wonder that the Romans subsequently built temples, the Jews their Synagogues and others their churches and mosques in what they saw as a tolerant land.

Until of course Lord Krishna came along in the guise of the Brahmin dwarf, Vamana, obtained by trickery a boon from the kind king and in three gigantic steps sent Maha Bali into the nether world. Sankaran often wondered what Lord Krishna had against such a kind and benevolent king. He also wondered how the wise king fell for that trick. All that the Brahmin dwarf had asked the king for was a piece of land as much as three strides of his stumpy legs. But when it came to measuring the land, Lord Krishna assumed his godly size and with two strides took his entire kingdom with no ground left to place his third step. Poor King Maha Bali then offered his head. Of course, in return he extracted the boon of immortality from Lord Krishna too. A kind of immortality that allowed him to visit his beloved subjects, the people of Kerala, every year during the Onam festival for eternity.

As he sat on the sofa of the gorgeous waiting lounge at Dubai's exquisite airport, Sankaran consulted the time on his mobile phone. He had at least four hours before his flight to Kozhikode. The two-hour drive from Abu Dhabi to Dubai to meet his Arab boss on Al Rasheed road before his departure home had become routine practice these last twelve years. Only this time his boss had sent his own prized car, a Bugatti Veyron 8.0 litre W16 Super Sport that made the journey in an hour and fifteen minutes, riding on the most powerful automobile engine in the world. The Arab was a kind soul, a fatherly man Sankaran could speak freely to. And from the very first annual vacation that Sankaran had applied for ten years ago, the old man always and unfailingly greeted Sankaran with, "Please Sankaran, you did not come to tell me that you are leaving me for good?"

To be fair to the narration, it didn't sound like that at all. It was more like, "*Blease Sankaron*, you *deed* not come to *thel* me *dhat* you are leaving me for *goodh*?" But barring his accent he spoke English well for a semi-literate second generation migrant from Ras al Khaimah.

Except this time Sankaran wondered if he had any reason to return to the UAE again. The construction of his house behind the emerging coconut grove was almost complete while a good sum of money had accumulated in various bank accounts which he intended to freeze into fixed deposits to live off the rest of his life on the interest accrued.

Twelve years in the *Gelf* ! Had he planned it well? Should he return? Need he?

He smiled to himself as a familiar voice bellowed inside his head. "*Blease Sankaron*, you *deed* not come to *thel* me *dhat* you are leaving me for *goodh*?"

Sankaran needed to reflect. He had web-checked in and surrendered his precious luggage to the Etihad Airways bound for Kozhikode.

He still had about three and a half hours to go before boarding. The softness of the high-backed sofa enveloped him with a comfort he couldn't imagine ever leaving. He closed his eyes and remembered reading somewhere that "the best laid schemes of mice and men go often askew."

It was then that the "ridiculous happenstance" I began to speak of in the beginning of my narration took place. Right there in the departure lounge of the Dubai International Airport.

Sankaran noticed a slightly balding and portly man, with a demeanor reminiscent of the late Dom DeLuise, waddling towards the departure counter, peeking over his shoulder as if afraid he would be recognized or followed. He was dressed in a smart silk shirt, corduroy trousers and suede shoes. Perhaps shy by nature, he approached the uniformed lady, the mannequin-like ground staff behind the Etihad Airways counter with hesitation and whispered an enquiry. The mannequin replied politely that the flight to Bangalore would certainly be on time. "Three hours to go, sir. But you may check-in your luggage if you wish. Your name, sir?"

"M B Virochana." The man replied.

"And you're coming from?" the mannequin enquired.

"Patala."

Sankaran stirred out of his comfortable sofa ever so slightly, quite certain he had heard wrong.

The rotund man looked over his shoulder again, this time at Sankaran. His handle-bar moustache was unmistakable. A twinkle escaped his eye. Then a wink. Memories of a thousand and more years jogged and raced through Sankaran's mind like the Bugatti Veyron 8.0 litre W16 Super Sport car engine he had just ridden in.

"My God! What the hell are you doing here?" thought Sankaran leaping up and striding purposefully towards the man he had known for eons. "Maha Bali! Our dear Maveli here in Dubai?"

King Maha Bali Virochana (as I explained, another immortal of sorts) pivoted around to meet him, a hand involuntarily raised as if to defend his balding patch.

"Ende Vamana!" he exclaimed, protecting his head. And even before Sankaran could greet his king he was being ushered away from the Etihad Airway's counter by His Highness.

"Shhh! Back-up! Back-up!" the stout man whispered in a voice of urgency. "I don't want to be on CCTV. Some smartass security personnel will definitely notice an anomaly. Here, come this way, let's indulge at the Duty Free for a while. I know exactly which cameras are blurred here. Hurry!"

"But what is Your Highness doing here?" Sankaran followed the quick-stepping mass of royalty furtively entering an empty corner of the duty-free section.

"I'm on my way to Kerala!" Maveli replied over his shoulder. "The same reason why you're going! The same reason why every Malayalee is going home! It's good old Onam!"

Sankaran followed the twinkle-toed, suede-shoed king into the Duty Free section. "You didn't answer my question, Your Highness!"

Maha Bali spun around again, almost knocking over an entire glass display of Vat 69. "Oops! That would have been expensive!" he smiled with the twinkle returning in his eyes. "Okay, let me tell you! Now, what am I doing in Dubai? What am I doing in Dubai? Okay, actually it's been some decades, just a couple of decades, mind you, since I've been coming to this part of the world during Onam. Of course I visit my beautiful Kerala every Onam. Unfailingly. But I prefer to make it there via the *Gelf.* Heaven knows why, but most of you are so entrenched here. You see Sankara, my people are all over the *Gelf.* There's more celebration and feasting here than in Kerala! Besides, you people are quite united here! Hindus, Christians and Muslims, all feasting on Onam." Maha Bali suddenly put on a conspiratorial tone. "Have you seen the women decking up here? They are more traditionally attired here in the *Gelf* during Onam than in all

Kerala! And the size of their *pookalams*!" He waved his fat arms once again threatening to knock over a shelf of bottles, this time no worse than a row of Chivas Regal.

He's like a bull in a china shop, thought Sankaran. "Your Highness! Can we not go elsewhere to talk this over?"

"Okay, but the CCTV! You don't understand Sankara! I'm not afraid of what the airport security will see! It's what they will *not* see that worries me." He pointed across the shop. "You see that monitor over there. Look at it closely. Observe! I don't feature in it. You appear to be standing alone doing some kind of mono-act. The security will be here for *you* when they see you talking animatedly to a rack of imported liquor bottles."

He stopped to catch his breath and feel the ends of his handle-bar moustache. "They've grown since you last set eyes on them, haven't they?" he tweaked their ends. "Okay, now tell me Sankara, do you really want to return to this place? I came by a cab to the airport today and discovered that even the taxi drivers don't know the city. The driving skills of the locals are even more pathetic, the cost of a drink prohibitive. And the expats, especially the white-skinned ones. They think they own the place. And have you ever been to Sonapur, the unofficial name for a work camp on the outskirts of Dubai? Sonapur! Ha! Hah!" he laughed aloud. "What an irony? The name means 'City of Gold' in Hindi. It is home to more than 250,000 workers, mostly from India, Pakistan, Bangladesh and China who are virtually held in a bonded condition. Modern day slavery effected by a simple act of confiscating their passports and holding back salaries. I wanted to advice Sheikh Mohammed that poverty in one part of the world does not justify exploitation in another. He's a good man. He'll eventually clean up the mess they're in. But look at you, Sankaran! Your children have virtually grown up without you. And your Ammu? Like so many Ammus of my beautiful Kerala? She's spending the best years of her life as a..... what do they call them?.....Ha, yes! As a, *Gelf*-widow!"

Sankaran looked deflated for a moment. "I do owe something to the *Gelf,* Your Highness. I made my money here. Not in Kerala. That place isn't that wealthy since you left millennia ago. Have you seen the men-folk there lately? Need I explain! They wake up late, often with a hangover, bathe religiously, apply Cuticura or Yardley talcum powder on their neck and armpits, put on a freshly ironed shirt and a white *mundu,* eat off the fat of someone else's income and end up in a bar by the evening for a *small,* to ponder over the state of international affairs. Lazy Commies!"

The ancient monarch nodded sagaciously. "The Commies became a necessity to deal with some evils that had crept into our society. Not that I condone their ways. Their's is an ideology based on envy. Their need is long over. Their numbers are fast dwindling. A number of those comrades with newly acquired wealth from the *Gelf* have chosen to quietly buy property in Bangalore and other less conspicuous places to settle down. A tough monarchy as well as a strict religion is keeping the countries of the *Gelf* intact. Otherwise, given their human rights record, these Commies would have wreaked havoc in the *Gelf* too."

Sankaran tried to change the topic. "So then, I hope Your Highness will be home on Onam day as usual." Sankaran interrupted. "That's just two days away. I couldn't but help overhear the Etihad girl confirm your flight to Bangalore. Why Bangalore?"

"Oh, I thought I'd better go see my co-immortal Ashwatthama for a day. I did send him a message. He should be awaiting my arrival."

"In Bangalore?" Sankaran's voice sounded incredulous.

"Believe me, Sankara! Bangalore has enough garbage to hide Ashwatthama for eternity and enough Malayalees to search for him if I need to. Have you seen the city lately?"

"No! Not in the last 220 years," replied Sankaran. "I returned through that place with an East India Company detachment after we laid siege on Srirangapatanam in 1799. After Tipu's fall, I remember marching through a picturesque cantonment with crystal-clear blue lakes, flowering trees and a handful of English bungalows."

"Oh of course! How could I have forgotten?" exclaimed Maha Bali, placing his palm on the balding patch of his head. "You too are a *chiranjivi*, an immortal."

"Of sorts!" Sankaran replied. "Your Highness is immortal in that you are able to emerge from the netherworld once a year to meet your subjects during Onam. Ashwatthama is immortal in that he roams the land as an undead. But, I. I have a mortal body. It dies and I need to take birth again. My immortality is in my memory. I can remember every one of my past lives. That was a boon I received from Parashurama."

"That arrogant jackass!" muttered Maha Bali under his breath. Sankaran ignored him.

"You remember that occasion don't you, Your Highness? Your Highness was ruling the land then. And I had just five days to warn the population of the catastrophe that was to come from the sea when he threw his axe to reclaim some land for us. How effectively we communicated then! How instantly we net-worked to evacuate the population to higher ground before the tidal wave hit us! What a man that Parashurama! An immortal too!"

"A jackass nonetheless," insisted Maha Bali. "Immortal does not mean eternal, as all physical bodies are foretold to become immaterial at the end of time, with the final destruction of the Universe." He patted down the denser hair on the sides of his head. "Well Sankara, I hope you make the right decision. Kerala needs you. Kerala cannot survive without people like you. I will certainly be there by Onam. Just one more thing...." His voice took on a serious tone. "Does anyone in Kerala even remember what a real *Sadhya* was like? I mean a really authentic one. Sixty-four dishes all served in a special sequence on a large banana leaf? Sixty-four distinctly different dishes when we last counted, you remember? That was our last record, wasn't it? Before that Vamana came and stomped all over me? Oh Sankara, do you even remember the names of the dishes?"

"We consider a cuisine of 24 items a fairly good Sadhya these days, at a stretch 28 tops," explained Sankaran.

"Twenty-eight? What a shame!" exclaimed the king looking distressed. "A dozen Punjabi *dhabas* on the Grand Trunk Road up north make that many."

"Malayalees have stopped eating many of the fancy dishes we did in those days, Your Highness! Since that other Shankaran, the Namboothiri of Kalady expounded his theories we have gone all vegetarian. Today the Kodavas and Tulus have monopolized the pork and wild-boar dishes. Even the ingredients are not grown in our gardens any more. Many are too expensive to procure. Have you ever been to one of today's Malayalee restaurants, my King?" complained Sankaran.

"Yes!" retorted the king with a look of incredulousness. "Yes! And I like to know since when did gobi-manchurian and fried mushroom become one of our dishes? By God's own country, that oily, rubbery and incomprehensible substance people chew on endlessly, which they christened *Kerala porota!* In my time I wouldn't serve that horror even in a famine!"

"We never knew famines in your time, Your Highness!" Sankaran tried to placate the irritated monarch. "Today we still have some of the old and amazing food on our menu. "Take *Kootan!* Curries like, *inji*-curry and *puliyinchy*. Others like *sambar, rasam, parippu, pulisseri, pulinkurry, kootucurry, kaalan, avial, thoran, olan, kichadi, pachadi, naranga*, etc. An assortment of pickles like mango, gooseberry, lime as well as some chutneys….not to speak of *pappadum*, buttermilk, curd and plantain chips… and for dessert, six varieties of *prathaman*…"

"Enough, enough!" some spittle had emerged from the corners of his royal mouth below the handle-bar moustache which he quickly removed with his thumb and forefinger. "Have a heart! I've just emerged from the nether world! Okay be it twenty-four or twenty-eight. I will be there on Onam as always. But Sankara, tell my people, I really think I'll just come out of exile, alive and ready, to rule over our land permanently again, if you could get just a hand-full of Malayalees to rustle-up all our sixty-four." The spittle now elongated into helpless dribbles, like shoelaces on each corner of his royal cheeks. He needed his pocket handkerchief to wipe it.

"That's some challenge!" remarked Sankaran.

"I have a flight to catch." The old king announced. "Ashwatthama awaits me somewhere. I will find him somehow. Somewhere, soon enough before my arrival for Onam at Kerala. So, be off lad! Farewell! I bless you, your wife and children on the occasion of Onam!" He raised a hand to bless Sankaran. "Hold on a second. Make that sixty-six. I hear that *Thalassery biryani* and *Kozhikodan Haluva* are doing fairly well too."

"That's a later innovation, way past your reign," explained Sankaran. "It doesn't feature among the original sixty-four dishes of the Keralites."

"Of the what?" The king looked bemused. "Of the what? Keralites? Since when did we become Keralite? Like Naxalite and cellulite! It even sounds impolite!"

"Sometime after Independence, You Highness," admitted Sankaran. "At least it's better than Madrasee. That's an inexcusable howler by our very own Indians up north. Everyone south of the Godavari is for some unknown reason called a Madrasee."

"In Bengal they took me to be a Keralian!" complained Maveli, slapping his palm against his forhead. "Keralian is terrible. Reminds one of reptilian and chameleon."

"In the *Gelf* they call me a Malabari," complained Sankaran.

"Malabari – That's an Arab booboo!" explained the king. "Ever since they began trading with the people of Malabar all speakers of the Malayalam tongue were labelled Malabari. They haven't yet worked out that the Malabar region only refers to the north of Kerala. It's only a poor understanding of Geography."

"Then there's "Mallu" – a more recent urban terminology," pointed out Sankaran.

"I still love the term Malayalee," confessed the king. "Rhymes nicely with Galilee and Jubilee."

"And Maveli," Sankaran added waving farewell to the king.

Thus the benevolent king of Kerala, His Highness, the ancient and immortal Maha Bali Virochana, fondly called Maveli by his extremely diasporic subjects, walked the Dubai International Airport terminus in his suede shoes and corduroys, to join the Bangalore passenger traffic. Sankaran watched with a feeling of sadness as the stout figure disappeared at the far end through a gate indicating the Etihad Airways flight to Bangalore.

Sankaran arrived without further incident at the Kozhikode airport to take his customary cab home where his family was awaiting him anxiously. As his suitcases rolled ahead of him into the doorway where a beaming Ammu stood in her new, frilly housecoat, he removed his Ray-Ban goggles to gaze at his aging landlord's compound, particularly up at the profusion of coconuts ready to be harvested.

"Poor old souls," Sankaran made a decision even as his children pestered him for attention. "I'll rest for a day. Then perhaps I could begin scaling these palms to harvest the coconuts for the old folks. Who else will do it for these poor old people?" He had also brought some preserved dates, two Chinese rechargeable torches and some clothes for them. He also hoped the T-shirts would fit his elderly landlord.

Thirty-six hours later, on the eve of Onam, as he climbed to the top of a swaying coconut palm in the landlord's grove, from somewhere in the locality Onam songs were being played aloud on a mike, carrying an ancient and familiar melody in the wind.

> Maveli reigned in the Malayalee's land,
> A casteless society with justice at hand
> Food was in bounty, clean water and air.
> Free from all harm, the people were fair.

No anxiety, no sickness, no boredom
No children ever died in his kingdom
There were no lies, deceit or even theft
Sparing pseudo-intellects who went Left

Truthful in speech, letter and pact,
Weights and measures were exact;
They loved and lent neighbours a hand.
When King Maveli ruled the land.

THE BOY AND THE WARRIOR

They made an odd pair. The boy and the warrior. Just the two of them on the western sea coast early in the morning. Sankaran, high up, swaying atop the slender and lofty palm tree watching the lone figure of Bhargava down below, impatiently pacing the rocky black and red laterite path that skirted the ocean.

The boy crouched atop the palm was slender, adolescent muscles rippling his torso and limbs. He sat with a reptilian comfort at the top of the coconut tree, poised in a minimal red loin cloth that barely covered his genitals. A human fly, who seemed as comfortable on this slippery perch, forty feet above the ground, as he might on level ground. A casually tied turban was the larger and only other cloth he donned.

Below him Bhargava flaunted reinforced silk, bronze chainmail, breastplates as well other assorted body armour that glittered in the morning sun. A heavy bronze-plated helmet was placed on a rock as he let down his long grey hair, shaking it so often to dry the perspiration that clung to it. His fair skin was a contrast to the tawny tan of the boy on the coconut palm.

It was dawn. But today there appeared no trace of the grey vaporous ambience that preceded the rising sun. Instead a heavy blanket of darkness hugged the craggy coastline. The choppy sea glinted anxiously in the barely visible sunrays that broke through the thickly forested, mountainous landscape behind them.

Sankaran who never felt any awe at human size found the exceptionally tall soldier rather overdressed and comical. "A foreigner, no doubt!" he thought. "But what a nut to dress up like that in this heat! He'll have blisters and prickly heat all over before the morning is over. And does he think he can stand up against the water surging closer and closer every minute? What is happening? He appears to have infuriated the sea waters somehow!"

"Careful!" the boy yelled out aloud at the bearded soldier as he clung on the palm. "She can throw a fierce wave or two in this sort of weather,"

"I don't need you here!" rebuked the tall lithe figure below in response, as he paced up and down the laterite path. Bhargava had arrived at Gokarna, battle-axe in hand and a single purpose in mind. He had already set-up devices that would cause a series of catastrophic explosions along the coast.

"I am simply saving you the discomfort of getting salty water down your disproportionate attire," Sankaran shouted down.

"Get off your perch, native!" Bhargava yelled back at the youth. "Ask everyone to retreat into the *ghats*. I'm triggering off a minor seismic event here that will initially send a few shock waves and sea water into your fields and houses. It can cause some inconvenience and even deaths."

"Aiyo!" the boy let out a shout of panic. He felt alarmed by the words of the tall warrior. Bhargava in turn looked amused at the boy's spontaneous reaction as he slithered his loin-clad naked body down the palm tree with the dexterity of a primate.

"What on earth are you doing that for?" Sankaran queried in bewilderment.

"To teach your Nair clan a lesson!" came the ominous reply from the man in battle-fatigues. "And besides, I will also need a new expanse of land to resettle some Brahmins I have brought along from the peninsula.

"But I'm only Sankaran, the coconut gatherer. My ailing mother lies in her hut down near the paddy fields. She'll drown! Do you have King Maha Bali's permission for what you intend to do?"

"No. I don't have your King's permission. But knowing Maha Bali, he'll only be too happy to govern the new lands that will rise from the sea when I'm done."

"But the king must be informed!" retorted Sankaran. "And the people! What about the people?"

"Be off then!" Bhargava grimly waved the youth away. "Inform the king. Save your mother and all those who will believe and regard your words when you tell them of what I intend to do here today. Ask them to retreat to the hills. The deluge will last but for a day. By tomorrow morning they may return and pick up their lives once again from whatever is left of their homes."

"What about their household belongings and their cattle?" the boy paused to ask, standing where he assumed was a safe distance from the warrior. "And there are other people apart from your abominable Nairs in the villages and towns. What have you got against them?"

Bhargava leaned on his axe as he weighed the matter in his mind. "Alright then. I grant you two days to warn them and have them shift out of their homes and move temporarily higher into the hills. Go on now. Be my messenger. Do the needful."

The boy didn't budge. He shook his head vigorously. "Not enough time. There are women and children. Senile elders, the sick and the ailing. We can't all make it up to safety in just two days! Even if I was to use every runner and drummer it would take me five days just to send out a warning down the coast."

The warrior looked extremely impatient for a moment. After some thought he offered, "Boy, I'll gift you a boon if you will do this in five days. Five whole days. Not a day more. Will you be capable of warning this population away in five days, boy?

"A boon? Spell it out, my good sir..." the boy took a negotiator's tone. Once again annoyance passed over the weathered face of the tall warrior but it soon passed.

"What is it you require, my child?" the warrior enquired. "Name it. It's yours.....but only when you have accomplished what I have just asked you to do."

"Immortality." the boy replied. "Like you, I wish to become a *chiranjivi*, an immortal. That's what you are, aren't you?" He sounded more defiant than pleading.

Bhargava could not suppress the smile under his bearded face. "Which district of Tamilagam do you belong to?" he asked with curiosity.

"Right here, to these hills," the boy replied. "This is my home. My *Mala Pradesham*."

"And what made you believe that I might be immortal... or even that I might be able to grant you the same?"

The boy replied slowly as if weighing the situation he found himself in. "I was taking a chance."

After a long silence during which the enormous blade of his axe twitched and glinted like a living creature, Bhargava broke the silence. His voice emanated in a low timbre, just audible above the impatient and noisy hiss, murmur and pounding of the waves as they challenged the shore about his large feet.

"I do not wish that innocents die during the first and inevitable deluge that Mother Ocean will let loose when I strike at her. There will be a very sudden upheaval, as Mother Ocean does not give up her lands easily. No man has ever attempted this before. But I have identified the fault-line that will yield to the forces I unleash. I will cause a substantial portion of the waters to sink into great caverns in the sea floor many miles away. The land along the shore will rise but will remain uninhabitable for some time due to the stench of dead fish and rotting seaweed. It will take another ten monsoons before the salt leaches out of the soil for any of you to grow crops here."

He was silent as he raised the ornate handle of the axe and held it vertically in front of his face. As if it somehow aided in balancing his thoughts. "Heaven knows Sankara, what will eventually occur, as the waters I displace here find their own level elsewhere... on some other shore far from us that will have to contain the overflow. A land somewhere that will need to submit and sink below the sea to accommodate the waters I displace here today. But I need to raise this land and mine the *deva jala*. In it is contained an element whose atom is the *anu* of endless possibilities in times of both war and peace. It contains the energy to fuel *vimanas* and the *brahmastra*. I will mine a small portion of it for my own use. The rest of the element will be left scattered in these sands, awaiting a time in the future when this subcontinent will unite under more peaceful rulers."

Sankaran shook his head enthusiastically in understanding. The warrior looked at him in confusion.

"Does that mean you disagree with me?" he asked, his axe still held high.

"Why, I certainly agree with you," Sankaran again shook his head vigorously from side to side.

"Where I come from, when one agrees, he nods his head up and down," Bhargava demonstrated the motion by lifting his chin and bringing it down again a few times in a bowing motion.

Sankaran once again shook his head in a quick side-to-side quiver. "I don't know about that, but I completely agree with you that the waters that recede here must find someplace else to flood."

"Then why don't you nod like the rest of humanity?" asked Bhargava in amusement and curiosity.

"I will answer that question as soon as I have my boon." Sankaran replied to the great warrior from the North, barely batting an eyelid. Bhargava, now axe on his shoulder, approached the boy in long strides that left giant footprints on the sand. The boy stood his ground.

"A tough customer, aren't you?" Bhargava's eyed the boy sagaciously and spoke slowly. "And a great one at bargaining and parleying! Good for you, son. I grant you this boon, my boy. Be the first and last Malayalee of this Mala Pradesham. Guard this land that I will create. Distinguish yourself in all endeavours as you march through time. Make this little province which I bestow you today the pride of this peninsula and this continent."

Sankaran bowed in reverence, holding his hands together as the blade of the warrior's axe lifted and poised a few inches above his turban. The soldier's eyes were closed in meditation as he spoke. "Immortal shall your name be when we meet again at the end of five days. Be off now. Warn the province. When the waves crash on to the shore let not a man, woman or child be harmed by the enraged Mother Ocean. For she will seek reprisal and the winds that accompany her waters will also wreck mayhem on the hills that border this coast. Save everyone you can. For this is my battle. And I shall not be vanquished. You have but five days!"

Sankaran bolted into the hills as fast as his legs could carry him. Shouting, screaming, hooting and yelling to one and all to spread the word that a great tidal wave was on its way to strike Mala Pradesham in a few days. "Evacuate, move to higher ground! Women and children first! Carry the elders! Herd the cattle! March, march, march! Don't pause in doubt! Inform the king. It is the truth! Mark my words! Hang me if I prove wrong!" Many more urging and urgent lexis spewed out of him as he sped past friends, relatives and strangers. Fellow villagers, townsmen and farmers. Merchants, soldiers and weavers.

The reaction of the community that dwelt in this countryside who had always seen Sankaran climbing, rarely running, was initially muddled.

"Is he running away from something or is he chasing something? What is that poor boy shouting about, anyway?"

"Did someone stuff something unimaginable into his loin cloth?"

"What did he see? Hey, Sankara! What is the meaning of this uproar you are causing?"

"Whatever it is, Sankaran must be right." proclaimed an octogenarian. "He has the best view of the world among us. He must have seen something. You see, he is always on the coconut tree."

"Someone inform King Maha Bali. Inform the chiefs. Let them decide and give orders as necessary."

"I say we stop asking questions and start moving uphill. We can belt him later if he turns out to be wrong."

"Now who has got the drums pounding? Can someone translate the beat?"

"It says- *Danger. Head East. Up the hill.*"

"Why?"

"You know the rule. You don't ask questions when the drums begin to play."

"Okay, I'm not arguing. I'm moving up too. But that boy will hang when all this absurdity is over."

And so it took, as Sankaran had envisioned, much more convincing before the denizens of Mala Pradesham began their exodus into a safer altitude. He had run many miles before an anxious trickle soon became an angry mob of refugees; the angry mob after due convincing became a larger procession of uprooted and sullen marchers. The crowds became mammoth swarms that filled the roads and pathways up the *ghats* carrying their provisions and driving their cattle before them. In at least two places a stampede was barely avoided as strong winds suddenly began to blow and cause panic.

Sankaran climbed a coconut tree many times to look into the distance and feel the reassurance of people moving to higher ground. Many volunteered to pass on the ominous message by runner, horse and drum beats. The clamour that had begun at Gokarna, now on its second day reverberated on the boundaries of Kanya Kumari. Even rival kingdoms between Gokarna and Kanya Kumari decided not to take any chances. In the far south, at the tip of the peninsula, their chieftains and rulers issued orders to subjects to move sufficiently inland if there was not enough high ground. "It's either a tidal wave that is of uncertain proportion or a false rumour that is of certain consequences to that coconut gatherer," they summarised. "If we do not see any water from where we take refuge, the king will crush his head under the feet of his prized war elephant. That Sankaran is incorrigible!"

When the fifth day came to pass, Sankaran returned to Gokarna. He had more or less accomplished his task. He now needed to carry his ailing mother up the *ghats* to safety for there remained only an hour before the *parashu*-wielding warrior awaiting Sankaran on the beach detonated his warhead against the western sea.

On entering his little house amongst the paddy fields he discovered to his astonishment and dismay that she wasn't there. His mother appeared to have left taking her belongings with her.

"She could barely walk. Where could she have gone? Have the villagers helped her up the *ghats* to a secure place, knowing I would be late in arriving here?"

He ran up and down the mud-banks that outlined the paddy fields yelling aloud for an hour – "Mother! Mother! Where have you gone to, Mother! This is your Sankaran, Mother! Where are you?"

Sombre empty homes greeted him all around where only a few days ago there teemed noisy and cheery neighbours. Now there were no children. No cattle. No dogs. Only the wind blowing powerfully from the direction of the sea answered his call. Good God, was all this his doing? He stood exasperated and gasping, the wind on his back, looking towards the hills in hope.

His voice now trailed into a whisper. "Mother, so you left without your Sankaran! At least you had the good sense to evacuate."

He decided to now return to the coast and claim his immortality from the remarkable soldier in bronze, armed with the *parashu*.

Bhargava, who was sitting on a rock, waved at him impatiently to come closer. "Observe carefully what I show you!"

The boy stood by the soldier who pointed to a domed device floating miles away in the distance. Like a buoy, rising and bobbing in the waves, the silhouette of the object danced in the orange glow of the setting sun. It appeared to be at the very point where the faint horizon dissipated, where the evening sky touched the waters.

"What is it?" asked Sankaran, protecting his eyes from the fiery sun.

"That Sankara, is my primary *yantra*, my 'little boy'," Bhargava replied, now standing up. "That is the point where my axe sets off the first detonation. It will lead to a chain reaction deep beneath the sea-bed, along the fault lines running south along this entire coast which I have identified for my purpose. The rest is *Bhuvijjana*! Geology! Now if you will please excuse me, I have work to do."

He tied his long hair into a top-knot that allowed the heavy helmet to slip over his head. A visor snapped shut with the firmness of a well-crafted mask over his bearded face.

"Be off now!" he ordered. "The typhoon will be upon us within seconds of my striking that floating device." He walked to an expanse of sand on the beach.

"My boon!" cried out Sankaran. "The shores have been evacuated. What of my boon?"

"It has been yours from the moment you showed up," replied the warrior without turning back.

Sankaran smiled and shook his head.

"Immortality is yours already even as we speak. But not in a way you imagine," he continued, placing his legs comfortably apart, the blade of his double-edged battle-axe on the sandy floor between his legs as he prepared to pivot his enormous frame - a run-up before releasing the great *parashu* from his grip.

Then firmly holding the end of the long leather encased haft, he turned his head to look at the boy one last time.

"I see you once again shake your head vigorously instead of nodding as we do in the north."

"For us who so often find ourselves atop a coconut palm, hugging its trunk for dear life, a nod would cause us to strike our foreheads on the trunk of the tree. We prefer to twiddle our heads side to side in acquiescence. That's a Malayalee's "Yes". Would that suffice for an answer?"

Masked by the warrior's bronze helmet, Sankaran did not see the amused grin behind the visor of the great figure that stood on the sand before him. Neither was he prepared as the giant form suddenly spun in a pivoting motion, circling the axe with a speed that made him startle and blink. Sunlight reflected like lightning off the great *parashu* as it spun in a wide circle. Once, twice, thrice, before it suddenly shot out of Bhargava's grip, travelling like an arrow shot from a long-bow into the air in the direction of the sea. Its flight path was visible as it cruised in a great arch towards the horizon descending upon the floating device the warrior had described as his "little boy."

As it found its target, a great plume rose into the sky in the distant vista, followed by a deafening thunder and a scorching white light more brilliant than the setting sun itself.

"Don't look!" screamed Bhargava. "Run! Run! The surge will be here in seconds. Water-currents that are impossible to resist, a deluge so powerful that it will rise to great heights and engulf everything in its path. For here Sankara, I gift you God's own country!"

Sankaran bolted toward the tallest coconut palm he could see on the beach. He heard the thunderous waters approaching over the sands as he scrambled to reach the tree. With the ease of long practice, he slid up the tree in quick motions even as the waters encircled and rose, threatening to dislodge him however high he climbed. It rose behind him. It surged up beneath his feet as he frantically climbed, slipped and climbed again. He could now see miles of sea water and surf pounding deep inland, tentacles of foam crawling up the hills. The palm he scaled swayed dangerously, bending against the force of thirty feet high waves, dunking Sankaran a few times into the surface of the raging waters. As the initial pressure of the tidal wave subsided, the tree almost dislodged him as a catapult would when it straightened up again suddenly.

Bhargava, the cause of all this tumult was not to be seen. He must have a plan. And a safe place to escape this inconvenience, thought Sankaran. He felt gratitude to the man for having at least allowed him to warn the population all of whom had been given time to escape with their lives.

More than two hours would pass before the waters appeared to be retreating. There were no fresh waves from the sea. The tide that had reached nearly forty feet high, almost touching the tips of the long coconut leaves that formed a canopy around him now began to descend. A dry branch of the palm suddenly extricated itself and was swept away at the blink of an eye in the direction of the sea by strong returning currents.

It was dusk and the sky was darkening very fast. Sankaran removed his long turban and used it to fasten himself to the tree as securely as he possibly could in order to give his limbs a little rest. As the waters receded, it would be a long time before he could safely descend to the ground below again. The sandy beach was gone. The coastline had shifted miles away. His favourite perch was suddenly deep inland.

He was exhausted. His head felt heavy with the fatigue of his efforts during these last five days. He needed sleep and rest. He could sleep up here. For he had never fallen off a coconut tree.

SULAYMAN'S BRIDE

"Sankara! Sankara!" from the distance his mother's otherwise melodic voice now took an urgent tone. "Sankara! Can you please come down and attend to matters here? Where do you disappear every time someone needs you?"

Sankaran blinked and peered over his shoulder in the direction of her voice. Sliding down, he removed the coir anchor-rope from his feet and threw it over his shoulder. Slipping his curved Malabar chopper into a loop of rope around his waist he turned to walk in the direction of his thatched house at the far end of the paddy field.

As he approached, a group of colourfully dressed men became visible in the compound where the house stood. They formed a tight circle around the front door and seemed to be busy in some discourse with his mother and perhaps some others seated inside the house. Sankaran headed for the well on the side of the house to wash and refresh himself before being seen by the strangers. And having done that, he removed his copious turban, unfurled the fabric and wrapped it neatly around his waist allowing its full width to fall right down to his ankles. He brushed back his long wet hair and shook it about his shoulders.

An uproarious laughter emanated from the house, followed by a voice that spoke in a thick accent. "His Highness, the great Sulayman will be pleased."

More foreigners! This time inside his mother's house!

But as he arrived on to the front of the house, the foreigners were already departing. Their long nosed countenances wore great mirth and satisfaction. They were, without exception all long-bearded men with clothes that completely covered them from their necks to their ankles with decorative ropes and tassels around their waists that served to hold their garments together. They didn't take much notice of him. So he hurried towards the front door, barely rubbing shoulders with the last overdressed foreigner as he walked past them.

"Mother, what's all this about?"

"Oh Sankara! Where were you?" his mother complained. "Up which tree do you disappear when I need you the most?"

Sankaran gazed upon the remains of a variety of refreshments that the visitors had consumed. "Who were they mother?"

"I wanted you to bring down some fresh tender coconut water for our guests. Don't you know your sister Paru has been chosen?"

"Chosen? For what?" Sankaran reached for a snack, a large ball of grated coconut bound sumptuously with jaggery.

"To become a queen, my son! The great Sulayman has chosen her for a bride!" His mother now moved about energetically gathering and stacking the innumerable copper and brass vessels scattered about the grass-mat laden floor of the large hall.

"Sulayman!" Sankaran sounded incredulous. "Which Sulayman?"

"Sulayman of Judea, son. A king! He that built the temple of Yerushalayim we hear so much about. Whose merchants have been for years buying our peacocks, ivory and pepper in exchange for gold! Why, he is as great in Yerushalayim as Maha Bali was in our lands."

"Rama! Parashu Rama!" exclaimed Sankaran. "And you, mother, agreed to this alliance?"

His mother shook her head determinedly. "Paru is nearly eighteen. She is beautiful and as pure as a fresh lotus. No raja in this land deserves her."

"Do you know anything about this Sulayman, Mother?" Sankaran dropped to the floor to look at his mother in the eye.

"They tell me he is powerful, wise and..."

"No! Not what *they* tell you, mother? What you should have heard spoken among these merchants before they laid eyes on Paru! He probably already has more than five hundred wives. And he is not a patch on our Maha Bali!"

His mother tried to look away, carrying the stack of plates into the washing area of the house.

"Iddo, the great Sulayman's ambassador just visited us with his entourage...." she began.

"Iddo - addo, I don't care, mother. Paru is my sister too. How could you do this?" Sankaran followed his mother into the kitchen.

His mother soaked the plates in a small stone tank of water and leaned against the kitchen wall preparing herself for an arduous dialogue with her son. "How could I marry her off to a king, you ask? Sankara! Did you ever wonder why your father died so peacefully? It was with the knowledge that a woman of this land was capable of managing her own affairs and those of her children too. Banu, your elder sister is happy in the Achaemenid country, married to a rich merchant. She dines with the nobility of the land every other day. And has she not visited us twice in the last decade along with her husband, children and chests of gifts?"

"Oh Bagadata the Achaemenid was indeed God-sent," Sankaran tried to sound sarcastic. "Banu visited you to avoid her husband getting himself conscripted by the king! Mother, the two occasions she visited us from across the sea, there was war in that kingdom. He was afraid of being recruited. They would rather risk the voyage through pirate-infested waters to visit you than offend their king." His mother closed her eyes in a gesture that was meant to convey that she wasn't listening.

"Don't you remember mother, Bagadata returned with Banu and the children only after traders brought good tidings of the end of the war," reminded Sankaran. "But this Sulayman, mother! I have heard much spoken of him. Among the sea-farers. And not all of it is good. Please do not compare him with our Maha Bali. Sulayman already has innumerable wives. Besides he is very old and feeble."

"Very well then. She can nurse him," his mother retorted.

"Since when did the world need nurses from our part of the world?" Sankaran exclaimed in an exasperated voice. "With Paru too leaving to nurse some old Judean, I'd rather remain on the coconut tree for the rest of my life!"

"Sankara, my son," his mother pleaded. "Understand this: that neither Banu nor Paru were meant to live with us forever. They need husbands and a life of their own. You were the one born to live here with me." her voice softened. "One day, you Sankara, will bring home a delicate darling who will be of company and great assistance to me. Please understand. I have to do this as a mother. Your father is gone. I have to see that my two girls find themselves in good, nay great stations, in life. It may seem like a bitter separation. But they have to find happiness elsewhere."

"But couldn't you find anyone in the whole of Keralaputra or even our own Malabar? This Sulayman is a foreigner!"

"I didn't go looking for the king of Judea," his mother answered coldly. "It was they who discovered her. Spied her in the market place in their last visit to Malabar more than a year ago. They spoke to their king and his astrologers who responded favourably. Sankara, this is a proposal from a king."

"What if she is carried away by one of those long nosed individuals who showed up at your door just now? What if they intend to keep her for one of their harems? Who is to know?"

His mother sighed emphatically dragging him by his arm. "Come, Sankara! Let me show you the gifts that these Yehudis have brought for me from the great Sulayman himself. That will perhaps convince you." She led her doubting son into her bedchamber and uncovered a carved wooden chest that was placed on her bed draped in satin. It was embellished with the figure of a lion, a six-pronged star and gleaming copper fixtures. She threw the wooden lid open to unveil a heap of precious stones. There were emeralds and rubies of unusual size and cut, diamonds of superb clarity, topaz and sapphires of astounding beauty along with bridal jewellery of the most outlandish kind.

"What does this Sulayman have in Judea?" Sankaran exclaimed, his eyes lighting up. "Mines? I've heard traders speak of his mines. But I thought Sulayman's mines were copper mines!"

"And this is not even her dowry. It is only a gesture of the great Sulayman's gratification! Now do you doubt me?" His mother sounded triumphant.

"Bribed up to her hair-buns!" thought Sankaran in dismay. "What does Paru feel about all this?" Sankaran queried, looking around for his little sister.

Paru was seated beneath a tamarind tree behind the house in exquisite finery staring dreamily into the sea. Her luxurious black wavy hair streaming behind her in the breeze.

She wiped a tear trickling down her cheek as Sankaran approached and managed to smile. He put his strong arms around her. "I don't want to hear what the big nosed Yehudis told you nor do I want to hear what mother wishes you to do," he ruled. "I want to hear what you think, Paru. What does your heart say about all these developments?"

"If it is my destiny, I have to find my happiness there in Judea with the king," she whispered. "I am quite happy here, Sankara, but I have to be somebody's wife sooner or later. It is like a throw of the dice. Mother is ambitious in her strange ways. But I cannot really say that she is not acting for our good."

"Every time she gets a girl married off to some foreign nobility, she advances her status here locally." Sankaran complained. "Is that her sole motive?"

"Hush! Do not speak of her like that," Paru placed a finger on his lips. "We were brought up well. At least I will be happy that I leave her behind me wealthy and respected in her own country. Sulayman, I believe is almost 80 years old. At least my knowledge of medicine may help him live a little longer. Even our own king will become aware of the eminence of our family following my marriage to the ruler of Judea."

"What was so deprived or wrong with our family before all this?" countered Sankaran. "When father was alive."

"*When* father was alive," she cut him short. "Things were very different when father was alive, Sankara. There's no denying that. Mother finds herself now in quite a new set of circumstances. I feel she's only trying to make the best of it."

"She's no doubt succeeding," Sankaran granted wryly. "What more would she want in this lifetime I wonder?"

Paru stood up excitedly. "Don't you know? Has she not hinted to you? We are buying a tract of land at Vanchi near Muziris. Where mother has some relatives. There are noble families in that neighbourhood. She has plans to build a grand house of stone, timber and tiles with a smooth floor. The grounds will have orchards and walls and the gate will be guarded. We will live there for a few happy months before I depart with the king's merchants.

Sankaran paid scant attention to Paru's narration of his mother's plans. His attention was drawn to the road in the distance where palanquin bearers now carried the prosperous looking Yehudi visitors in a small procession back to their camp near the mouth of the river some miles away.

"I need to have a word with them," Sankaran told Paru as he began to run towards the road.

"Don't upset them, Sankara!" she cried out. "I won't, I promise you!" he yelled back at her.

He knew they were observing his approach as he neared them. When it became obvious that he intended to speak to them, someone yelled at the palanquin bearers to halt. Two interpreters turned to face him. The language of Judea was known only to an Arab. He would interpret what had been said by Sulayman's agents to another Arab who spoke and understood Tamil. The second Arab prepared to further translate all that was said into Tamil for Sankaran. And vice-versa.

Sankaran stood before them and cleared his throat politely. "Does your king not require the blessing and consent of his intended bride's elder and only brother?" he asked hesitantly.

The Arab turned to his compatriot and spoke disparagingly in Arabic. "Looks like the brother of the girl too wishes some fine goods as inducement before he can allow the matrimony. The beggar!"

The Arab who knew only Aramaic now translated to the Judean guests. "Your Excellency, this man is here to stop your king from marrying his sister until his demands are met."

The bearded Judean official jumped off his palanquin, visibly infuriated. "Who, by Abraham, does he think he is?" he raised his voice. "I represent the mighty Sulayman. His mother has given her consent, hasn't she?"

Sankaran was perturbed by the Judean's demeanour. "It's a custom of the land from the bygone days of our great king Maha Bali..." he began to explain.

"It's a rule," the Arab translated.

"It's his order," the Arab who spoke Aramaic further interpreted.

King Sulayman's ambassador now looked furious. "How dare he?" he yelled at Sankaran and appeared to be in the mood to draw his sword.

"Now listen," yelled Sankaran at the Tamil-speaking Arab. "Are you translating this correctly? What is the king's representative so angry about?"

The Arab turned to his compatriot. "He wants to know what right the great Sulayman's agent has to show his temper."

"Your Excellency shall not show your temper here on this land," his fellow- Arab compatriot further interpreted to the Judean official.

Sankaran did not quite know who was playing mischief here, but when the Judean official took two steps towards him with his hand on the hilt of his sword, Sankaran knew something had been lost in translation or misinterpreted deliberately to cause this overwrought situation. For a fleeting moment he considered drawing out his crooked Malabar blade from his waist in self defence, but the king's official suddenly stopped in his tracks.

"Inform this Malabari that I am Iddo the Seer. Today is no day to spill blood. No! I shall not attempt to hurt one who is to be tomorrow a relative of the king. Let the wise Sulayman decide this man's fate." He returned to the palanquin in a flourish and indicated to the rest of the party to march on. The two Arabs smiled slyly at each other.

Sankaran was furious despite Paru's plea not to antagonize the visitors. "Come back when your king learns to respect the traditions of our land," he yelled at the departing men. "Go tell your king, his Judea will be torn open like a coconut before you can have the hand of my dear Paru."

"He curses! How he curses, Your Excellency!" translated the Arabs as their voices trailed down the path as they accompanied the agents of Sulayman the Wise back to camp.

"It will be at least a year by the time preparations are made and the royal barges from Judea arrive," thought Sankaran. "A lot can happen in a year's time."

It was about five months later that Sankaran and Paru accompanied their mother to Vanchi, where a new house had been built. It was a fine piece of masonry work that was roofed with tiles baked in a kiln. The compound offered a view of the sea and Sankaran was overjoyed by the profusion of coconut trees that lined the edge of the beautiful bay.

And there in their new house Paru and her mother anxiously awaited news from Judea. Within a few months of their stay in Vanchi, it arrived in the form of rumours from Achaemenid and Arab sailors. King Sulayman was thought to have died and there was talk of civil war in Judea and Yerushalayim over succession. Now two kings Jeroboam and Rehoboam ruled the erstwhile kingdom of Sulayman the Wise from the North and South. The kingdom would not despatch traders to Malabar for some years now. Judea was in chaos.

Sankaran's mother was adamant. "We have used their gifts and benefited from the wealth bestowed upon us by that dynasty. Paru shall one day need to fulfil her obligation. Iddo the Seer will certainly come again to these shores and claim her for some surviving prince of Sulayman's empire."

And so it came to pass in about three years. One sunny morning in the month of July, Sankaran spied a fleet of royal barges steering into the bay. From aloft a coconut tree he could clearly see the sails and flags that bore the standard of the Star of David.

"Now what have we here?" wondered Sankaran as he slid off the palm to convey the news to his mother and sister.

Later that day, the man who entered their compound with his royal entourage turned out to be a personage of great humility and age. Iddo the Seer had indeed returned, but appeared subdued and grey. He wore no sword and greeted Sankaran first with a passive bow. To Sankaran's relief the two Arab interpreters were not among the men that accompanied him today. This time he had a new pair of translators.

Iddo spoke first, sounding submissive and sad. "Before he departed to his heavenly abode, the great Sulayman in his wisdom had understood the grave error in our estimation of your family and your country. As a result, the heads of the two Arabs now rest on spikes outside the gates of Yerushalayim. They paid gravely for their waywardness. Our country has been divided, split open like a coconut! We have paid our price too. The great Sulayman is gone. We are here to claim the bride for his grandson Prince Abijah."

This time there were gifts for Sankaran too. Iddo flung open a chest of red Judean woven cloth, brightly polished armour and an assortment of gold jewellery. It also included a sword with a two-inch-wide double-edged flexible blade that uncoiled out of a round casket, and displayed the characteristics of a metal whip rather than the stiff conventional knife blade. Iddo was quick to convey that "this sword in the hands of the trained in unassailable by any adversary with a contemporary weapon. Nobody but the great Sulayman knew the use of it. But its mastery requires courage. The great Sulayman is said to have injured himself four hundred times, often severely, before he learnt to dodge its twisting and convoluting blade. It is like a blade made of water with a hilt."

Sankaran shook his head. Iddo, though confused by the gesture watched Sankaran examining the finely curved ivory hilt. "This is like receiving a cobra for a pet. How many coconuts can I lop off with a swing of this?" he enquired, mocking the curious weapon that dangled noisily in his hand.

The day for Paru's departure drew close. The Judean royal barges, built by the skilled engineers of Tyre at Ezion-geber on the Red Sea, had dropped anchor at Muziris where carpets were laid out on the beach leading all the way to the principal barge. This heavily guarded boat, also housed the most sophisticated and dignified eunuchs of the empire. Two leading ladies of the court of Abijah also awaited Paru to give her company on the long voyage. Their brief meeting with Paru's mother had been both pleasant and meaningful. Somehow, women understood each other better in momentous circumstances than men.

The road from Paru's home to the beach was decorated with specially styled coconut leaf canopies and arches of fresh flowers. Incense burnt in thousands along the route. People thronged both sides of the route in gossipy curiosity. Some women wept while everyone threw jasmine and marigold petals at the bride. Some of the chiefs and rajas of Keralaputra arrived with their entourage on elephant, horse and palanquin while some were represented by their ambassadors. Their gifts and largesse were loaded on to a second barge dedicated to the secure storage of royal goods. The hold reeked of an assortment of spices packed in massive jars, baskets and linen bags.

Much to Sankaran's amusement, a final feast on the shores of the harbour displayed a flamboyant populace whose raucous songs and appetite for food and drink left the Judean guests quite intimidated. For the occasion, Sankaran wore a beautiful red tunic that the tailors of Vanchi had sewn upon Paru's instructions with the red Judean cloth he had been gifted. Iddo the Seer and his entourage felt honoured.

"Perhaps we ought to build a synagogue here along this coast sometime," Iddo mused. "The Greeks and the Phoenicians already have a temple or two in Keralaputra."

A Judean fleet of galleys awaited the barges a few miles away in the Arabian Sea. With the blowing of bugles, the barges indicated their readiness to receive the royal bride.

"Mother, this is your *asa*. Your wish," whispered Paru. "I shall prevail upon the great prince Abijah to name our child Asa in memory of you, were I to bear him a son." She wiped a tear before embracing the old lady. Sankaran blessed his little sister who now cried brazenly.

With Paru on board, the barges lurched forward against the current. Iddo the Seer bowed again one last time at the multitude. Then almost instantly, the shores of Muziris began to clear as the crowds retreated inland.

Only Sankaran remained on the deserted beach. He found the tallest coconut trees close to an incline on the far north, which submerged in the high tide and deposited fertile sand at the foot of the palms. Scaling one of them he frantically waved a bright red tunic knowing that Paru, far out at sea, would certainly be looking out for him one last time.

RETURN OF A NATIVE

Winter in the Malabar region is always followed by a period of unbearable heat and humidity that lasts for nearly four months. The strip of land that Parashurama had reclaimed lies parched beside the very waters from where it rose, yearning for rain. The pitted red laterite rocks of the region absorb the heat sending it up in shimmering waves. Even the sea breeze laden with moisture and salt gives no relief. Only a rare pre-monsoon shower resulting from a localized thunderstorm would occasionally spray modest droplets, almost like an act of kindness. Water levels in wells drop drastically, flies from ripening fruits multiply and all forms of creeping and crawling creatures from scorpions to centipedes and cobras are out in the open, constantly shifting location for air, shade, water and relief. Until the south-west monsoon, driven up from the Indian Ocean and the Arabian Sea, strikes the palm-lined coast in a thunderous rapture.

But before the arrival of this year's rains, a pair of fully-battened sails were visible on the horizon headed for the harbour, driven by winds and currents that preceded the violent storm of the oncoming monsoon. It was late afternoon.

From his lookout, Sankaran saw the easily distinguishable Chinese vessels of enormous size. It was low-tide and the heavily laden junks could not reach the harbour without being beached. Sampans or smaller boats would have to be deployed to bring anyone ashore. But no such boat left the junks for the remaining of daylight. It was past sunset in the evening when one such boat finally left the leading junk, rowed by two oarsmen. From his perch Sankaran saw a lone figure seated in the centre, in a meditative posture that neither bore the resemblance to a trader or a ship-hand.

As the sampan skimmed on to the sandy beach, the oarsmen bowed respectfully at the old man who alighted. Though he appeared to be a Buddhist monk he did not look one bit Chinese from his features. He was dark, his baldness having receded all the way to the back of his head, sparing only a strip of long grey hair at the back and on the sides of his head. He had a bushy beard of considerable length, stood erect despite his obvious age and alighted carrying a bundle of personal belongings on one shoulder and a single wooden slipper or *paduka* in the other. Sankaran watched as the two Chinese youth prostrated themselves on the sand for his blessings before they started back.

"Stopped by Muziris only to bring this strange man ashore?" wondered Sankaran. "Or are they intending to drop anchor here?"

Even as he wondered about the two strange crafts bobbing far out in the sea, Sankaran was startled by the behaviour of the old man with the *paduka*. In the growing darkness he stood very much at the same spot where he had alighted on the beach, but appeared to be staring directly at the very point of the coconut tree on which Sankaran was perched.

"How, by Parashurama, did he spot me?" wondered Sankaran. "I haven't moved an inch and I thought all this foliage had me sufficiently camouflaged...."

The old man's eyes appeared to glow with a greenish-blue light. He made no gesture, no motion. He only stared steadfastly at Sankaran as if he was trying to penetrate the darkness of the entwined branches of the palm foliage. Sankaran became convinced that the old man had spotted him, strange as it might seem even for a cat or an owl to have discovered him perched motionless behind the heavily overlapping pinnate leaves of the palm.

For a moment Sankaran averted his eyes from the man below to the sea in the distance. Against the darkening sky he could see lanterns begin to glow on the junks. This was characteristic of most Chinese vessels that docked at Muziris. They prided in their variety and array of oil and wax based lanterns and kept their vessels well-lit through the night.

When his glance returned to the beach he was again startled to note that the stranger was suddenly gone. Instantly, as if he had vanished into the sand where he had stood a moment ago.

Not sure if the darkness was fuddling his vision, Sankaran silently slithered down the tree. As his feet hit the ground he searched about him in all directions. The man was nonchalantly walking away from him at the far side of the grove in the direction of the road to town leading out of the harbour.

"He must know someone here," thought Sankaran still trailing the lone figure in the Buddhist attire. The man led Sankaran to a small Hindu temple that offered a little thatched shanty for pilgrims to rest. Nobody appeared to pay much attention to the ascetic looking figure who squatted in one corner of the shed, now back in his meditative posture.

Sankaran returned home that night a little disappointed. And he might have forgotten the old man in a day or two but for a chain of events that began an hour before dawn broke over the town of Muziris.

It began with a heart-rending scream that woke up most of the neighbourhood followed by a commotion of loud urgent voices. It had woken up his mother and little brother. Peering out of his window he could see confusing silhouettes of running men and a fire that appeared to have broken out in the town far away.

His mother was at his back in an instant. "You are not venturing out," she spoke firmly. "Someone's house or shack is on fire and there are enough men out there to put it off."

"We'll know in the morning," his little brother intervened, squeezing his head through the wooden lattice. "From here it looks like the fire might be close to my *gurukula*."

"Okay, I'm not going out," Sankaran assured them. "But I am going to accompany you to the *gurukula* in the morning. We need to know what happened, don't we?"

They did not quite fall asleep again after that. The first light of the sun had barely broken through the cashew and mango trees around the house when another commotion brought grave news from Muziris. News arrived at Vanchi that the port had been attacked by pirates. Chinese pirates who had dropped anchor off the coast. The local chieftain's sentries had been alerted the moment the raid started and several Nairs had rushed to the harbour to protect the town and the stockpiles of goods stored near the quay for export. A sword fight had broken out in which a number of the Nair militia and pirates were injured but the Chinese had managed to load at least four bags of pepper, a basket or two of cardamom and a sack of cinnamon on to their sampans. They were pursued by local fishermen ferrying Nair combatants in war canoes and snake boats that could have easily outpaced the slow moving sampans. But as they approached the Chinese ships, a rapid volley of arrows from sharp shooting Chinese archers kept the native boats at bay.

Sankaran's thoughts went back to the previous evening. Was that old man who had come ashore in the Buddhist garb a spy? A veteran pirate in the guise of a dark-skinned local who had been disembarked to reconnoitre the area before signalling to the Chinese to raid the harbour?

Leaving his little brother at the *gurukula* he headed to the small temple where he had last seen the dark stranger. As he had expected the man was not there. Sankaran could not rest until he had reported the matter to the Nair chieftain.

A band of about a dozen armed Nairs soon followed Sankaran through the streets of Muziris in search of the elusive monk. Armed with swords and shields, daggers and spears, the warriors marched through the town, surveying and enquiring at every possible crossroad and exit-ways of the town. Sankaran was just coming to the conclusion that having achieved his purpose, the old man must have ferried back to the junk much before the pirates raided the dockside, when a Nair suddenly pointed towards a coconut grove. They all saw him. The monk appeared to be meditating again, this time under the shade of young palms that grew bountifully just outside the town.

"Let's nab him!" yelled the leader as they broke into a run towards the grove. Sankaran followed the energetic Nair warriors as they spread out to prevent their quarry from escaping.

"Don't hurt an unarmed man!" Sankaran yelled at them fearful of what the well trained band would do to the pitiable looking ascetic.

As they approached closer, the old man opened his eyes. It was a strange and penetrating pair of eyes that stared at the oncoming onslaught, but the man himself appeared to be calm and did not move from his meditative posture at the foot of the tree. A pair of Nairs made a grab for him. Still seated, the old man made a flurry of movements with his hands. To Sankaran's astonishment both Nair warriors were flung a few feet into the air, landing hard on the sandy ground in cries of pain and shock.

Recovering from that initial surprise, three more Nairs surrounded the monk, swords drawn to inflict a debilitating injury. The old man was up on his feet in an instant, easily evading the sword blades that were aimed at him. With the grace of a dancer he suddenly bounced back and disarmed each of the swordsmen with intricate movements of his hands, locking their arms and trapping their wrists so painfully that they screamed before dropping their swords to the ground.

Sankaran was aghast. Five of among the best Nair warriors he had known in Muziris lay on the ground writhing in severe pain while the old man calmly dusted his yellow robe and looked enquiringly at the remaining seven.

In a voice that was grim and coarse with age, the old man spoke. "We could talk, if you wish," in clear and lucid Tamil.

But despite Sankaran's attempts to stop the Nairs from attacking the old man again, one more assault was made by the leader of the band, a skilled soldier who had never been beaten in single combat by anyone in Keralaputra. Spear in hand he approached the monk feinting and manoeuvring in quick darts and thrusts as he closed in. For a moment the old man appeared to have become impaled at the end of the spear, but in the next moment it became apparent that he had trapped the sharp end of the spear in the folds of his robe, making it impossible for the Nair to retrieve it. Abandoning the spear, the warrior plunged a machete at the old man's neck. The monk side-stepped with ease and landed a blow with the palm of his hand on the young warrior's temple. He crumpled to the ground unconscious, leaving the old man to calmly disentangle the end of the spear that was thrust at him from the folds of his garment.

Sankaran trembled. "Please, please stop this violence…"

The six Nairs who watched their leader fall now slowly placed their weapons on the ground in astonishment and surrender.

Sankaran spoke immediately. "We…they…we believe you are one of the pirates who raided the dockyard early this morning!"

The old man looked at Sankaran with amusement. "And you look like the one who instigated these men to suspect me," he spoke sardonically to Sankaran. "The meek and the unarmed once again proves to be the most dangerous, as the great Maha Bali found out at a dear cost many, many years ago!"

Sankaran remained speechless.

"It is true, I requested the Chinese captain to take me aboard their ship when I heard they were sailing to Malabar. That they were pirates was not my concern. My purpose was to reach here."

"They seem to show a lot of respect towards you," Sankaran remarked remembering the little drama at the beach the evening before.

"Oh, so it was you on the coconut tree?" the monk now regarded Sankaran with more amusement. "I would not loot and plunder my own land now, would I?"

"Are you from these parts?" enquired Sankaran.

As the six Nair soldiers went over to help their compatriots back on their feet, the Buddhist monk spoke to Sankaran. "I am a Buddhist as you have probably guessed. I will heal your friends. But I wish to be left alone after that. I shall then let these men go unharmed despite what they intended to do to me. You have my word. I am not a pirate nor have I brought the pirates here of my own accord. I was merely a passenger in their ship."

He walked across to each fallen man on the ground and applied pressure on specific points on their bodies with his hands, sometimes rubbing his palms together vigorously to generate heat, sometimes applying pressure with his fingertips on their temples and spinal cord. They all stood up one by one. Then following a stern gesture by the incredible stranger they picked up their weapons and walked away silently, mystified by the old man's dexterity and composure.

"I am not a pirate," he told them as they departed. "The pirates do not speak Tamil. Certainly not as well as I do. Be off. Your target should have been those ships that raided your dockyard. Not this unarmed old man."

Sankaran apologized to the retreating band of Nairs whose scowls and grimaces made him exceedingly uncomfortable. When they had left the old man smiled at Sankaran. "Not your fault for having done what you did. I was the only suspect the Nairs could have unleashed their fury upon after the wily Chinese got the better of them."

"Now they do have a bone to pick with me," admitted Sankaran with worry, wondering what the reaction of the chieftain would be once word got around that he had led the unwitting Nairs into an unexpected defeat at the hands of an old and unarmed man.

"Where did you learn to fight like that?" Sankaran asked, his eyes wide with wonder.

"In this very land where I was born," replied the monk. "Except that I have practiced every technique a hundred thousand times more than anyone I know. I have improved, evolved and honed my skills to a level that my own teachers may never comprehend.

"You were born here?"

"My name was Jayavarman when I left these shores many decades ago," replied the monk. "Yes, many years before you were born. It must be over forty years ago, abiding by my teacher the great and venerable Pragyatara. I was her favourite student of Mahayana Buddhism. The *Sangha* named me Bodhitara but as she departed for Lanka she blessed me with a new name, Bodhidharma. It was her wish that I travel to China. I am the third son of your king who rules from Kanchipuram. I am now back after having established the *dharma* in the Chinese kingdoms."

Sankaran bowed. It was well known that the old Pallava king that ruled from Kanchipuram had a son who had left for some foreign land many years ago.

"Your father, the king and all your brothers will be pleased to hear of your return," Sankaran remarked.

"It is of no consequence, anymore. I am in no hurry to seek them," Bodhidharma replied. "Come let us walk across to your house. Perhaps you can provide me with some nourishment. I have not eaten for a while now. Is there any generosity left in the land of Maha Bali?"

Sankaran felt elated. The joy showed on his face. "It will be an honour," he exclaimed.

"Why do you carry a single *paduka*?" Sankaran enquired with curiosity. Are you searching for the other?"

Bodhidharma laughed. "It is a long story. But let me explain briefly. At the age of six, I was sent to Mahodayapuram where I was to learn both Hindu texts and the teachings of Buddha. As a prince I was also expected to learn combat and techniques of warfare. However, my mind was inclined towards Buddhism and medicine and I excelled in these two areas of study. But as a prince, I could not avoid or reject the martial traditions. One day, when I was about ten years of age, I listened to a discourse on the protection and preservation of life and came to the conclusion that as much as medicines cure and heal, the nature of society was such that no learning, indeed no peace was possible without quelling violence by means of experiencing the nature of violence itself. This sparked my interest in every form of human and animal aggression and the means of subdueing it. Having gained some proficiency in the various subjects of study, I ventured out to teach. I travelled as far as Persia, Mongolia and China, teaching meditation and healing people. I finally retreated to an excellent monastery on a mountain in the forests of Shaoshi. The people in the region revered me as one would revere a teacher. But their tradition also constitutes some age old beliefs that were very inconvenient for me. On of them being their belief that, in the event of my death, they would continue to receive my blessings only if I was buried in their soil. I had been among these people for many years, and by then, was preparing to leave for home, satisfied that I had completed by duties as the venerable Pragyatara desired of me. Someone in a moment of desperation thought it necessary to poison my food so that I die in their soil. I was forewarned of the conspiracy as well as the nature of the poison that was mixed in the food I would partake. I went into a state of *samadhi*. Presuming me to be dead, they buried me. Twelve hours later I dug my way out of my intended grave, but could not retrieve one of my *padukas*. I left it there for posterity to discover, if such an event was to come to pass, of my having departed from China. On the other hand, as long as they do not discover I am gone, their belief that I lie buried in their soil must give them some contentment. So, what I carry with me today is one *paduka* which I was determined to bring back to Mahodayapuram as a reminder to myself of the nature of man and my close shave with death, in a way neither my study of religion nor my expertise in combat had prepared me for. Look at the paradox. I was being murdered for the sheer love they had for me."

"A final lesson from the very people you reached out to, all your life to teach," Sankaran remarked. "Will we ever understand the nature of the human being? Learning has no end!"

"And while I reside here at Muziris, perhaps you can begin to learn how to defend yourself," Bodhidharma suggested, joining Sankaran for a long walk to Vanchi. "You appear to be a peaceful kind. I am sure you will need to learn some skills before you run into the Nairs again."

"For which I shall forever remain grateful," replied Sankaran with sincerity. "In fact, I have always wondered how one learns the use of a sword. Especially a strange sword that I possess, inherited by my forefathers. A sword that has a flexible blade. The story goes that it belonged to a wise king from some kingdom in the western seas. He was the only one capable of using it."

"That is interesting," replied Bodhidharma. "I have long heard of a rare weapon called a "wave". An *urumi*. Its blade is said to imitate the waves of the sea. A weapon that is more liable to kill you unless you tame it first. Its flexibility is its drawback and a detriment to the user. Once you master it you turn the litheness of the blade into an advantage hundred-fold. Let us see if I can find a way to wield it. You may in the beginning wish to stay a safe distance from me while I attempt to swing and brandish it."

"Oh, don't you worry about that, sir. I know where I will be most safe while you try out my sword, as long as the *urumi* doesn't cut down the tree." replied Sankaran as they walked home.

A Boy With A Mission

"**O**ur teacher Chanak is leaving along with his family for Nalanda," announced Sankaran's little brother Vasu, crestfallen by the prospect of losing his dear friend and schoolmate Vishnugupta, son of master Chanak.

The siblings were seated on the beach watching fishermen setting out into the sea, pushing their long canoes against the tide. It was mid-morning and the fishermen were on their second foray. Vasu was expecting Vishnugupta to show up any moment and dreaded the thought of parting with the Brahmin boy for what might be the last time in their lives.

Sankaran tried to console his little brother. "Guru Chanak has never considered himself sufficiently learned to teach all of you through your adolescence. He yearned to learn more of the subtle philosophies of the Vedic traditions. This, as you know, could take many years to study and imbibe. So he has decided to take his family along to live with him for the many years that he requires to spend at the University of Nalanda."

The little boy continued to look forlorn. "But I will miss Vishnugupta."

"Oh, but you always had me believe he was a bit of a bully, Vasu," Sankaran countered.

"Well, a kind of learned bully. He has radical ideas as to how things ought to be. He has a choice of words and an enviable vocabulary which he flaunts. But for a twelve-year-old he is very intelligent."

"So how does he believe things ought to be?" enquired Sankaran patiently.

"For example, he believes we could do better if the residents of Keralaputra ruled this strip of land all on their own instead of being vassals of the Tamilagam. From Gokarna to Kanya Kumari we have, over the years, developed a distinct language, lifestyle and culture. This reclaimed land is Parashurama country. Distinct from the Tamilagam."

"And you believe that too?" Sankaran looked at his little brother with curiosity. "Do you realize what you're saying is paramount to defying the Chola King."

"The Tamil Chola king," Vasu pointed out.

"What young Vishnugupta is suggesting is sedition. The Tamil rulers won't take it kindly if they were to hear even a whisper of this kind of talk. They are not very different from us. We only speak a slightly different dialect," Sankaran tried to explain.

"Vishnugupta believes that in the ancient days a very benevolent king called Maha Bali ruled over this region. He was no Tamil king. He was a Malayalee like you and me. During his reign this region did not know any poverty. He was just and powerful. There was peace and prosperity."

"That was many, many years ago. Oh, maybe even some millennia ago. From where does little Vishnugupta get these belligerent ideas today? Catch a Malayalee dynasty coming to power in this day and age. As long as our chieftains pay the annual and seasonal tribute we are allowed to live in peace within the Tamilagam. What is wrong with that?"

"Vasu!" a shrill voice came from behind them, from the path that led to the seafront. A shaven headed boy appeared in a smart starched *mundu* with a gold embroidery along its border. The *poonool* or sacred thread over his left shoulder and the sandalwood paste on his forehead showed him to be of the highest caste in the land. But his pock-marked face, determined jaw and lithe muscular body made him look older than his twelve years.

"It's Vishnugupta! Come to say his farewell," cried Vasu as he stood up to greet his schoolmate.

"We start tomorrow," Vishnugupta cheerily announced. "The caravans have gathered in town. We will join them at dawn and we will be somewhere high up in the *ghats* in some forest shelter by nightfall. The morning after we will descend into the northern kingdom of Mahishasura. It will be over four months before we reach Pataliputra in the Magadha kingdom far towards the north where my father will seek the king's permission to study and teach at Nalanda."

"Who rules Magadha?" enquired Sankaran.

"The Nanda dynasty, my father tells me. A very young but mighty king, Dhana Nanda has an army of 200,000 infantry, 80,000 cavalry, 8,000 war chariots, and 6,000 war elephants. Dwarfs the army of our Tamil king by 1 to 10 in every division." Vishnugupta laughed aloud.

"So it is true what the Yavana and Farsi merchants speak of at our Muziris harbour!" remarked Sankaran. "They say that Al Xandre and his Yavana army panicked when they realized they were nearly decimated by a minor tributary serving under the mighty Nandas a year ago. When they finally signed a treaty with Purushottama of Paurava, I've heard it said that the Yavana soldiers rebelled and ran scared when Al Xandre tried to convince them to march further east into the Magadha kingdom."

"Had Al Xandre done so, they say no Yavana would have returned alive from the campaign. Such is the might of the Nandas." Vishnugupta added, clearing a patch of sand of dry seaweeds and shells before satisfying himself that it was clean enough to sit.

Vasu dragged himself on the sand towards his Brahmin companion. "Vishnu, I have wondered why our ancient king Maha Bali was punished by God. He was a benevolent ruler. Pious and generous."

"Politics," murmured Vishnugupta, causing both Vasu and Sankaran to laugh out aloud.

"Never underestimate the strength and intentions of the meek," Vishnugupta continued in his usual candour. "It is metaphorically believed that God disguised as the poor and docile Vamana placed his foot on our poor Maha Bali's head to vanquish him into the underworld. But before that happened, Maha Bali begged of God to allow him to visit his subjects in Keralaputra once a year. Today we celebrate Maha Bali's annual visit to this land as Onam, arguably the best day in a Malayalee's calendar. I am sure my father will celebrate Onam at Pataliputra every year that we live there, which will be of much curiosity to the locals. That was smart of Maha Bali. He caused every Malayalee from then to eternity to remember him and feast in his name wherever on earth they may be."

"That is true. Onam will be celebrated by a Malayalee in any place that he finds himself," Sankaran confirmed. "I do know that Malayalees throughout the Tamilagam celebrate Onam. Even an atheist Malayalee will celebrate Onam day with a feast. It is not about religion. It is about his roots. Maha Bali certainly saw to that."

"Maha Bali appears to have achieved a kind of immortality in the bargain!" Vishnugupta remarked. "The festival of Onam transcends religion. So it is bound to survive as long as there are Malayalees on earth."

"Like the coconut tree," Sankaran quipped. Eighteen of the twenty six different dishes cooked for the Onam feast require the coconut kernel or its oil to prepare. Maha Bali and the coconut tree are inseparable."

"So it is to a powerful kingdom that your father has chosen to take you," Vasu remarked. "How do you think they would treat outsiders from the south?"

"How should they treat a Brahmin? They should know that better," Vishnugupta retorted haughtily.

Sankaran tried to placate the proud youth. 'Be that as it may Vishnu, but when you reach Magadha, please keep your seditious ideas to yourself. Magadha is not Keralaputra. The Nandas will have you and your father packing as quickly and surely as their sheer might had Al Xandre and the Yavanas retreating back to Persia over the mountains."

Vishnugupta regarded Sankaran and Vasu for a while. A slow smile appeared on his countenance. "So you have been discussing my ideas of a Malayalee nation have you? Well, I will have to forsake that brilliant idea as I am going away to Pataliputra. But it is an idea, isn't it?"

Sankaran was the first to respond. "Fighting the Tamil king would require a large army. You are being reckless and impulsive with that kind of talk."

"You don't need a large army," Vishnugupta countered. "All you need to do to begin with, is to simply plant a seed in people's minds. A seed. A fertile idea. An idea whose time has come. Your idea must become a convincing and viable propaganda. Turn the tide of people's thoughts and you will have already won more than half the battle."

Vasu raised his eyebrows at his brother to take note of the unusually mature and radical doctrine of his schoolmate.

"You think we have leaders of that calibre and the resources to stand up against the Cholas?" Sankaran sounded incredulous.

"Leaders will sprout on their own," Vishnugupta raised a hand in a classical gesture that indicated an innate ability at oratory and drama. "You need only to harness their energies towards a common goal. The war machinery in the form of resources, men, weapons and field-rations will begin to pour in and accumulate once the strategy for the campaign is identified. Your idea and doctrine must be lucid and appealing. Anyway, why should I go on with this? I will not be here to see such a thing happen and neither of you have the necessary will to follow through with my idea."

"It is not even necessary," Sankaran replied with an air of finality. "We are quite content as a people under the Tamil dominance. So far the Chola dynasty have not really been oppressive in the least. Changing the order of things does not behove us well."

"Things change all the same. Times change. Circumstances change. And with time so will our opinions and needs," Vishnugupta seemed to be talking to himself staring at the horizon. He was silent for some time, playfully twisting the sacred thread running across his torso around his forefinger. He appeared disinterested in continuing any discussion about any seditious plans for now. "I do hope the Nandas of Magadha are kind to us. My father has great hopes in that kingdom. To be able to study at Nalanda and teach there has been his greatest dream since childhood. He has had long discourses with every sage, seer and Buddhist monk who travelled from Nalanda to Keralaputra."

The fishermen once again appeared in the horizon, their boats tactfully dragging the nets towards the shore.

"Looks like a good catch," Sankaran remarked as he left the two boys and walked towards a coconut palm to get a better view of the sea.

"Brother Sankaran. He belongs to the old school, Vasu," whispered Vishnugupta. "Drastic and dynamic ideas do not sit well with him. It is a kind of complacency."

Vasu was not sure. This fiery son of Chanak was the most rebellious Kautilya Brahmin he had encountered. Logical and practical as his ideas sounded they were always a little unsettling.

"I cannot bear the sight and smell of dying fish," Vishnugupta remarked, suddenly standing up. "Come, it is time to say our goodbyes. Father will be waiting for me. Mother will be expecting my to help with the packing."

Vasu felt a lump in his throat as Vishnugupta hugged him one last time before departing.

"God willing, we shall meet again," was all that Vishnugupta said.

Kautilya Brahmins were few in the region, serving only as teachers and most of them, like Vishnugupta, had migrated north. Namboothiri Brahmins were rapidly replenishing the temples of Keralaputra with new priests and adherents of the Malayalee way of life. Staunch in their practice of religious tradition, they would not expect a Nair to hug or even touch them.

But Vishnugupta Kautilya embraced his dear classmate Vasu before departing. And as he passed beneath the palm, the Brahmin boy waved up at Sankaran.

"Keep well and safe, son of Chanak!" Sankaran waved back at him. "Be mindful of what you say and do as you travel from Keralaputra to Pataliputra. Your ideas are nothing short of upheavals. The Nandas won't take kindly of your queer ideas. But come back one day to this land. We will miss you dearly."

"At least I know where to find you when I return, dear brother," Vishnugupta smiled as he disappeared down the sandy path.

"Time for us to head home too," Sankaran tried to make some commonplace conversation with his tear-stricken little brother. "A nice haul these fisher folk have made today."

"There is something very appealing about Vishnugupta," Vasu exclaimed not responding to his brother. "His mind is always on to something larger and unachievable by people like us. And he always sounds so sure of himself."

"If they ever cross paths, God help the Nanda king!" Sankaran muttered under his breath as he led Vasu home.

HEALING HANDS

S ankaran loved the comfort, the privacy, the shade, the breeze, the magnificent view, the gentle rocking, the cool tender-coconut water and the toddy, all of which his perch on a single tree provided. Harnessed firmly, his limbs were free to re-tie his turban or drum-up a beat to sing the many Malayalam songs he knew. The songs were ballads that extolled everything from the size of a local Jewish merchant's nose to the jiggly behind of the neighbouring village's belle.

On an uneventful day, his raucous voice could be heard many miles down the sandy beach irrespective of which direction the wind was blowing. But then again, very few days of Sankaran's life remained uneventful.

"I doubt if they have doctors here."

This uncertain statement was made in a hoarse voice by a middle-aged gentleman as he disembarked from a Roman ship with the most sea-worn men Sankaran had ever seen.

"Pickled in salt and as ravenous as rats," thought Sankaran as he slid down from his coconut tree perch, his Malabar machete in hand.

"Son, my brothers need medicine," the man tried to explain to Sankaran. "I doubt if they will live if they are not treated immediately."

Sankaran could barely discern what the man was saying as he seemed to be suffering from some kind of throat infection. His voice hissed like a loud whisper in his struggle to communicate.

The ship that lay anchored in Muziris harbour between two Phoenician vessels that midday had seen a perilous voyage due to a minor maritime miscalculation. Though the passage to the Malabar Coast was a well-known sea route to the Yehudis, Yavanas, Farsis, Romans and many other seafarers from the west for over a thousand years, they would only set out from the African coast at a time of the year that provided the most favourable eastward winds. The size and speed of their ships, the weight of their cargo and the experience of their sailors all played a part in the expert navigation that the Arabian Sea demanded of them. They understood that the principal season to avoid being caught in a storm was when the South West monsoon swept over the sea in May and June.

The Roman ship that came ashore that day had set out from a port somewhere in the Sinai Peninsula. It had lost itself at sea following a monsoon storm and drifted aimlessly north for over two weeks before it found the company of two Phoenician vessels that were proficiently steering for Muziris. Stating their plight and begging for food they were guided eastward once again by the Phoenicians, coming ashore in the middle of a raging monsoon.

The man who had lost his voice was bearded and his long hair fell in locks over his shoulder. He appeared to be Yehudi from his clothes and appearance but spoke several other languages.

Sankaran gestured and pointed in the direction of the town and accompanied the travel-worn men to the road that led to the Yehudi quarter of Muziris. He hoped his young Yehudi friend Matan would be able to take care of the men.

Matan was at home. But one look at the men convinced the young Yehudi that they required immediate treatment. They looked pale, depressed, and had difficulty walking. Some had open, suppurating wounds, had lost teeth and appeared jaundiced and feverish. Sankaran was familiar with these symptoms. He had witnessed many voyagers landing at Muziris with the same sickness. Something the sea did to them.

"Perhaps the Nair *tharavad* down the road would be able to help them," Matan advised. "They have mendicants and are knowledgeable in the use of herbs and medicines. This is not a contagious disease as far as I know."

They marched slowly again, their bearded leader leading them chanting some kind of prayer.

"What prayer is that Yehudi chanting?" enquired Sankaran.

"Not anything I've heard before," replied Matan walking alongside Sankaran. "He may be a Yehudi, but his prayers are not anything akin to what we recite. I perceive that he is calling upon his father in heaven and his dead friend Yesu."

"That's unusual," remarked Sankaran. "A dead friend called Yesu to come to their aid? Strange are the people this sea brings us. What is his name?"

Matan spoke briefly to the elder leading the procession, then turned to Sankaran. "His name is Yehuda. He is also called Tauma for I think he has a twin brother elsewhere."

Following the duo, the twelve men dragged themselves wearily to the gates of a large Nair house set deep in a heavily foliaged and well-guarded compound. The armed guards spoke to Sankaran and obtained permission from within for the foreigners to enter. They were then ushered into a large, sprawling shed that was roofed and water-proofed with intertwining coconut palm leaves and provided with cushioned seats to recline on. Erected in the Nair compound set apart from the main house, it was a place where the *tharavad* elders interacted with traders, foreign visitors and the public in general. Plumeria trees and jasmine bushes provided a sweet aroma whenever the wind blew. Cool drinking water was served from an adjacent well.

Sankaran spoke to the Nair elders who had assembled in the courtyard curiously looking in the direction of the bedraggled foreigners in the shed.

"It's nothing contagious," Sankaran reassured them. "It's the same disease these sailors pick up in the sea. The one the Romans suffered from some months ago."

"Aha, *pitham!*" exclaimed one of them. "A deficiency arising from a lack of green vegetables and fresh fruit."

"They need a decent, well balanced meal and perhaps some medication," suggested Sankaran. "A day or two more at sea might have been too late."

"Whatever, our *vaidian* will correctly diagnose their disease however bad it might be," spoke an elder. "Do not worry. This *tharavad* does not lack charity. But they will have to wait awhile. The *vaidian* is attending to the head of the family right now. He has been injured in a duel and is in great pain. In the course of defeating his adversary he was injured by the opponent's sword in three parts of his body. The wounds have internal consequences and require some complicated surgery."

Matan was informed of it and the tired dozen in the shed were requested to wait. While they waited warm medicated water was despatched in a number of enormous bronze vessels from the main house for the visitors to wash themselves. Servant boys were despatched to help the men in their task of cleaning their weary bodies and wounds beside the well. The process lasted over an hour, but the foreigners looked relieved. In the meanwhile, hot rice gruel, stir-fried vegetables and pickled goose-berry were served in the shed for them to eat. Sankaran watched them devour the simple warm meal with relish.

Tauma their leader watched in silence. His sore throat did not allow him to speak but he appeared pleased with the developments. When they had eaten the *vaidian* appeared in the courtyard. He looked troubled as he engaged the Nairs of the household in deep consultation.

Sankaran, Matan and even the foreign travellers in the shed could gather that all was not well with the wounded patient inside the house.

"Could I see the man?" came a hoarse whisper.

Matan turned to Tauma. "The injured man is lying inside. His condition has worsened."

"But could I please see the man?" Tauma insisted again. Matan spoke to Sankaran.

"Impossible," Sankaran replied. "Why would the Nair household allow some miserable visitor to attend to their family head? What does he wish to do?"

Matan debated for a while with Tauma.

"He might be able to ease the man's pain," explained Matan. "It might be worth a try."

Sankaran stared in disbelief. "You want me to put this proposal to the family?"

Matan nodded shrugging his shoulders neutrally.

The discourse on the courtyard was now getting louder as Sankaran strolled up to them.

"The Yehudi foreigner offers to help the *karnavar* in whatever way he can…" began Sankaran causing the multitude to stop their animated debate abruptly. They stared at him in silence.

"I thought it was they who needed our *vaidian*," retorted one of the Nairs.

"If it is to deal with pain, he insists he might be able to help." Sankaran explained.

Another silence followed. It was the *vaidian* who spoke now in an incredulous voice staring at the shed that housed the visitors. "A dispossessed and deprived lot they appear to me. Are they carrying medication of some foreign kind? I must examine the ingredients before they are used or consumed by the *karnavar*.

The Nair group now approached the shed peering at the bearded men seated inside. All but Tauma stood up respectfully. The *vaidian* entered and looked about him enquiringly, raising his eyebrows at

Sankaran. Matan immediately spoke to Tauma and announced that they carried no medicine of any kind.

"Then how does he expect to rid the *karnavar* of pain?" the *vaidian* wished to know.

Tauma raised his two bare hands open-palmed at the Nairs. "With these."

A disbelieving and distressed expression crossed the *vaidian's* face.

"A masseur?" he enquired finally. "This is not a case for a masseur. There are deep open wounds that are beginning to fester."

Tauma's hands remained in the air. His eyes unblinking, almost challenging the *vaidian's* disbelief. The rest of the Nairs looked on incredulously.

Finally, it was the *vaidian* who relented. "Bring the *karnavar* to the courtyard outside and let us see what our Yehudi friend can do."

The *karnavar* was conveyed out on to the courtyard on a palanquin. He was squirming in pain and groaning. His naked muscular body was wrapped with innumerable cotton bandages soaked in herbal extracts. Coagulate blood and pus oozed through the fabric. His attendants carried him off the palanquin and laid him on a grass mat that was rolled out on the courtyard. For the first time a number of anxious and tear-stricken women stepped out of the house. The atmosphere was funereal.

The sagacious looking Tauma stepped out of the visitor's shed and bowed humbly at the feverish *karnavar*. Kneeling beside the warrior he meditated and seemed to be in prayer for a few minutes. Then he placed the palm of his right hand over the incapacitated man's head and held it there as if attempting to transfer some unseen force from his own body into the prostrate figure writhing on the mat.

Minutes passed. The audience remained silent observing every move that foreigner made. Tauma's lips moved in silent prayer. His hand moved slowly to the patient's forehead, then his throat, chest and groin. The struggling and twisting stopped and the *karnavar* began breathing more easily. His eyes opened as if he had begun to feel some kind of relief. Some more anxious minutes passed before Tauma finally announced to Matan. "He will rest peacefully now. The pain has subsided. Let him sleep."

To the astonishment of Sankaran and the Nairs the *karnavar* stopped moving and appeared to have fallen into a deep sleep.

"I will see him yet again," Tauma spoke as he stood up. "The worst is over. Continue to give him water for he will thirst for it all night. Tomorrow this man will be up and walking."

When Matan translated Tauma's words, the women muffled their wails of relief. The Nairs in the courtyard gazed upon the bearded Tauma with renewed respect and awe. The perplexed *vaidian* sat down to feel the patient's pulse. "Yes, I believe it is working. He is indeed in deep and restful slumber."

As the *karnavar* was carried back into the house, the *vaidian* followed Tauma and Sankaran back into the shed. His voice was now reverential and nervous. "A nice *mantra*. Indeed, a divine *mantra*."

Matan tried to translate for Tauma. But the Yehudi ignored the interpretation. "It is not I. It is our father in heaven and his son who sends the Holy Spirit to heal. My hands only spell my intention."

The *vaidian* looked sceptical. "Eh, then you could have spared your men this detour and healed their sickness too, could you not?" he enquired obliquely.

For a moment Sankaran wondered about that too. But Tauma spoke without hesitation. "My men don't suffer from a disease. They suffer from a deficiency. Weeks of deprivation at sea has depleted essential nutrients from their bodies. I sought the help of our father to keep them alive. And thus they have survived and lived. It is for timely and correct nourishment that I have accepted the kind hospitality of the *tharavad*. In the hope that cure would be affected as nature intended, with the right balance of a special variety of food and water. I knew that they of the *tharavad* who have knowledge of the malady that afflicts seafarers would not go wrong in the treatment of their guests. Do not compare it with the inflicted injuries of a soldier whose wounds are causing his life to ebb away. Infection was setting in and poisoning his system. I have the ability to cleanse a human body by the mere laying of my hands. For the Holy Spirit that pervades all of us is a benevolent one."

It had been another eventful day for Sankaran.

THE ASCETIC

A few kilometres west of the village of Sasalam flowed the river Poorna. While deer, hog and bison occasionally came to drink water here, they steered clear of Sasalam, where the deep mud-banks posed a veritable threat. For in the currents of the Poorna lurked fearsome crocodiles, invisible to man or beast. The animals found it safer to drink from the shallow shore of the river further upstream where the stream curved, where wide sand banks sprouted grass to graze upon and the waters were clear as crystal.

It has been said that crocodiles and human beings shall never mix. Crocodiles are known to be cold, innately impulsive reptiles, motivated purely by hunger and self-preservation. They are aggressive by nature and one of the few animals who perceive human beings as food. But our Sankaran was about to learn that this belief was not wholly correct.

It all began one summer morning about the turn of the 8th century CE. Sankaran was atop, lopping coconuts for a local Nair landlord. The bare-bodied, pot-bellied landlord stood with his back to the edge of the river, flanked by armed guards, shouting instructions to the gatherers below filling bamboo baskets with ripe coconuts. From his vantage point Sankaran suddenly observed a large crocodile stealthily skimming the water, approaching the oblivious landlord, in a bid to drag the man into the river. Sankaran shouted out to the landlord to alert him of the danger, but it was his two bodyguards who reacted. With the ease of long practice and expertise the guards discharged six arrows in quick succession, penetrating the approaching creature's eyes, snout and the side of its neck. The crocodile trashed about in agony, rolled over once in the ensuing bloody, muddy murk, before disappearing from view altogether.

But not from Sankaran's view. From that vantage point thirty feet above the river he could see the crocodile swimming desperately to a deeper part of the river, at a bend below the steep embankment of the village of Sasalam, coming to rest beside some logs and driftwood that had wedged in the sand.

It was late in the afternoon when everyone left the grove, having completed the coconut harvest. Sankaran scampered over the sand banks towards the driftwood to see what had become of the crocodile. Stepping carefully into the water and wading up to the soggy, moss-laden logs, he saw a heart-breaking sight. The crocodile lay on its side, perceivably dead, its mouth partially open and a floating eye-ball being picked at by small fish. He felt a sense of overwhelming guilt. Through the open mouth and around its long snout swam its babies, three of them, each hardly a foot long, bewildered at the smell of their mother's blood and her lifeless body bobbing buoyantly in the current. Sankaran removed his turban and opened out the cloth on to the surface of the water. Picking up the three wriggling hatchlings, he carefully wrapped them in the turban and headed home, determined to feed and nurture them to adulthood. He somehow felt responsible for their care, for having alerted the landlord's bodyguards and causing the death of the beautiful female crocodile.

It took him some days to find a sizable pond in the neighbouring forest to release the brood. Every evening since that day he would visit the three orphans at the pond bringing them locusts, small frogs and fish to eat, often carrying them out of the pond and placing them on his lap to familiarize himself with their behaviour and habits. In the beginning they snapped harmlessly at the sight of his fingers, but as they became accustomed to his voice, body-warmth and touch, they showed less aggression. Day after day they depended on him for food and looked forward to his visit. He noted the unique and individual markings on their bodies sufficiently to be able to identify and give them names. He called them Viru, Showry and Kalian, constantly using their names in his conversations with them and especially while feeding them. Within weeks they stopped snapping at him, instead happy to nuzzle up to him as he waded waist deep in the water. He appeared to have replaced the mother they had lost.

As they grew to about three feet in length he knew it wasn't long before he would need to carry them back to the river, their natural habitat, to hunt on their own. He had been bringing them larger game, fowl and rabbit-meat as well as small fish, but their appetites were reaching a point that would soon defeat his capability to procure sufficient quantities of food to feed them. They would need their natural diet of live fish, snakes, turtles, birds and small mammals. He however decided to keep them in the pond for a month more. Any heavier, it would be difficult to transfer them to the river Poorna.

Despite their primitive brains Sankaran was amazed at how they formed a bond with him. A reptile he thought incapable of any emotions. He had developed an intimacy with them and could feel their love, loyalty and affection. He understood their moods. The manner in which their eyes blinked when agitated or excited. He sensed their heightened hunting instincts especially at night. He communicated effectively with them, slapping the surface of the water while he called out to them. He realized they were able to sense vibrations in the water over great distances. They responded to their individual names while he acknowledged their shoving and nuzzling by repeating their names, touching, patting and rubbing their snouts. Viru was the more aggressive and unpredictable. Kalian, shy and distant. Only Showry was the completely obedient and gentle of the three, always eager to please him. But they all hissed their approval and rolled against him in joy. By the end of that last month in the forest pond the three crocodiles were over four feet in length, capable of inflicting severe injuries to human beings. But Sankaran had somehow penetrated a forbidden boundary and become intimate friends of these three antediluvians.

One late night, unseen by the inhabitants of Sasalam or her neighbours, Sankaran carried Viru, Showry and Kalian one by one from the forest pond to the Poorna, releasing them gently into the warm currents. Kalian was the last to be leave his arms and as he watched the three adolescent creatures hesitatingly glide towards the deeper waters he hoped they would be able to hunt fresh fish, snakes, turtles, birds and even mammals. They would grow to more than double their length and weight as their mammalian prey altered from small to medium-sized animals, such as monkeys, squirrels, chital and otters, eventually growing brawny and ferocious enough to target cattle or even bison that dared to venture into the waters.

For many months to follow, Sankaran often walked on the sand banks of the Poorna to take a quicker route to his home, situated just outside the village. If it was sufficiently dark, it also became convenient to wade into the water for a discreet rendezvous with his reptilian friends.

"Viru! Viru! Viru!" he would call out softly in an almost inaudible baritone, slapping the surface of the river water. In a few minutes as if awaiting his cue, monstrous eyes would emerge glowing eerily in the dark, gliding purposefully towards him, only to frolic in joy at the sight and smell of him. "Showry! Showry! Kalian! Kalian!" and unknown to the sleeping residents of Sasalam, a most implausible ballet would ensue between man and reptile in the dark waters of the Poorna.

Sasalam was predominantly occupied by the elite Namboothiri Brahmin caste whom Sankaran wished to avoid running into. He was in awe of their power, their knowledge and their strange customs. Since Parashurama departed, the Namboothiri had settled all along the new lands the sea had given up since that illustrious warrior forced the waters back and gave Kerala so much more land. Sasalam's small population mostly kept to themselves, rarely crossing paths with Sankaran whose caste was that of an untouchable. The Namboothiri never visited the sand banks he crossed, while he found no reason to enter their village.

Except once.

One monsoon, some years after he had rescued the crocodiles, Sankaran walked down the sandy bank of the river, when ahead of him, he noticed a few startled deer darting into the thicket that grew copiously on the rich river silt upstream. Some dark clouds were gathering over the horizon. The group of white spotted deer were too far to have sensed his arrival, which made Sankaran wonder what it was that had startled the herd. He saw bison dung too, along with footprints and remnants of other creatures that had visited much earlier at dawn.

He suddenly halted at the sight of human footprints. Rare. But not unexpected. A single pair of footprints, they seemed to have been left by someone coming from the direction of Sasalam. They were small prints, perhaps of someone not much older than Sankaran himself. So he placed his own bare foot into one of them and then into the next. A seamless match both in size and stride.

"Perfect *kalady*. Now who could you be?" Sankaran muttered under his breath as he walked on mimicking the strides of the proprietor of the footprints. As he stepped on footprint after footprint, the horizon upstream lit up momentarily with a flash of lightning. The clouds had darkened and a low rumble could be heard. Sankaran pranced on, noting that the sand was getting siltier, the clay displaying the mark of each foot in deeper imprint.

"You there!" a voice called aloud. "Move up the bank, there's a flash-flood on its way!"

Ahead of him a figure appeared to have suddenly materialized. A Brahmin boy about his own age, a large palm-leaf parasol in hand, bare-bodied, save his pristine white mundu and the marks of a Brahmin: the holy string over his shoulders and an assortment of ash markings on his forehead, arms and body.

Sankaran stopped in his tracks. "How do you know that?" he enquired.

"I chanted a mantra, that will cause the river to change course and flow inland after the flash-flood." Even as the stranger spoke, it began to drizzle, filling water into the footprints Sankaran had been following. "Come with me, come up here unless you want to drown and become a crocodile's meal." The boy holding the parasol climbed higher up the bank in the direction of Sasalam.

Sankaran hesitated. He had never entered the Brahmin village. Not that Namboothiri Brahmins would harm him in any way, but they would never allow him into their homes.

He was again in awe of the Namboothiri. A mere chant of a Brahmin boy to move the waters of a river? Should he listen to the boy's warning or rush back home before the foretold tide of waters arrived? Moreover, should he believe the boy?

"I am not afraid of crocodiles. I can handle them," Sankaran yelled back. "But a flash-flood caused by a mantra is something I haven't seen before."

He continued to hesitate.

That morning it was the river Poorna that helped him decide. The first small wave of water suddenly lapped at his feet, followed by a stronger gush that indicated it was too late. If he attempted to run back along the sands the river waters would soon engulf him. It was already rising rapidly up to his knees, climbing up, increasing in level and speed even as he stood there in hesitation.

The boy with the parasol waved at him frantically. "Run, run! This way. It is higher ground here."

Sankaran suddenly remembered the herd of spotted deer that had darted in alarm into the thicket. They must have heard the roar of the waters coming this way. He trusted animal instinct. He impulsively bolted in the direction the boy indicated, watching the river swell behind him, its currents uprooting small shrubs and tufts of grass that barely held roots in the soft sand. Free of the menacing waters, he was soon climbing the slope that led to the boy under the parasol. The drizzle intensified. On noting that Sankaran was now safe, the boy walked away in the direction of a small house in the centre of the village. Sankaran followed cautiously. Nobody in the village was about as it had begun to rain. He followed the boy to the house, but chose to remain outside. He was an untouchable.

The boy threw the parasol at him. "Here, hold on to this while it is raining. I know you cannot come inside. I will be with you in a minute." He pushed open a teak-wood door, stepped over a high teak-wood threshold and disappeared inside. Shankaran stood outside in the courtyard, sheltered under the large canopied umbrella the boy had given him. He shivered. A large stone-slab seat, a basil plant and a milch-cow tethered to a coconut palm was all the wealth visible outside the house. He must be the poorest Brahmin in the village, thought Sankaran.

The boy soon emerged with a dignified middle-aged lady clothed in white. She smiled on seeing Sankaran. "And who's this, son?" she enquired of the boy. The boy ignored Sankaran.

"Mother, look!" the boy spoke. "I have caused the river to flow as near as our courtyard. You will never have to walk such a distance to the river again."

"That is just a flash-flood," Sankaran interposed. "It will soon recede away."

The boy's eyes flashed at Sankaran in an exaggerated expression of annoyance. "No it won't recede!" he snapped. "The currents are furrowing deep channels here that will keep the waters flowing by the very mark of my footprints. Where my *kalady* has marked a path for the river to follow."

Of course, the mantra, Sankaran suddenly remembered and fell silent.

The boy's mother looked impressed and held her son close to her body. "He's all I have, since my husband died when he was just three years old. He cares for me." She kissed the boy's forehead. "I fell down exhausted a few days ago trying to reach the river. My son has now brought the river to my doorstep. Have you eaten? Shall I fetch you some curd-rice?" the mother addressed Sankaran turning to enter the house again.

"As easy as that!" thought Sankaran. "Look at the nonchalance of this Brahmin woman and her son! Order a river to one's doorstep? Have currents furrow a channel where your *kalady* was imprinted? Followed by curd-rice? What other powers do these people possess?"

The mother appeared again at the doorway carrying a small areca-palm bowl, placed it on the stone slab and disappeared into the house. Sankaran squatted on the stone-slab and devoured the curd-rice with his fingers, watched by a detached and dispassionate son. The boy appeared lost in thought, hardly noticing Sankaran, gazing at the inundation that the flood accompanied by rain was causing on the edge of their courtyard. No words were spoken until Sankaran had eaten, thrown the areca-palm bowl into the river and washed his hands and mouth.

"Did I hear you say you didn't fear crocodiles?" the boy addressed Sankaran. "Do you possess some kind of mantra too?"

Sankaran nodded in a small gesture of triumph. The Brahmin boy, he thought, now ought to respect him for that. An untouchable who could touch crocodiles like no human can. "They do as I order them to. They dare not bite me. The hungry and ferocious crocodiles listen to my call and I turn them docile with my mantra," he expounded.

The Brahmin boy looked unimpressed. "Try your mantra on a crocodile that has taken a bite at a human being and tasted human blood. Then see what control your mantra has over the creature," he quipped.

Sankaran was thoughtful. The Brahmin boy appeared to have thrown a challenge, a trial to test his mantra, if indeed he had one. "Is it of so great an importance to you that I claim I can control crocodiles?" he asked.

"Not really," the boy sounded dismissive. His eyes were set somewhere far in the horizon beyond the river. "I have a severe task I have set myself to accomplish. It transcends all trivialities such as your crocodiles, this village, indeed even this kingdom. I have far to travel one day. Perhaps this I will accomplish only as an abstinent and an ascetic."

A loud exclamation ensued from within the house as his mother rushed out, startling Sankaran. "Don't say that again, my son. Please don't start that again," she cried. "What on earth will I do alone here? You are everything I have."

The boy hung his head in an exaggerated gesture of exasperation. "We are all alone, mother," he patiently explained. "Relationships are accidents of birth. Not chosen, not planned and never owned. It is an arbitrary occurrence. You can hurt yourself clinging on to it. I love and revere you mother, but if you do not believe it is random chance that you gave birth to me, here is a boy who claims congenial relationship to crocodiles. What have you to say to that?"

"But an ascetic! A sanyasin!" his mother appeared to find that thought hard to swallow. She held her son by his shoulders. "Who will see to my funeral rites, son. Tell me, who? These untouchables?"

"Hush, mother!" the boy tried to calm her. The curd-rice in Sankaran's belly did a roll threatening indigestion. The boy suddenly gestured to him to leave and Sankaran, who now regretted having entered Sasalam, dropped the parasol and walked into the rain in the direction of the river.

He noted the currents had furrowed a deep gorge right outside the young Brahmin's compound, all indication that the river was here to stay, much as the boy had specified to him. The Poorna had indeed changed course. He was keen to meet the reptilian brood today, especially following the flash-flood and the Brahmin boy's challenge.

As he waded into the water, he experienced a mild sense of nervousness and uncertainty for the first time. Of the three, Showry had always appeared to be the more obedient. Instantly obeying his commands and showing no aggression whatsoever. Sankaran therefore decided to first summon the now 12 ft long Showry to test his faith in them. Using the sharp blade of a toddy-tapping knife, he slashed his own forearm. Blood flowed down along his arm in a small trickle as he awaited the crocodile's arrival.

A few weeks ago he had seen Showry grab a thirsty deer that had accidently stopped at this part of to the river to drink. He had seen Showry execute the death-roll, the most terrifying of crocodile behaviours, dragging the deer into the water while simultaneously separating its entire hind limb from the hip. The swift and continuous rolling had torn the flesh and wrenched the limb off the hip-joint in a profusion of blood. The odour of hot gore had instantly attracted both Viru and Kalian making short work of the living, kicking meal.

Showry now glided up to Sankaran, hissing aloud at the smell he could sense from across the river. The crocodile hesitated a few feet away from him. Sankaran waited, holding his breath in uncertainty for the first time. As he immersed his bleeding arm into the water he noticed that Showry was blinking rapidly and arching his back, a clear sign of excitement or distress. But it left him unharmed and swam away. In the next instant he saw all three crocodiles swimming in his direction as if some sort of communication on Sankaran's status had transpired between them. Within seconds Viru and Kalian were close up, sniffing and hissing. Sankaran extended the injured arm. It was the unpredictable Viru who opened his mouth and bared his teeth. But instead of snapping those horrific jaws shut, he closed his mouth gently over the arm as if he was attempting to soothe the pain of the injury in some way. A tear flowed down Sankaran's cheek. "Viru!

Viru! Viru! Viru!" he repeated almost inaudibly, feeling a lump in his throat. All three showed their pleasure at his voice and gambolled in the water, bounding and frolicking about, splashing water with their tails and snouts.

"Love! Ultimate Love! Unconditional and absolute love! That is the mantra, my dear Sankara!" he assured himself as he extricated his feet from the deep river silt and stepped on to the bank of the Poorna.

After that monsoon day he encountered the Namboothiri Brahmin boy and his mother only one more time. And not without incident.

One evening as dusk approached, Sankaran was returning home along the river sand, his eyes wandering over the surface of the river, looking out for signs of his beastly companions in the vicinity. He could not spot them. Instead, it was the Namboothiri boy he saw in the distance, walking towards him, a complaining and clearly distressed mother in tow. Sankaran moved closer to the waters to clear the way for the approaching pair who belonged to a higher caste. But that was not to happen as the Brahmin boy headed straight towards Sankaran, who seeing this, promptly halted in his tracks.

As they drew closer, Sankaran noticed that the boy had shaved his head and was garbed like an ascetic with ash covering his body and wrapped in a single length of cloth.

"Tell her! Please tell her, crocodile-boy!" the Brahmin boy gesticulated at him in a vexed tone, that seemed to have worked up into a shrill tenor over hours of debate and argument, "What is the most powerful mantra in the universe?"

"Absolute, unconditional, all-pervading, all-encompassing love!" Sankaran replied promptly.

A mischievous smile of utter surprise and admiration shone on the Brahmin boy. "See, there you are mother! Even an untouchable knows that. Not selfish love! Not clinging, possessive love! Not selective love, mother. Love everything and everyone around you and you will never be alone."

Dusk had set in and it was getting dark. It was a moonless night. The Brahmin boy, quoting something in the Sanskrit language only Namboothiri Brahmins understood, perhaps still preaching love to his mother, walked casually to the edge of the river, splashing his foot, agitating the waters that flowed dark and deep near the embankment.

"In your love for everyone and everything, you even petted and played with a mangy dog today in the market, son." His mother continued in her complaining voice. "Love, it might be, but is it not filth too?"

"But that's what I have come here for, mother!" the boy replied. "I will wash and cleanse myself." Holding a stout amla plant that grew on the river-side, he stepped knee-deep into the water.

That dark, dusky evening, in the milieu that followed, Sankaran could not immediately fathom whether it was Viru, Showry or Kalian who showed up. But it certainly was one of them. As the Brahmin boy splashed about, a large snout appeared out of the water, grabbing the boy by his leg, rather gently compared to the deer that he had seen seized, dragged into a roll and torn into shards of flesh. The grip must have been in jest or play, for the boy looked rather composed even as he was dragged a few feet more into the water, a hand still clutching the amla plant firmly.

"Sankara! Sankara!" the boy's mother screamed in terror. Sankaran bounded into the river to disentangle the boy's leg, fearing the crocodile would commence the death-roll.

"Mother!" the boy called out. "Allow me to be an ascetic and the crocodile will let go of me. You see mother, that is my destiny!" The amla plant he held on to was slowly uprooting.

"Yes, yes, son. You have my blessing!" screamed the mother, "Be an ascetic but please don't die tonight! Oh Sankara! Sankara!"

Sankaran had in the meanwhile resumed his own mantra in a low baritone, "Viru, Viru, Viru!" fearing it was the unpredictable one, but now recognizing Showry he felt at ease. "Showry, Showry, Showry, Showry", he muttered under his breath as the jaws opened to let go the

Brahmin boy. The crocodile splashed about in joy at seeing Sankaran before once again disappearing into the deep.

"Son, are you hurt?" the mother fussed over her boy. "Come! Let us go home. You have been granted your wish! But I must immediately perform a special puja to thank and appease the gods." She turned to walk towards Sasalam.

Sankaran stood on the bank of the Poorna realizing suddenly that the Brahmin lady had screamed out his name when Showry had grabbed the boy's leg. At least four times. Her shrill voice still rang in his ear. But he had never revealed his name to them. They had always referred to him as "the untouchable." How had she figured out his name?

The Brahmin boy, feeling sufficiently cleansed turned to leave. "It will be a long, long time before I will be seen in these parts. I am an ascetic now." He walked away following his mother's footsteps.

"How, by Maveli, did your mother figure out my name?" Sankaran enquired.

In the last of the dusky light Sankaran saw the boy turn to depart, smiling that mischievous smile again. But while Sankaran stood there mystified, it was a realization to the new ascetic that he and the untouchable shared the same name, mantras and an innate understanding of love.

And for the rest of their lives both would wonder why one of them had been born an untouchable.

A Mariner And A Traveler

Trade with the fierce, narrow-eyed sailors who came to berth at Kozhikode had been profitable for the kingdom for some years now. China had been sending fleets of merchant vessels from time immemorial. They were a tough, but gentle lot. Well attired, polite and full of culture and etiquette. They prided in their kings and emperors as much as the Malayalee. They admired the arts and architecture of the land, took part in the local feasts and festivals and even dared to learn what they once regarded, an intricate and tongue-twisting language. They were as wary of the Nair swordsmen as the Nairs were of the Chinese broadsword. But the Chinese easily identified with the philosophy of humility and quietude, of ritual hygiene and spiritual cleansing that was practised in Kerala. Above all, they felt enthralled to visit the land of their very own Bodhidharma.

The Siddha and Ayurveda systems of medicine aroused their curiosity to such an extent that the emperor of China sent a delegation of his own personal physicians to study both the systems. Stories abounded of martial arts that did not require even the touching of an opponent. Apart from the visibly spectacular *Kalaripayattu*, the secret arts of *Marmakkala, Nokku Varmam* and *Choondu Varmam* had them dumbfounded.

Over centuries, their sailors stayed awake many nights to observe the incomprehensible festival of *Theyyam*. They believed there existed black arts and demon worshippers in the Malabar region of whom they wrote extensively about in their travel journals. However what genuinely terrified them was the possibility of an encounter with an impish spirit called *Kutti-Chathan*. They believed that at least twice in the last century, the spirit had climbed aboard their vessels berthed at Kozhikode and wreaked havoc in China before quietly flying home to Kerala.

Yet they overstayed every time they came ashore. They would first be granted a period of berth at the harbour based on their time requirement for trade, repairs, procurement of rations, wind and climate conditions and the health of their crew and slaves. Two weeks to two months.

But it became routine affair for Sankaran to have to visit the trade representative of the Chera king on their behalf, to request the extension of the visas of the Chinese merchants. Though Sankaran knew that the real reason for their extended holiday was the local palm toddy, the sweet white beer called *kallu*, the distilled and stronger *charayam* along with the accompaniment of fried or sauteed spiced mussels popularly called *kallumakai*-fry. The other item that anchored them to Kozhikode for months on end was the tapioca gruel called *kappa* eaten with fish-curry.

Admiral Zheng He, the greatest navigator the world had ever seen, a eunuch who stood seven feet four inches tall, with a girth of four feet and a voice that was as loud as a bell from hell, dropped anchor at Kozhikode in his treasure ship for the seventh and last time. Zheng He was born a Mongol Hui Muslim, who entered the third Ming King Yongle Zhu Di's service. He commanded the largest Chinese fleet that ever set sail from China, captaining the Chinese treasure ship, the largest wooden vessel the oceans had ever seen. Zheng He was well versed in the art of war, possessed great knowledge about combat strategies and was accustomed to battle. But above all else he loved food. He made it his personal agenda to taste every cuisine from China to Hormuz. In the course of one of his voyages he was compelled to attack the king of Ceylon whom he defeated, imprisoned and carried away to China. But not before he had tasted every menu on that island. Of course, he had also destroyed the ships and subdued innumerable bands of pirates along the various sea routes his fleet voyaged. Before walking the plank each pirate had to confess to Zheng He what he had eaten for lunch. In the total absence of sex, food was the eunuch's obsession.

But the rulers of Kochi and Kozhikode received special treatment. The Chinese knew the value of keeping cordial relations with the western coast. The wealth of the land and the opportunity to trade had Zheng He wrest special concessions from the Yongle Emperor of China, conferring special status to the Kerala kingdoms. They exchanged artisans, architects and ship-builders, teak-wood, silks and fine cotton, medicinal herbs, knowledge of their use, prescriptions and innumerable kinds of consumer goods and spices. As a result, untold wealth accumulated in the households and temples of Kerala.

It is said that due to Zheng He's naval expeditions, about twenty-four kingdoms became vassals, paid tribute, maintained diplomatic relations or at least granted trade licences to the Chinese emperor. Zheng He was undefeatable. It is said that it took a regular nocturnal addiction to *kallu, charayam, kallumakai,* followed by a breakfast of *kappa, idli, dosa, appam, idiyappam, puttu,* and *pathiri* soaked in curries and stews of chicken, lamb, beef, pork and fish to finally do him in. When he finally died under Sankaran's coconut grove in Kozhikode, the Chinese felt humbled.

"They have in this country, food to die for," wrote an emissary to their Chinese emperor. Enough reason for us to believe they relished chicken Malabari many, many years before we did chicken Manchurian.

But over a hundred years before the great Chinese fleets of Zheng He arrived, China was under the Mongols, with Kublai Khan, grandson of the great Genghis Khan at the helm. In those days they sent smaller fleets for the purpose of trade. Sankaran particularly remembered one of those visits, for among the Chinese trade delegation that discharged on the Kozhikode shore was the most disparate and incongruent human being he had ever met.

Sankaran always found it difficult to describe this man. He was certainly not Chinese, but spoke the language with a distinct accent. Obviously a well-travelled sailor, he spoke a smattering of Arabic and Farsi too, but with the *same* distinct accent. A quick learner, during his sojourn at Kozhikode, he even tried his hand at Malayalam. But that accent never changed.

It was the winter of 1294 AD when that memorable fleet anchored at Kozhikode. The Chinese and Mongols in formal silk gowns and embellished tunics stepped out of the boat, carefully treading the sand in their embroidered shoes. Bowing gracefully at Sankaran and other Malayalee officials they walked towards the customs and berthing offices on the pier. Following them emerged this conspicuously outlandish one, walking with a swagger Sankaran had never seen even among champions of Kalari *ankams*. He could barely stand still, continuously poised and posturing as if he were preparing to commence a ceremonial speech or fend off an attack on his person. It was so outlandish that soon the man became the cynosure of all eyes on the jetty. Displaying long black hair with streaks of brown under an over-sized red cap, sporting a neatly trimmed beard covering an impassive face, he looked over Sankaran and the officials as if he were examining goods heaped for export. Sankaran and the officials looked at one another quizzically. One of them choked in an effort to stifle an impulse to laugh out loud and uncontrollably. A passing senior Chinese merchant, sensing the reaction of the hosts at this particular inconsistency in their entourage, drew up to Sankaran and whispered apologetically, "A friend of our emperor! Insisted he wanted to join this voyage! I had little choice in the matter!"

Sankaran nodded sympathetically watching the Mongol emperor's large contingent march away from the landing-stage on to the sands in their customary, orderly fashion not failing to notice the only head that bobbed and swayed, especially the red cap that was constantly on the verge of blowing away in the wind. On an impulse Sankaran left the Malayalees on the pier and decided to follow the traders from China.

When he walked up to them, some of them began a conversation with him. Sea farers had a language that combined the common and essential local words they had learnt with some universally understood language like Arabic or Farsi. In the process, sentences formed may include four to five known languages, spoken patiently enough for the listener to comprehend. It was a language that varied from port to port, kingdom to kingdom, but it was understood. A dialect of the mariners, some called it the language of the salt.

In the course of his conversation with the Chinese, which mostly included polite greetings, small talk about each other's families, news of few births, some deaths and a couple of weddings in their respective households, Sankaran was momentarily left speechless by a sudden interruption by the swaggering foreigner.

"Yo, piasano! Coulda you tella me vare isa da pepper bazaar at?" He gesticulated with both his hands as if he was grabbing hands-full of peppercorn.

Vaguely grasping what the man enquired, Sankaran pointed to the large thatched sheds deep inland. "You need to walk in that direction to see or buy pepper."

"Along waya? OK, fora you walka no problem, piasano," replied the emperor's friend waving a hand skyward to exaggerate the distance. "Tella me, do you know vare isa da stable at? I aneed horse to ago."

"Where, by Maveli, are you from?" Sankaran enquired incredulously.

"Venezia!" the man exclaimed tilting his head to smile. "Veneto? Capisci? Yo comprehendere?" He now waved both hands to indicate some shape he had in mind.

He wigwags his hands in ways that resembles our *mohiniyaatam*, thought Sankaran.

"Oh, a merchant of Venice?" Sankaran had heard of them. This was the first time he had met one.

"Si! Si! I'ma so prouda ma Venezia. He maka the sil-vare coin *grosso*. Da Moors call it *matapano*. Pure sil-vare. Hesa genio! Yo comprehendere?"

"Venetians are geniuses," admitted Sankaran remembering stories he had heard of their naval and architectural accomplishments. "What are you doing with the Mongol emperor?"

"Viaggio fora…." He made gripping and tossing gestures with his hands. "fora denaro."

Sankaran understood. "You voyaged for money. Well, have you earned enough? Abbastanza? Enough?"

"Never abbastanza!" the stranger laughed, "But anow time to go ahome!"

"How do you like the food in China?" Sankaran enquired.

"Everything is food in China," the Venetian explained. "Yo wanta locusta or ratti, yo got it."

"Disgusting!" exclaimed Sankaran.

"Yo wanta cani fora dinner, yo got it! Yo know cani?" he made a barking sound and pranced about.

"Dogs! That's ghastly! You ate a dog?" whispered Sankaran, slowing his pace and falling back to stay out of the Chinese traders' earshot.

"Ha! Ha! Yo wanta gambe di rana?" the Venetian squatted and hopped, pointing at a puddle on the beach.

"Frogs!"

"Si! Si!" he nodded. "Gambe! Gambe!" he held his thigh.

"You mean frog's legs?" Sankaran laughed. "This certainly is getting to be funny!"

"Si! Si!" he seemed happy, his swagger getting dandier. "Leta me tella yo, uno scherzo, a joke! Ma father he cama back froma China. He sit ina ristorante in Venezia. Ma father he say - Inn keeper! Inn keeper! Do yo hava froga legs? Thena Inn keeper he say No!... I always walka this way!" He made a bandy-legged walking motion with his two forefingers.

Sankaran burst out into loud laughter. Men from the Chinese delegation, walking ahead of them turned to look what the sudden familiarity between the two was about. It almost sounded rude. But the red capped Venetian continued unabated, his hands poised for action.

"Wella, another time ma father he sit ina ristorante in China. Ma father he say – Inn keeper! Inn keeper! Do yo hava froga legs? Yes Sir! the inn keeper say. Ma father he say to inn keeper -Then hopa over here and geta me some water!" He pointed his forefinger down at an imaginary table.

The two dissolved into another round of laughter.

"Oh, my dear Venetian, your hands never seem to stop gesticulating. What would happen if someone was to tie both your hands up?" Sankaran asked, still caught in a rapture.

"I woulda go mute!" he replied, palming his mouth with his hands,

"What is your name?" Sankaran needed to know.

"Marco. Marco Polo," the Venetian replied.

"You're unbelievable, Marco!" Sankaran exclaimed.

"Sama day I will write ita all adown!" Marco replied, "And when yo read it, it will be unbelievable fora everybody. But yous better show some respect fora the book."

CHRISTAINS AND PEPPER

"I see a fleet of vessels on the high seas," came a shrill warning from the top of a coconut palm one late morning.

"Do you recognize their flag?" A Mappila Muslim youth repairing fishing nets on the sands below shouted back at Sankaran.

"Looks a lot like my sister's *pavada*," Sankaran replied, at which the Mappila laughed aloud.

"The frayed old one," described Sankaran. "The white one with the orange border, yellow and blue flowers. Aiyo! This looks like a fleet of new foreigners."

"You mean a new fleet of foreigners?"

"No! A fleet of *new* foreigners, by the look of it," emphasised Sankaran. "Four vessels as far as I can see. Damn! They have some kind of firearms on those vessels."

The Mappila looked up from his fishing-nets alarmed. "What are you talking about, Sankara? What firearms?"

"The sides of the ships appear to be bristling with many appendages that look to me like firearms. If they had been lower and more numerous I would have taken them to be oars. But the size and position of these indicate that their purpose is of explosive nature."

"I'm going over to the Nair constabulary to alert them," the Mappila youth shouted, dropping his net.

"Aiyo, Khadir! Relax!" Shouted out Sankaran. "All bulls have horns. They don't all gore people! It just might be for protection against pirates!"

"They may be pirates themselves!" Khadir was unconvinced. "We need to inform somebody. It's *Jumma* today. We will all be gathered at the mosque for prayers at midday, in an hour's time. I'll announce it there. I don't have a good feeling about this."

"On the other hand, you could be right," Sankaran reconsidered. "It's bad timing. It's at *rahu kalam* time that these foreigners chose to land here. And that too on a Friday!"

Sankaran watched until ladders and row-boats were lowered from one of the vessels. "A party of emissaries rowing this way," he remarked. Then hearing no response from below, he stared at the fishing nets abandoned below. Khadir had already departed to report the new development.

It took less than half an hour for a dozen Nair guards to arrive, led by an excited Khadir. Sankaran slid down the tree to join them. Two row-boats bearing about a total of ten men had left one of the ships and were progressively rowing towards the beach, heading to the sands some distance away from the regular dock. A few regular Mappila and Moor interpreters joined the Nair guards as the foreigners glided expertly towards them on the surf.

Bearded men in tight pantaloons, brass-buttoned tunics, buckled leather belts and long swords stepped out on to the sand, smiling, bowing and making sure it was understood that they had come in peace. One of them held a flag at the end of a long pole, the sight of which caused Sankaran and Khadir to exchange a smile. The Nair guards reciprocated to the visitor's tributes with a native salute of joined hands and a reverential bow.

Everyone halted in their tracks. An awkward silence followed as each party studied the other to discern who their interpreters were.

The chief of the Nair guard, Achutan, spoke up with a single worded query, his fingers pointed at his own lips. "Malayalam?"

It elicited no response from the newly arrived group. So he enquired again, "Arabi? Arabiyah?"

A thin Tunisian youth from the boats was stepping up to utter something but he was immediately restrained from speaking by a man who appeared to be their chief oarsman. Instead the chief oarsman enquired, "Língua Portuguesa?" pointing his fingers at his lips in the manner Achutan had gestured. "Castilian? Genoise?" His queries were met with silence and incoherence.

"We can safely discuss matters in confidence. None of these visitors know Malayalam," muttered Achutan to his own guards. He tried again. "Arabi? Farsi?" now looking directly at the thin Tunisian youth, "As salam alaykom. Hal tatakallam al-lughah al-'arabīyah?"

This time the gaunt youth was allowed to speak. "Yes I speak Arabi! And how many speak Arabi amongst you?" he enquired in Arabic.

"Ask us who doesn't speak Arabi among us? It might be easier to count," Khadir broke the ice with the visitors. The Nair guards laughed along with him and the Tunisian joined them with a look of satisfaction. He immediately translated the interaction along with Khadir's jibe to the rest of the boatmen, who nodded in unison and smiled in understanding.

"Now we can safely discuss matters in confidence. None of these natives know a word of Portuguese," Pedro Escobar, the chief oarsman announced to all the men who had arrived by boat. The Tunisian was about to speak, but he was immediately halted by the chief. "Idiot, don't you dare translate that." The Tunisian swallowed and fell silent. The chief oarsman smiled beatifically at Achutan and the Nair guards.

"I sense they're playing the same game," Sankaran mumbled to Achutan. "Khadir, can you ask them where they are from and what it is they want here at Kappadu?"

At this stage an official interpreter interrupted. "I will require to report to the king when he returns from Ponnani. So, if you gentlemen don't mind, let me do the talking." Then addressing the Tunisian, the king's interpreter enquired. "*Ahlan!* Of what nation are your companions and what is the purpose of their landing on our shores?"

After some exchange in Portuguese with the boatmen, the Tunisian explained, "They are Portuguese. They come looking for Christians and spices."

"Only one of those two commodities is available for sale," Sankaran teased aloud, drawing an amused glance from the King's interpreter.

The chief oarsman raised a hand to draw the attention of the King's interpreter and announced, "His Excellency the Ambassador, representative of our king, together with the Captain-major of our fleet, the venerable Vasco Da Gama," he pointed to the fleet, "await the principal ruler of your land to invite him to the shore so that he may pay his respects and present his credentials on behalf of our king His Royal Highness, the Fortunate Manuel, King of Portugal and the Algarves."

As the Tunisian translated the chief oarsman's formal announcement, there was a sudden moan of dismay coming from two Moors standing among the Nair guards. The Portuguese boatmen frowned and raised their eyebrows, trying to decipher what the sudden resentment was all about. But keeping to the local Malayalam language in which he was quite fluent, one of the Moors explained the reasons for their apprehension and dismay.

"Do you know who these are? They are the consumers of our spices which they buy from the Venetians. Arabs and Moors have been traditionally buying these goods from Malabar and selling them to the Venetians. Today they are here to bypass the Venetians and the Moors. These are a fanatical race of people. Their king, their religion and their way of life leaves no room for Jews and Muslims to exist in peace. I have heard of them from other sailors. Doing business with them will lead to no good. It will destroy the livelihood of a large number of people. Ask the Tunisian. He should know of this."

"He appears to have been kidnapped along their journey for the sole purpose of serving as an interpreter," remarked Sankaran, continuing in Malayalam "He is an Arab. A poor, crestfallen Tunisian Muslim who now finds himself in a very awkward situation. I will get around to him later to extract the truth."

"Not until regular traders arrive from the ports that these sailors have touched will we know what atrocities they have left in their wake," remarked Achutan. "They look like pirates in fancy pantaloons. Anyway, let the king decide."

"Our duty to our king, the Samoothiri, is to be hospitable to our guests," remarked the official interpreter of the king. He turned to the Portuguese sailors and addressed the Tunisian in Arabic.

"Our king is fifteen leagues away, otherwise occupied with matters of the realm. Thus, I, official interpreter of the king hereby welcome you to this land. Retire now to your ships, save for two messengers who will accompany the Nair guards to the king. Having presented your letters, the king will make a decision and, God willing, will meet your captain and ambassador at an appointed day and time soon enough. Until then, be at peace and rest." At a cue from Sankaran, he added. "We require the Tunisian to accompany the two messengers. They will all be delivered safely back to you by this hour tomorrow."

The official interpreter's words were met with nods and approval. The veil of uncertainty lifted, replaced by a sense of peace and purpose that settled upon the visitors.

A scroll was passed to the bearer of the flag, who was then joined by the chief oarsman to act as the first emissaries of Portugal to meet the Samoothiri. The Tunisian youth was ordered to join them, nervously stepping out of the boat at a signal from the chief oarsman. Following a ceremonial salute, the two boats commenced rowing back to the ships, leaving only the three visitors on shore.

As the Nair guards escorted the three inland, a throng of curious onlookers were already gathering in the bazaars and street-corners.

"I do not intend to wait. I will march them to Ponanni immediately. What's your agenda?" enquired the chief interpreter of Sankaran.

"If I have your permission to accompany this delegation, I have a plan," replied Sankaran. "It will be late when we arrive at Ponanni. The king will give audience to them only some time tomorrow. At supper this evening, while the Nair guards eat with the two visitors, I require you to order the Tunisian to eat separately for being a servant and a slave. I will take the Tunisian aside and in the course of dining with him, do some interrogation. There is a lot the boy is not revealing. The local Moors are apprehensive. They have obviously heard much of the nature of these visitors who call themselves Portuguese and appear very cultured. The Moor people abroad bring stories of all that which transpire in their kingdoms, the neighbouring kingdoms and the high seas whenever they berth at Kozhikode. They have heard much about these Portuguese. It is time we educate ourselves and our king."

"That would be useful," agreed the chief interpreter.

The day's march to Ponanni was accomplished with ease as the Nair guards were able to requisition fresh ponies and palanquin bearers at the required halts in their journey.

Pedro Escobar, the veteran sailor, rode along with the bearer of the Portuguese standard. "They wear much gold here," he remarked. "It does not seem to serve a religious purpose, nor does it seem an embellishment to enhance their beauty. Both men and women have pierced their ears. They have gold around their necks, arms, ankles and waist. The streets are full of gold. Yet they are barely clothed and their clothes are plain and colourless."

"I wonder what that ghastly thing is that I see many elders chewing?" the standard bearer exclaimed. "They appear to be bleeding from their mouths. They keep spitting too."

"What was that fruit we were given in the last halt? I've never eaten anything so divine."

"*Manga*. I think that's what they called it," the standard bearer replied. "We could take a few seeds to Lisboa. Perhaps try and grow a whole grove there."

"I hear they don't have potatoes and tomatoes in this land," remarked Escobar.

"With the variety of spices to flavour their meat, do they need our potatoes and tomatoes?"

"But they certainly require better clothes," laughed Escobar.

"They appear comfortable," responded the standard bearer. "The heat is making me sick. Our clothes are not suited to this climate."

"But their ponies are pathetic," continued Escobar. "Which is surprising considering the number of Moors in Kozhikode. The Moors and Tunisians in Africa have the best horses."

"Which reminds me, we'd better keep an eye on that Tunisian we picked up at Melinde. We don't want him to shoot his mouth off."

At Ponanni the visitors were subject to a disconcerting hour's tuition in the manner of washing and cleansing themselves before they could meet any member of the royal household of the Samoothiri. The two sailors were soused and soaped with perfumed *thailam*, doused with heated herbal water before being liberally drenched and washed with cool water drawn from a well. The Tunisian was shown another well and was free to bathe any way he wished.

Supper at Ponanni, or at any port in Malabar, especially prepared for foreigners, was a deliberate and subtle marketing gimmick. It was a departure from the Malayalee way of cooking, utilizing every herb and spice available for trade, in distinct dishes of food, causing the foreigner to raise his eyebrows each time he smelled or tasted a new dish. Meat and fish of various kinds were spiced, marinated and prepared skilfully to arouse their interest in many more exotic items of trade, apart from pepper. As standard practice, a meal served to a foreigner was also his introductory education to spices, a sampling of all that was available in the market. The meal served was aptly named *pareeksha*, meaning "test", and its success was measured by the host and cook, while the foreigner sniffed, snivelled, hiccupped, sneezed, burped, got teary-eyed, yet ended up overeating and thoroughly enjoying the meal.

However, on the evening in question, the *pareeksha* was successful in two ways. The recently disembarked Portuguese drank toddy and ate food they had never seen before, oblivious to where their Tunisian servant and interpreter was spirited away by Sankaran and Khadir.

In a room, some distance away from the dining hall where the Portuguese guests and the Nair guards ate, the emaciated Tunisian was served on a plantain leaf. Seated on a grass mat, he ate the gravy soaked rice and vegetables served to him with gusto, but hesitated to touch any meat.

"Try some of this mutton. It is *halal*." Sankaran prompted, drawing himself close to the boy. "The cook is a Mappila."

On hearing this, the boy served himself a sizable quantity of meat. There was delight on his face as he devoured the mutton, spiced with pepper, clove and cinnamon.

"What is your name, Tunisian?" Khadir began in Arabic.

"Karim," he replied.

"Are you really from Tunisia?"

"Ifriqiya we call it," replied the youth. "But there is constant trouble in our land. Our Hafsid rulers are weak and fight among themselves. So some years ago we migrated to Melinde, on the eastern coast, two day's march from Mombasa, where my father was a tradesman."

"So then, is it at Ifriqiya that you learnt to speak Portuguese?"

"My father was a descendant of the great Ibn Khaldun. He was an educated man and had travelled far and wide. He traded in silks and carpets when we lived in Ifriqiya and was a frequent visitor to Lisboa across the sea, for the purpose of serving his clients, mostly the Portuguese nobility. From the age of twelve I accompanied him and in due course learnt Portuguese."

"Try some of this fish, Karim." Khadir continued, as Sankaran watched in amusement. "What made you accompany these men on this voyage? Are you to be paid on your return?"

Karim choked, and was delivered some water by Sankaran. A tear appeared on the corner of one eye. Khadir ate slowly stealing a glance at Sankaran.

"Your father," enquired Sankaran. "Where is he?"

"With Allah," the tear became more prominent.

"And your mother?" persisted Sankaran.

"She awaits me at Melinde." this time tears flowed from both eyes. Sankaran knew it was not caused by the spices.

"Eat. While the food is warm, eat," continued Sankaran indifferently. "Karim, if we were to arrange your return to Melinde by some other ship would you choose that option?"

The youth stopped eating. "I see you have understood something about my situation!" His voice became a whisper. "I curse the day I began to learn Portuguese."

"So you have been brought here against your will?" Sankaran enquired triumphantly.

"To work as interpreters," Karim whispered. "Two of us. Kais my friend from Mombasa is at present held on one of the ships. He too is a Tunisian but hides behind the pseudonym of Jean Nunez. He speaks Castilian which many of the Portuguese sailors understand. His father was from Toledo. Kais also interprets a language that is spoken in some parts of your land, called Hindavi or Hindustani. I hear they intend to use him later."

This sounded like a break-through. Khadir dragged his own plantain leaf closer as the three suddenly began to conspire.

"What do you mean by "held"? Is he too here against his will?"

Karim surveyed the room they were seated in. His eyes wandered to the door. Sankaran rose to shut it. Looking more at ease, Karim whispered, "Can I trust you?"

"You must," Khadir emphasised. "Go on and eat while you talk. When the sailors finish their meal they are going to be looking for you. Tell us your story while there is this opportunity."

"Kais is older than me by a few years," continued Karim. "He too lost his father some years ago and we share a house and some farmland in Melinde. About a month ago, at Melinde, we were both summoned by a rich merchant called Kanji Malam. He comes from the Jadeja kingdom that we traded with for many years, some week's voyage to the north of your coast. He was a friend of my late father. He spoke Hindustani. He has seen our fortunes dwindle since the men in our respective families died. It was he who suggested that he could raise us from our poverty if we made this voyage to Kozhikode as interpreters."

"And your mothers agreed?" asked Khadir.

"Kanji promised our mothers that we would be returned to our homes in six months. My mother was apprehensive of the Portuguese, but Kanji convinced my mother that all was well and that we would be sailing in his own ship and treated as his very children. He paid my mother handsomely in gold, surely wrested from the Portuguese for the purpose. Anyway, after much hesitation we agreed and set sail from Melinde. Kanji had six ships far larger than the Portuguese. But he had more goods and merchants than fighting men and firearms. I could tell he was a good navigator for we sailed smoothly with the wind behind us. And very steadily, in a North-Easterly direction. All went well until the eighteenth day of our journey here, when Kanji ordered us to be transferred to one of the Portuguese ships. We protested and rebelled against the idea. He was adamant and when we resisted, he was compelled to hand us over, virtually as prisoners."

"And what of Kanji and his fleet?" Sankaran wanted to know.

"They departed north along the coastline as soon as your towns became visible to the Portuguese. He has headed to his hometown, to some place called Mandvi," replied Karim. "I think he still believes Kais and I will be returned to our mothers waiting in Melinde."

"What causes you to doubt that?" Sankaran enquired.

"These Christians, these Portuguese are very different in their treatment to people not of their own kind." complained Karim in a whisper. "They are contemptuous, surly and conceited."

"Then they certainly ought to meet our Samoothiri, the king," Sankaran sneered. "He has a way of putting such upstarts back in their place." Khadir coughed in an effort to laugh silently.

"I fear we will be enslaved and retained for their purpose for an indefinite length of time. Perhaps years," Karim sounded grave. "They are merciless in their treatment of the slaves on their ship. I have heard that condemned prisoners intended for exploring the beaches of unfamiliar country have been abandoned, killed and even thrown into shark-infested waters before they arrived at Melinde. I was myself witness to one such atrocity a few days before we arrived here."

"Are they really looking for Christians and spices?" Khadir questioned doubtfully.

The Tunisian boy shrugged. "From what I hear they appear to have voyaged here for spices, especially pepper and medicinal herbs. Even as I speak, the fools believe that all save the Moors here in your country are Christians. They know nothing of the existence of Hindus."

"They cannot all be so ignorant," Khadir contended. "We haven't met with the others on their ship."

"My only concern is my friend Kais," Karim declared. "Once our work is done, I know for certain that they don't intend to return via Melinde. We will either become their slaves or food for the fish. I cannot trust them."

"They do have some strange ways we are unaccustomed to," Sankaran accepted with a shrug.

"They are always unwashed and urinate standing up," Karim added, causing all three to laugh conspiratorially.

"So Karim, we understand you are certainly not looking forward to returning with the Portuguese. What instead is your plan?" Khadir was curious.

"If I could rescue Kais from their clutches we could go into hiding somewhere here in Malabar and await some other vessel headed for Melinde," declared Karim. "However, it is important that we reach Melinde before the Portuguese decide to give us chase. As much as I doubt that they would care about two miserable interpreters, our mothers must be warned and shifted to a place of safety if that happens and should a single Portuguese ship berth at our harbour at Melinde."

Karim appeared either to have lost interest in the food or satisfied his hunger. He rose to wash his hands.

Meanwhile, in the dining hall where the sailors sat dining with the Nair guards, there was an uneasy silence. The chief interpreter of the king had delivered the letters to the Samoothiri and also received a royal response. That His Highness saw no need to meet or give audience to these two sailors. He was preparing to depart for Kozhikode.

"Where the hell is the interpreter?" Escobar enquired aloud.

Karim was quickly ushered to the doorway of the dining room by Sankaran and Khadir. The Samoothiri's message was translated into Arabic for him. In turn he translated it for the two sailors. "His Royal Highness is unwilling to grant audience to the newly disembarked sailors of Portugal as he is proceeding tonight to the capital city Kozhikode. His Royal Highness would rather give audience directly to your king's ambassador and to the captain of your fleet Senhor Vasco da Gama at Pantalayani Kollam, some distance away from the capital."

Pedro Escobar's face wore a slight expression of exasperation. The long ride from Kappadu to Ponanni had been made with nothing substantial to report to his captain.

As the chief interpreter continued, Karim translated, "We hope you are happy with our hospitality and will forgive this minor inconvenience. You will now require to ride back to the beach where you came ashore and direct your fleet to a dock at Pantalayani Kollam where the sea-floor is low and less rocky for your fleet. The dock is less crowded and His Highness will give you audience there. This has been done for your convenience. Some fishermen will be instructed to guide you to Pantalayani Kollam." Then controlling his nervousness Karim added a falsity. "His Highness will require your interpreters in Arabic and Hindustani."

In the brief silence that followed, Karim held his breath to trace any indication of doubt on the faces of the two sailors. It was Pedro Escobar who spoke. "Then so be it. It has not altogether been a fruitless evening. We will depart at dawn and deliver your ruler's message to our venerable captain and the honourable ambassador awaiting us on the ship. We thank you for your hospitality and, God willing, shall meet you and your good king at the designated place of his wish Godspeed."

"I think Karim is attempting to ferret out Kais," whispered Khadir to Sankaran. "The two of them will be together tomorrow in audience with the king. Karim's effort at ferreting out Kais is so that we may identify Kais and know him by sight. He is begging to be rescued. Do we have a plan?"

As the three visitors were led away to their sleeping quarters by the Nair guards, Karim stole a glance at Sankaran and Khadir, hope writ large on his face.

The chief interpreter turned to Sankaran. "His Highness is aware of the resentment and apprehensions of the Moors and the Mappilas. As a result, he considers the dock at Pantalayani Kollam suitably unobtrusive."

Another thirty-six hours would pass before the Portuguese fleet docked at Pantalayani Kollam. A grand reception was underway even as the first vessel dropped anchor. Pedro Escobar stood on the deck keenly watching the natives thronging the causeway to the pier, holding baskets of flowers. He breathed a sigh of relief as he noticed drummers and musicians lined along both sides of the boardwalk while two caparisoned war-elephants with enormous tusks carrying men bearing colourful canopies and parasols stationed themselves on either side.

"We appear to have made a good impression," he remarked in a vaunt that made no impression on the stern-faced bearded figure beside him. Vasco da Gama was least enthralled by the shindig on the harbour. His face was impassive as he studied the scanty town beyond the docks. This was far from the capital, Kozhikode. He could not understand the intention of the Samoothiri. Perhaps things would have been different, he thought, had he not exposed the guns his vessels carried. His eyes had not failed to notice at least five native cannons, pointing seaward, spread out inconspicuously among the thatched huts that lay interspersed some distance from the shore.

"Manhoso desgraçado," he muttered under his breath. Then addressing Escobar, he instructed, "Send a message to the shore that I will not disembark to meet His Highness today. Assign some reasonable explanation. Today is Sunday, a day of prayer. These Christians should know that. We will go ashore tomorrow. And order the crew to retract the guns. They must not look offensive from the shore."

Meanwhile, deeper inland, Sankaran and Khadir sat in deep consultation with the Nair guards. A decision upon the course of action, following Karim's plea, would have to be taken against the larger trade interest the Samoothiri vested on these foreigners. The antagonism that could crop up if the two interpreters were rescued could go against their king's economic investment, especially if parleys with the Portuguese were to be found profitable and feasible. They would have to await the outcome of the negotiations between the Portuguese and the Samoothiri before planning a rescue.

However, if an opportunity for rescue of the two interpreters was to come about, Sankaran, for the purpose, had already enlisted an adequate number of expert Nair swordsmen and *mukkuva* fishermen, champion swimmers of the king's coast guard. It was going to be an agonizing wait before they discovered the outcome of the Portuguese negotiations with the Samoothiri and the date of departure of the foreign vessels from their harbour.

But the Portuguese fleet was to be marooned in the harbour longer than they had expected. The southwest monsoon struck Malabar the following week. The ferocity of the winds and the deluge that followed discouraged anyone wishing to venture out into the sea. Even local fishermen stayed home till the initial squall, which lasted over a fortnight, subsided. Even the occasional foray by larger boats was a gamble as the waters were rough and unpredictable.

The two boys working as interpreters for the Portuguese were rarely seen. Sankaran and his Nair scouts peered eagerly every now and then at the four ships in anchor, but not once did the boys show up on deck. A clear indication that their movements were restricted, or like prisoners, chained in the hold of one of the ships. On very rare occasions would they come ashore along with a bunch of Portuguese sailors to buy food and necessary supplies, their faces looking hopeless, their eyes drawn and forsaken. Sankaran was frustrated even as he tried to reassure them that he would soon come up with a plan to rescue them.

As the weeks wore by things took an unexpected turn for the Portuguese. The initial reception and enthusiasm shown by the Samoothiri turned sour and trade negotiations all but ceased due to the Portuguese insisting on complete monopoly in their dealings and transactions, effectively propagating the complete extinction of the livelihood of the Mappilas, Moors and other traders who traditionally served as middlemen.

The gifts brought by Da Gama did not impress the Samoothiri either. The king found them trivial and laughed unabashedly at some of the goods he received from the monarch of Portugal. The Samoothiri and his officials treated each item that Vasco da Gama offered with disdain. They enquired as to why there was no gold or silver to which the Portuguese had no answer. They could not admit to their kingdom's poverty in such items of wealth. To add to their misery, the Muslim merchants who considered the Portuguese their rivals in the business even went to the extent of suggesting that these impoverished men might be just ordinary pirates and not royal ambassadors of a king. The Samoothiri roared with laughter at this pronouncement, joined by his court officials. Vasco da Gama and his delegation bowed and left the Samoothiri's palace seething with rage.

It did not take a day before the public and the marketplace began to hear of the ludicrous and outlandish gifts the Portuguese had presented the Samoothiri. A box of seven brass vessels, four cloaks of scarlet cloth, six hats, four branches of corals, twelve almasares, a chest of sugar, two barrels of oil and a cask of honey.

On hearing of the items on the list, an idea struck Sankaran. He was not quite sure it would work, but he decided to devise a plan. He engaged the services of a flautist and two drummers and composed a series of verses that he decided to sing the next time the Portuguese left their harboured ships and came ashore for supplies.

And when the fateful day came, it was Pedro Escobar accompanied by Karim and three other sailors who became his target. On their arrival to the marketplace on the beach, he greeted Karim casually, careful not to arouse any suspicion among the Portuguese sailors as they strolled into the bustling bazaar. After waiting some time for an opportune moment he whispered his plan to the boy. The Tunisian looked doubtful and nervous. But eventually shrugged and nodded.

Sankaran then signalled to his band of three impromptu musicians, who having taken their places around him, began to play a deranged tune with a nonsensical beat to which Sankaran sang his first verse in Malayalam:

> Aiyo Gama! Pompous pants
> Learnt a lesson in our hands
> Gifts from his King Manuel
> Are only suited for a funeral

A number of bystanders burst out laughing. Some joined in the singing.

> Aiyo Gama! Pompous pants
> Learnt a lesson in our hands
> Gifts from his King Manuel
> Are only suited for a funeral

Pedro Escobar looked pleased at the spontaneous outburst of singing. "Do they have a festival on today?" he enquired of Karim.

"I suppose they do," answered Karim innocently.

"Is it a song to their Gods? Or is it to a lover?" Pedro tilted his head to listen.

"Hard to say. I don't quite follow their language. It is definitely not Arabic," Replied Karim

> Aiyo Gama! Pompous pants
> Learnt a lesson in our hands
> Gifts from his King Manuel
> Are only suited for a funeral.

> Aiyo Gama! Your brass vessels!
> Toilets here have better essentials
> You are the palace's top lampoon
> For our king uses a gold spittoon

"Did I hear *da-Gama* and *Manuel*?" enquired Pedro again. "What is the meaning of *Aiyo Gama*?"

The sailors went about picking supplies for the ship, but Escobar looked distracted. "Is this a song of praise or otherwise?" He turned to Karim. "You think we should find out?"

> Aiyo Gama! Your six hats
> Are being used to trap rats
> This inverted silk-cloth pot
> Don't suit our king's top-knot

> Aiyo Gama! Your branches of coral
> Are almost close to being amoral
> You'll never impress our local girls
> They're already wearing pure pearls.

The singing picked up momentum, gathering more singers who clapped and rocked their bodies to the beat.

"I do think they're singing to poke fun at us," Escobar frowned. "Listen carefully! You will hear them calling our captain Gama's name."

Karim made a pretence of trying to understand. "There appears to be many Hindustani words in it. Kais should be able to decipher easily it if these songs are abusive or an insult to your king."

> Aiyo Gama! Your chest of sugar
> Made our king look like a beggar
> If you had bothered to reconfirm
> This is where it all went from

Pedro Escobar now looked irritated. "It's *Aiyo Gama* again. You hear them? I should have brought Kais here instead of you! Wish I could figure out this infernal language!"

Karim looked alarmed. He was doing the best he could. He hoped things would go as Sankaran had planned. He watched the singing and prancing of the multitude with anticipation.

Suddenly it was Khadir who now joined with a new verse of his own.

> Aiyo Gama! Your cask of honey
> Must have cost quite some money
> Sad! For look around at every tree
> This land has honey for us for free

The crowd laughed, some holding their stomachs, some even rolling on the floor.

Pedro Escobar looked frantic. "I've got to know what's going on. I'm sending a man to fetch Kais! You're sure this is Hindustani?"

Karim shrugged. "Does sound a lot like it," he lied. "Only Kais can say for sure."

Khadir now looked unstoppable, his voice singing at a very high pitch as the drummers warmed up to him. Not to be outdone, the flautist too took a high pitch as the next verse commenced.

> Aiyo Gama! Your barrels of oil
> Are of olive from another soil
> They will stay in their barrels shut
> We only use oil of the coconut

A Portuguese sailor departed for the ships in the harbour at a signal from Escobar. "I've sent for Kais. Let's get him to hear this before they stop singing."

But Pedro Escobar need not have feared on that account. Sankaran had no intention of stopping the singing till Kais was brought to the marketplace, especially now, as his plan was succeeding very well indeed. Besides, Khadir appeared to be in a deeply inspired mood, lyrics lucidly leaving his lips in the high pitch he was so fond of.

> Aiyo Gama, your twelve almasares
> Prayer books and Catholic wares
> Gave our deacons a strange allergy
> It does not seem to be their liturgy

A number of Saint Thomas Christians in the crowd laughed aloud. Pedro Escobar looked in the direction of the harbour. He waved frantically for them to hurry as he saw the sailor he had sent escort Kais out. They in turn saw him signal and broke into a run towards the marketplace just in time to catch the lyrics of the last verse that the stimulated Khadir spewed out.

> Aiyo Gama, finally your scarlet cloth
> Made our poor king retch and froth
> In Portugal it is sheet for your bed
> Here it's used only to cover the dead

The crowd cheered and laughed aloud as a breathless Kais finally took his place beside Karim. The drumming had reached a crescendo before the singing finally concluded. The flautist and the two drummers led by Sankaran moved towards Pedro Escobar. Sankaran briefly greeted Escobar with a raise of his hand. He could see a mild sense of nervousness in the man who quickly waved at the other Portuguese to join him. With a native crowd so large the air appeared thick with some kind of strange anticipation despite the festive mood.

"Ask him what the meaning of that song is," Escobar addressed Karim, indicating Sankaran with his hand. "I wish to know if it is about our captain or our king."

Karim drew Kais close to him while edging defensively towards Sankaran. His heart was beating fast and he swallowed in nervousness. Then with all the courage he could muster he spoke to Pedro Escobar. "Tell the captain that Kais and I are not a part of your crew or your voyage any longer."

Pedro Escobar's face wore an incredulous look. "What do you mean you are not part of the crew? Don't you know we are the champions who have found the sea route to this country? Champions of Europe who touched these shores? Oh I see, you have both managed to find some supporters here, have you?" His face reddened and his hand poised for a moment over the hilt of his sword, but quickly fell back to his side when he noticed a dozen enormously built Nair swordsmen led by Achutan step purposefully into the marketplace.

"Well planned! Well done indeed! Let the captain hear of this. He will turn every gun we have towards your city." Escobar's face was now a deep purple in anger and helplessness. "That song!" he stared at Sankaran. "That song was a ruse to bring Kais out! I should have known!"

"Ask him to save his breath!" Sankaran turned to the interpreters. "And if he is threatening us, remind him that his ships lie anchored in the harbour like sitting ducks and within range of our guns too. It will take little time to turn the fleet into a heap of burning firewood at the least provocation from him. He is free to leave with his captain."

After Sankaran's message was translated, Kais spoke for the first time. "You people enslaved us and kept us in chains despite our agreeing voluntarily at Melinde to do your work for a fee. We have had to wrest our freedom from you. There was no other way. You people cannot be trusted."

Pedro Escobar and his three compatriots left for the harbour in silence. Anger surged through his head at the native cunning of the people he had encountered on these shores. He knew it would require far more men and firearms to subdue this wealthy nation. On climbing aboard his vessel he turned and shook his fists at Sankaran standing on the beach. "You sir, will be singing another song when we come by again, by God!" he promised.

It was already two months since the hapless Portuguese ships had harboured at Kozhikode. Now despite adverse weather conditions, preparations for their return voyage had to be made in haste as the Moors and the Mappilas could easily storm their ships if they wished. That apart, the sense of insecurity and uncertainty the crew felt had grown into a kind of weariness and the tempers of the senior sailors aboard were frayed. Vasco da Gama's request for permission to leave an agent behind at Kozhikode in charge of the goods and merchandise he could not sell was refused by the King. The Samoothiri instead insisted that da Gama pay regular customs duty in gold like any other trader. He had to finally sell whatever he could at prices he had no control over, even abandoning some goods for want of time and space. His primary concern was the difficult navigation he would have to undertake against the South West monsoon winds in the Arabian sea on his way home.

On Monday, the 29th of August 1498, aloft a swaying palm on the beach, Sankaran watched four vessels leave the shelter of the Kozhikode harbour and head towards the open sea. He shook his fist at the fleet. "Champions indeed! Every other nation knew their way to these shores millennia ago."

THE CURSE OF ALAMELAMMA

One has heard of the Maharajas of Mysore. A kingdom of South India that has had a single dynasty ruling between 1399 and 1947 except for a period of brief interruption caused by Hyder Ali and Tipu Sultan. Post 1947, the dynasty continues to be part of the cultural heritage of the region with the Maharaja symbolizing an important part of the ethos and religious rituals of the region. However, what many are unaware of is that this dynasty was once cursed by a noble woman and the effects of the curse are still to be seen. There have been no convincing explanation todate as to how a curse could actually manifest and its effect made visible for all to see even today. This curse which was uttered sometime in 1610 by one Queen Alemelamma (of which one can read about in all the history of the Wodeyars in books, encyclopaedia and the internet) is taken very seriously in South India. And just as she had cursed, the place called Talakad did actually turn into a sandy wasteland subsequently, the river Cauvery did turn into a whirl-pool and every alternate Maharaja since 1610 could not beget an heir to the Mysore throne. Even the latest scion to the throne who passed away in Dec 2013 died heirless as the curse dictated. In this story we have a witness to the events that took place on that fateful day in 1610, someone who actually saw and recorded his eyewitness account of events that lead to the dreaded curse.

It begins with an interesting story about one Otheyoth Kannan of Malabar, a district of the Madras Presidency (British India) at that time. His name was referred to as O. Kannan or "OK" by his unit over the wireless radio during the South East Asian operations of the 2nd World War often to the confusion of the other wireless operators in the region. An intelligent and intrepid youth, before the war Kannan worked as an apprentice in the Cannanore Cantonment at Burnassery impressing the station British commander by his ability to read and speak fluent English. He was also adept at deep-sea diving and showed considerable skill in assembling radio equipment in the battalion's workshops.

Following a scuffle on the cantonment football field during which he dislocated the jaw of a local landlord's son and in the ensuing fracas even knocked out an Anglo-Indian youth, Kannan set sail for Borneo in 1936 aged 22. He was serving the British in North Borneo when the 2nd World War began and was subsequently deputed to the 11th Indian Infantry Division stationed there and later to the ABDACOM to repair WS19 radio sets. Not much more is known of his role during the Japanese invasion except that for some months he was believed to have roamed the jungles of Borneo with local militia carrying out guerrilla attacks on the occupying Japanese army rather than surrender as his division had done. Later he made a perilous journey to Dutch Batavia along with a group of bedraggled and injured Indian soldiers.

Between 1943 and the end of the war, in the rapidly changing political environment of the time, he hid in Batavia alternatively in the guise of either an Azad Hind Fauj member of one Dr. N K Menon's team, or a Karto Suwiryo follower, both keeping him above suspicion of the occupying Japanese officials stationed there. Following the defeat of the Japanese in 1945, Kannan felt a longing for home, and for the first time in nearly a decade since he left his homeland started sending regular despatches, mostly long narrative letters, to his family in Malabar. In one of his despatches he wrote a detailed account of his discovery in 1943 of what he called the "de Jong" manuscripts, which he had accidently come across in a half-burnt library in one of the abandoned Dutch villas of Batavia that had been bombed in the previous year by the Japanese and reduced to rubble. Among many Dutch books, papers and correspondences that he examined, he was intrigued to find a number of manuscripts written in ola (coconut palm leaves) which he instantly identified because it was written in an archaic form of Malayalam, his mother-tongue. Batavian locals reported the wrecked library to be the collection of an eighteenth century Dutch Commander of Cochin that had been archived in the villa. Many of the ola manuscripts were damaged by fire and subsequently by the dousing of water that put out the blaze. The rubble had not been cleared for over a year since the bombardment and rain water had seeped into many of the buried items in the library. A considerable number of furniture and artefacts appeared to have been looted by the locals. But the piles of rubble had somehow also preserved many of the books and documents from further damage. Out of sheer curiosity and being well versed in the language, Kannan studied the partially damaged manuscripts for weeks trying to make some sense of their origin and meaning. He deciphered that some of them were religious texts, apparently from the temple of Guruvayoor. In due course, what Kannan managed to translate from especially one bundle of the ola manuscripts was the most astounding. It appeared to be the writings of a Namboothiri Brahmin of Guruvayoor, who had once served the legendary Queen Alamelamma of Srirangapatna and even witnessed her death on the river bank of "Māyilangi."

How such manuscripts reached Batavia is not very hard to trace if one looks closely at the events of history many, many years before the 2nd World War.

By 1663 the Dutch had wrested control of much of Kerala's trading stations, ports and factories that had been earlier occupied by the

Portuguese. In the early part of the eighteenth century, they appointed Jacob de Jong to command the Dutch forces along the Malabar Coast. In 1731, dissatisfied by some of his actions and decisions and his involvement in the local politics of the region, Jacob de Jong the Dutch Commander was recalled from Cochin by the Dutch Supreme Government at Batavia. The ola manuscripts appeared most certainly to be part of the personal effects of Jacob de Jong that he had carried with him for some unfathomable reason all the way from Malabar to Batavia. For about 200 years the manuscripts remained among the Dutch archives in Batavia and for reasons best known to their keepers, lodged in the ill-fated villa at the time the Japanese bombarded the place.

Back in the early 1700s, Jacob de Jong had engaged the Dutch forces effectively to expel the Portuguese from the coasts of Malabar and gained enormously by monopolizing the pepper and other spice trade. But the Dutch officials of his time also eyed the enormous wealth stored in many of the temples of this region of India (now Kerala). In times of relative peace, the Dutch, using African mercenaries, often attacked and looted some of these temples. Anticipating such arson, temple priests, Brahmins families and local Nairs collaborated often to hide the hoard of gold, expensive idols and precious jewels deep underground in vaults beneath their temples or in other secret locations far away from the area. Despite this, intimidation and torture of temple priests or the translation of the temple archives often led the Dutch to the secret hiding places of the temple's treasure. Could Jacob de Jong have mistaken these manuscripts to also contain some clue or lead to temple treasures?

In 1716 the Dutch colonist army raided the Guruvayoor temple (present day Thrissur District). They looted whatever temple ware they could lay their hands upon and set fire to the western portion of the temple known as the Western Gopuram. Among a large number of ola manuscripts that were confiscated by the Dutch was a 100-year-old manuscript whose inscription appeared to have been started in the

Hindu month of "Sravana" in Saka 1567 (about August 1645) by one Sankaran Namboothiri, narrating events related to another kingdom, north of Malabar and referred to in the manuscript as the "Mahishuru" kingdom.

From the translation of the palm leaf document, it appears that Sankaran Namboothiri, the author of the manuscript, was an occultist, a sorcerer of some kind, an architect as well as a very learned Vedic priest. The ola manuscript claimed that he was thrice offered the position of 'melsanthi' (chief priest) of Guruvayoor, but that he declined to accept the position.

The first chapters or introductory portion of the manuscript read like any other temple archival manuscript of that time. It deals with a brief opening account of the author Sankaran's position at Guruvayoor. It then goes back to Sankaran's parents and a chronicle of his lineage from a Kerala Brahmin family that served the temple of Mookambika at Kollapuram in the Vijaynagara empire as well as some significant events that occurred during his younger years at the Kodachadri shrine where his family suffered isolation and hunger. But as it progressed, the narrative contained detailed accounts of how and why the Mookambika shrine became the royal temple for the Nagara Rajas. It also recorded the events that led to how the idol of Mookambika was adorned with rare jewels sent to Kollapuram by their Vijayanagara and Alupa patrons.

It can be speculated that Jacob de Jong may have managed to translate certain portions of the manuscript and discovering that it contained the names of many temples and especially a reference to a particular set of valuable ornaments innumerable times in the manuscript, thought it prudent to retain it until he figured out where these mentioned temples were located.

Half way through the manuscript a strange tale is narrated by Sankaran Namboothiri. Firstly, from Sankaran's account it becomes clear that it was the father (named Keshavar) of Queen Alamelamma who invited the author of the manuscript, a young Brahmin boy at that time, to reside near the palace at Srirangapatana and serve the Rayas as a family priest at Tiruvarangam (Sri Ranganathaswamy Temple). Sankaran was given 4500 "kuzhi" or 125 "marakkal vaedaipadu" of land and a house by Keshavar, which was later artistically rebuilt by him following Alemelamma's marriage to the Ranga Raya. The manuscript further states that Sankaran served Queen Alamelamma for fourteen years from the time she attained puberty, through her marriage to the Vijay Ranga Raya, Raja Thirumala, and until her death at Māyilangi. A later portion of the manuscript narrates Sankaran's meeting with Odeystan Raja at Cheluvanarayana Swamy Temple in Thirunarayanapura, and the strange series of events that ensued.

Throughout the manuscript the word "Odeystan" appears to refer to the Mahishuru kings. The word "odeystan" in Malayalam however means "owner." Why it is being used by Sankaran to mean "Wodeyar" (as the dynasty is known today) is not known.

This ola manuscript from de Jong's collection is the first evidence we have of how Rani Alamelamma got her name. In the manuscript, Sankaran states that her father Keshavar loved the musical compositions of a poet named Annamacharya, who lived more than a hundred years before their time. Keshavar especially loved the "sringaara sankeertanas", romantic lyrics that celebrate the love of Lord Venkateshwara for Alamel Manga, performed by courtesans, which he often listened to in Raja Thirumala's court. When his daughter was born, he named her Alamel.

After her marriage to Raja Thirumala she began to be addressed as Rani Rangamma or Alamelamma by the raja's subjects at Srirangapatana. Raja Thirumala was already married to Lakshmi Chellamma of Thalakadu for 20 years at the time, but she did not bear him an heir to succeed the Srirangapatna throne. Sankaran's manuscript records that it was on the behest of the queen that the Raya married a second time, but that visitors and guests from Thalakadu and Māyilangi were not pleased by the second marriage of the king. If the heir to the throne was to be born of Alamelamma, they felt that the

Raya would neglect their province. From calculations drawn from the Saka era (the Hindu calendar which Sankaran uses in the manuscript), the Raja was 53 years old when he married for the second time the beautiful 15 year old Alamel on a Wednesday in Saka Agrahayana 1526 (December, 1604).

Sankaran discovered that Alamel was a pious girl from the day he was given charge of the child. So much so that he suspected she was an incarnation of some Devi. In the years to follow he would teach her various sacred mantras and she in turn would engage in severe forms of meditation and fasting. She could speak Sanskrit, Kannada, Tamil and Malayalam with ease. She would read the writings of Kumara Vyasa that were in circulation at that time. Sankaran was astounded at her ability to recite the Krishna Paatu he had inscribed on ola in Malayalam while serving the lord at Tiruvarangam. She worshipped the Krishna Paatu ola and kept the bundle of leaves wrapped in a saffron cloth beside her even when she slept.

"On many occasions I have seen the "Devi" possess the young girl," Sankaran writes in his manuscript. "Occasions when she assumed the demeanour of a much mature woman than her years and spoke with great wisdom."

Sankaran states that Alamelamma has no illusions about her purpose in the palace. She remained subordinate to the senior queen Chellamma and knew that her purpose was to beget a son for the Ranga Raya. She was so detached from royal indulgences and extravagance that she would hand over her own jewellery received as gifts to the Ranganathaswamy temple to embellish the consort Ranganayaki's deity rather than wear it herself. She always chose a simpler adornment to the senior queen and often shied away from public appearances when the Ranga Raya and his royal entourage held court` or met their subjects during festivals.

When Alamelamma was about 21years of age, her husband the Ranga Raya developed a disease that had afflicted male members of his family in previous generations. The tissues on his back, chest and forearms grew into lumps that sometimes festered. Many physicians from Hampi and Malabar tried to cure the ailment but did not completely succeed. Whenever it festered the Raya became very feverish. Alamelamma was at that time pregnant with her first child and her health too was a matter of concern to the Royal family. Matters reached a head when rumours began to circulate among pilgrims arriving at Tiruvarangam that the army of Raja Odeystan of Mahishuru was gathering in their garrisons to march towards Srirangapatna. Further, intelligence reports confirmed that war preparations were afoot at Mahishuru as the Raja Odeystan was keen on conquering Srirangapatna before the birth of an heir to the Ranga Raya and instead place his son, the Yuvaraja (heir apparent) on the throne. Having many sons, he was keen on expanding his territories to place them as governors in the conquered provinces.

Sankaran Namboothiri writes that an invasion of Srirangapatna never really took place. Instead a general panic and consternation among the inhabitants at Srirangapatna ensued and an exodus began only when another group of riders, emissaries from Venkata Raya, the Vijaynagar overlord's court from Penukondapuram arrived with the news that they would not be able to send reinforcements to fight against the Raja Odeystan until after Navaratri owing to their own political problems and palace intrigues in Penukondapuram and Chandragiri. Some of the riders offered to remain with the Ranga Raya till the crisis was overcome. The rest returned to Penukondapuram.

Left to himself, a bed-ridden and very feverish Ranga Raya despatched an army to engage Raja Odeystan before he could enter Srirangapatna. But also as a final effort at peace the Ranga Raya sent a small delegation consisting of the Penukondapuram emissaries ahead of the army to parley with the Odeystan and salvage the situation somehow. It was thought that since the Odeystan was subordinate to the Vijaynagar overlords, the Penukondapuram emisseries, representing the mightier Vijaynagar, could play for sufficient time for the Ranga

Raya's recovery, for the birth of an heir and perhaps also for some reinforcements from his overlords at Penukondapuram or Chandragiri.

Sankaran notes that about this time, Keshavar, Queen Alamelamma's father disappeared from Srirangapatna on some secret mission entrusted to him by the Raya, carrying with him Alamelamma's jewellery that had adorned the Ranganayaki deity. It was not uncommon for Keshavar to take custody of Alamelamma's ornaments when no special festival or puja was being conducted at the temple. With the imminent invasion of Srirangapatna the priests did not think it unusual for the regular custodian to collect the royal ornaments and secure it in some place of safety. Even Sankaran, who was among the Brahmins that handed over the small silver chest containing the ornaments to Keshavar was at that time unaware how their action would precipitate a series of catastrophic events.

Sankaran also states that representatives of both armies met at a jackfruit grove called Keshari wherein the emissaries of Penukondapuram tried to influence a peace settlement, whereby Srirangapatna would be handed to the Raja Odeystan for a period of three months while Raja Thirumala received treatment at the Vaidyanatheshwara temple at Thalakadu. Raja Odeystan was distrustful of the Penukondapuram delegation and demanded a one-year charge of Srirangapatna. On the suspicion that the Penukondapuram emissaries were also buying time for the Ranga Raja to advance a march on Mahishuru, the Raja Odeystan arrested them. He also extracted information from the emissaries that confirmed that another viceroy was being considered by the Vijaynagar overlords at Penukondapuram to replace Thirumala until the heir expected to be born to Alamelamma was fit to rule. Further negotiations if any broke down when news arrived that the army of Tirumala Raya was already on its way to Mahishuru. The Penukondapuram emissaries were put to death by the Yuvaraja (heir apparent to the Mahishuru throne) at the Keshari jackfruit grove and an elaborate ambush was planned in which Tirumala Ranga Raya's army was routed completely.

Word of the defeat reached the residents of Srirangapatna by nightfall. Protection of the possible heir to the throne in Alamelamma's womb became the priority. In the darkness of the night, amidst fear and turmoil in the city, twenty-four heavily guarded ferries, one of which carried Sankaran Namboothiri and two other Brahmins set sail that very night from Srirangapatna along with the Royal family and innumerable treasures and food grains down the Kaveri River towards some destination unknown to the author at that time.

While the older queen Lakshmi Chellamma nursed the anguished and distressed king, the pregnant Alamelamma prayed at his feet throughout the journey. On two occasions they were required to disembark and travel along the banks of the river by foot and palanquin. It was on this second march on foot that Sankaran Naboodiri records a curse uttered by a tired and tear-streaked Alamelamma. As she was being carried in a palanquin she threw a handful of ash out on the road and cursed the Yuvaraja for murdering the emissaries of her husband. "No son of Raja Odeystan shall remain alive to sit on the throne of Srirangapatna," she uttered in anguish. "The Yuvaraj shall not see this Navaratri."

They reached Māyilangi the following day and Sankaran was surprised to find the old Keshavar, father of Queen Alamelamma, among the anxious people and physicians gathered to welcome the royal family. Security of the royal family being of utmost importance, severe restrictions were immediately imposed upon the population of Māyilangi so that no resident was allowed to travel out of the region and the visit of strangers was to be reported immediately to the ministers in charge. For some weeks the fugitive king resided in peace and received treatment at the Vaidyanatheshwara temple, but the residents of Māyilangi were hostile to Alamelamma. Sankaran records that the residents of Māyilangi and Thalakadu secretly blamed Queen Alamelamma and her father Keshavar for all the misfortunes that had befallen their king.

The town of Mayilangi is described brilliantly by Sankaran. The fertile silt of the Kaveri caused much of the land around to become lush paddy fields and orchards. Large herds of cattle were grazed in the neighbouring forest while herds of elephant, deer and peacock roamed freely between Gajaaranyam, Thalakadu and Mayilangi. There were innumerable ferries and fishing boats and the town had many large mud and brick houses with coloured wooden columns and courtyards surrounded by groves of fruit trees. Vegetables and fruits grew in abundance while the markets were well stocked with food grains, salt, incense, spices as well as cloth, copper and bronze vessels. A large and palatial house was reserved in the centre of the town for the royal family.

It wasn't long before arrows shot into trees and paddy fields of Māyilangi and Thalakadu by unknown horsemen in the night left messages indicating that the Raja Odeystan was aware of their refuge here. It was no more a secret than it was a safe hiding place any longer. Soon the injured and battle weary remnants of Ranga Raya's defeated army also began to arrive at Māyilangi. It became clear that many had changed alliance or had been killed or taken prisoner. Sankaran records in the manuscript that the sudden news of the death of the Yuvaraja of Mahishuru before the ensuing Navaratri festival did not surprise him at all. The "Devi" had already bespoken the event through Alamelamma. But Tirumala Raya's life was once again in jeopardy as it was never sure which of the returning soldiers might be carrying instructions from the Raja Odeystan to dispose of the defeated king or the pregnant queen Alamelamma for a bounty. The hostile attitude of the Māyilangi and Thalakadu residents became more evident day by day. Treachery or an assassination attempt became the major concern of the royal family.

However, none of this came to pass as the very depressed Ranga Raja Tirumala breathed his last following another bout of fever and despair after receiving news that most of his subjects had returned and joined hands with the Raja Odeystan in celebrating Navaratri and a rajya-abhisheka (coronation) with great pomp and pageantry at Srirangapatna.

Sankaran writes that an inconsolable Alamelamma, whom the Thalakadu priests and physicians prevented from entering their premises, cried before the Vaidyēsvara temple for an entire day and night, striking her head against and dislodging a lesser idol of Vaideshwara installed outside from its moorings. With a severely bleeding forehead, she carried the small idol of Vaideshwara, stained with her blood to Sankaran Namboothiri and uttered – "neither friend nor foe will worship him for a long time to come." Sankaran received the partially damaged and uprooted idol of Vaidyesvara with much trepidation. He also states that from that day the idol remained with him all his life as the temple priests were afraid to receive it back at the temple. The feet of the idol were damaged.

Following the demise of the Ranga Raya the funeral procession on the banks of the Kaveri saw outpourings of grief and anger directed at Alamelamma. It was only the senior queen Lakshmi Chellamma's intervention and pleas that prevented a direct attack on Alamelamma's person. The population of Thalakadu and Māyilangi were convinced that misfortune had befallen their deceased king by some evil wrought by Alamelamma. Sankaran, in his manuscript, even expresses a possibility that rumours instigated by Raja Odeystan's spies who had infiltrated Thalakadu and Māyilangi may have fuelled this opinion and belief. The possibility of an heir in Alamelamma's womb still posed a threat to their machinations. Alamelamma's last hope and resort was the protection she had of a handful of people that included the senior queen Chellamma, her father Keshavar and Sankaran Namboothiri.

With Ranga Raya's passing, more obvious attempts were made by the Raja Odeystan to monitor events at Thalakadu and Mayilangi. The first of them was a formal delegation that arrived to meet Queen Lakshmi Chellamma expressing the Odeystan's condolences at the passing of the Ranga Raya. The Odeystan's delegation also brought a number of chests and sandal-wood furniture that had belonged to

Lakshmi Chellamma and which had been left behind in their hasty departure from Srirangapatna. This gesture of the Odeystan was understood by all present, in that it was to deliberately convey to all that Lakshmi Chellamma had lost her seat at Srirangapatna and that her husband's palace had been occupied. Sankaran writes that the sight of the chests and furniture caused Lakshmi Chellamma to weep.

On another occasion, a group of armed horsemen arrived in search of Alamelamma's father Keshavar with orders that the Raja Odeystan had summoned him to a temple audit at Tiruvarangam. He was required to bring along with him all of Alamelamma's ornaments and declare their antecedents so that the priests of Ranganathaswamy temple may satisfy the Odeystan as to which ornaments were of the temple and which were Alamelamma's. This had to be done before the "Ghatasthapana", which, according to Sankaran the author of the manuscript, fell on 18th of September 1610 which was a Saturday. This order was deeply resented and strongly opposed by Alamelamma who declared aloud that the whole city of Srirangapatna and every priest of the Tiruvarangam knew very well whose ornaments had adorned Ranganayaki, Ranganatha's consort. "There is not a grain of gold or a single glint of precious stone in my possession that belongs to the temple," she declared. "But if it pleases Ranganayaki to have them I shall readily give it all up. But not because the Odeystan ordered me to do so."

Sankaran writes that these words, uttered by the queen, carrying the heir to the Srirangapatna throne in her womb was interpreted by the riders to mean that Queen Alamelamma still believed she had authority over affairs at Srirangapatna. It was a very tense and trying situation. While Alamelamma believed the ultimate target of these forays into Thalakadu and Mayilangi by the Odeystan's men was to eventually harm the baby in her womb, Lakshmi Chellamma on the other hand believed that the Odeystan was greedy and eager to possess the ornaments for himself. Sankaran states that he was even more confused when he heard that the priests of the Tiruvarangam at Srirangapatna had in fact been replaced by new priests from the Cheluvanarayana Swamy Temple at Thirunarayanapuram. On hearing of this Alamelamma became suspicious as to what purpose the ornaments were being summoned for. A decision was made to send Alemelamma's father Keshavar to Srirangapatna with a single piece of jewellery, the nose-ring of Ranganayaki and to meet the Odeystan and elucidate matters before sending any of the other ornaments. This decision, writes Sankaran was the most regretful one. They were never to see Keshavar again.

Some weeks passed before news arrived that the Odeystan was sending an army to arrest Alamelamma and confiscate the remaining ornaments. This spelt misfortune for Mayilangi as the residents would be seen as harbouring the fugitive queen. Alamelamma on the other hand was now willing to hand over all her ornaments only if her father Keshavar was returned to Mayilangi unharmed. However, this never happened.

Sankaran narrates that the next forty-eight hours became a period of extreme uncertainty and a battle of wits. It was not certain whether the army that was riding to Mayilangi would return to Srirangapatna with the ornaments if offered or press further to arrest Alamelamma and carry her also away with them. The delivery of her baby was almost due. The possible threat to the child, especially if it was a male child could not be ignored. There was also no news of Alamelamma's father. Had he been murdered? Was he being held hostage in return for the remaining ornaments or was it a ruse to get to the heir of the Srirangapatna throne by arresting Alemelamma? Surrounded by hostile residents at Mayilangi and spurned by an even more hostile temple community at Thalakadu where was this heavily pregnant queen to hide? Her whereabouts would quickly be pointed out to the soldiers of the Odeystan. Sankaran admits in his narrative that he wept for the poor lady in his charge, whose life had now become very pitiable.

That very night Sankaran Namboothiri and another young priest accompanied Alamelamma, two midwives and three trusted servants of the young queen into the nearby forest along with some food and clothing hoping to hold out long enough to frustrate the Odeystan's men. When the army arrived on the outskirts of Mayilangi they were courteously received by Lakshmi Chellamma. From fragmented reports received in the forest, through trusted runners, the small party in hiding tried to gauge what was happening in the town.

The first report that came was encouraging. It conveyed that the commander of the troops carried a written instruction under the seal of Raja Odeystan to surrender Alamelamma's ornaments as well as an invitation from him to the deceased Ranga Raya's family to come and live in Srirangapatna where they would be treated with respect and dignity. It also implied that Keshavar was still alive and in parley with the Odeystan.

The second message which arrived at dawn, according to Sankaran, was very conflicting and destroyed all hopes of remaining in hiding. Firstly, it was not brought to the hiding place by the same runner, but by a new man whom they did not recognize. The regular runner had been ambushed by Mayilangi's residents and handed over to the commander who had tortured him for information of Alamelamma's whereabouts. The new runner also revealed that he had reliable information that Queen Lakshmi Chellamma was under house – arrest in a heavily guarded compound in the heart of Mayilangi surrounded by a melee of local residents and priests of Thalakadu vying for compliments from the commander and swearing to bring the sorceress Alamelamma to justice. The fate of Keshavar became uncertain once again.

The little food that they had brought along was exhausted and Sankaran worried about Alamelamma's condition. She struggled for comfort on the forest floor with a child kicking in her womb. While she did not complain her hunger was evident in her eyes and the chances of procuring food from the neighbourhood became remote.

They had to remain content with a few sips of water, while below them they could see the rich fields of Mayilangi ripe and ready for harvest.

Sankaran records in his manuscript that it was at this point that he once again saw the Devi in Queen Alameamma take over her faculties. She became introspective and her demeanour became that of a sad but peaceful and mature woman. "What manner of queen am I?" she quizzed Sankaran. "An heir in my womb and God's very ornaments in my possession. Do you not see the intentions of the Odeystan? He wishes to kill this unborn child. They have robbed me of my father and now they are in pursuit of my son. Does the greed of the Odeystan so overwhelm his reverence for the father of a widow or her unborn child? Was he not begot of a mother? Oh, Hiriamma, may your sons learn in penitence for four hundred years what they have done to Alamelamma. Let their happiness in begetting an heir be afflicted again and again by remorse and repentance when they find themselves barren."

Sankaran raised his hands to stop Alemelamma from cursing for he knew the consequence of the words she uttered in this state of mind. For they had received information that the Odeystan's son, the Yuvaraja, had died since the last occasion when Sankaran had heard a curse uttered against him by Alemelamma. But she continued unabated. Sankaran witnessed the extreme pain and torment that Alamelamma was suffering. She continued to speak. "I am anguished that the residents of Mayilangi and Thalakadu could not shelter a recently widowed and pregnant woman. That they should readily surrender her to the enemies of her husband even as a young heart beats in her womb desiring only life. What life will these people allow this baby to live even if he were born?"

As dawn broke and a weak sun rose over the Kaveri river which was dense with monsoon clouds, the group huddled in the forest were alerted by the sound of alarmed birds that a search party was heading across the paddy fields. The river below them flowed gently. Though the paddy and other crops effectively concealed the approach of the search party, it soon became quite evident that a sizable group consisting of the Odeystan's men, led by local Mayilangi inhabitants, were traversing the fields slowly in the direction in which they lay hidden. In less than an hour they would reach the boundaries of the forest. "Were all this sand rather than these rich crops these residents don't deserve," uttered Alamelamma again in wrath. It began to rain heavily and Sankaran hoped it would slow down the progress of the search party.

"Devi, we do not fully know what the truth really is," pleaded Sankaran. "Please do not curse upon the lives of many who may be innocent and as yet unborn and whose lives will be afflicted by the words you utter."

But Alemelamma's rage was still relentless. "Did anyone show mercy to the unborn in my womb? Not the Odeystan, not a resident in Mayilangi, not even a Brahmin in Thalakadu!"

An important and high point in the manuscript as recorded by Sankaran is what Queen Alemelamma utters next. Cryptic as it sounds, according to Otheyoth Kannan, it appears to tantalizingly convey something that today's generation ought to decipher.

Standing in that torrential downpour in the forest she addressed Sankaran Namboothiri. "As uttered, my curse will endure only for four hundred years from today. Time flies but in a blink of an eye. I name you and place upon your shoulders to redeem this doomed dynasty. You will be reborn to restore the kingdom to the Odeystan's dynasty after four rulers have been enslaved by a servant of the state, a hundred and fifty years from now. You will be reborn yet again, seven and a half years after the 26th Odeystan in the Shravana Nakshatra and Makara Rasi and you shall bless the then Odystan on my behalf. After this unfortunate Odeystan of today, who has extinguished my husband's kingdom, sixteen more generations of the Odeystan's generation shall rule from a throne. The seventeenth, dispossessed of all power shall be the one humble enough for you to bless. For there will come a time exactly 400 years from the time of my departure today, and during the lifetime of the first dethroned king, when you shall enter the palace of the 26th Odeysthan. You will meet the Odeysthan. You will venerate and present me to him in writing. But your importance will not be recognized by the Odeysthan. In fact, when the four hundredth year has arrived you will have reason to enter the residence of the then Odeystan many times. He will not recognize you for he will be influenced by charlatans and pretenders who claim to bring him salvation. It will be some years before he learns of what I utter today, and through a much read man identifies you and seeks your blessing. For you shall not be a priest as you are today, but an ordinary family man. But you shall still possess the bloodied Vaideshwara with broken feet that I uprooted at Thalakadu. For you shall still possess the Krishna Paatu ola which I worship. For you will carry a sample of my husband's disease on your left shoulder blade and left forearm. May the then Odeystan be wise enough to recognize and identify you and invite you into his home. May he make compensation for your loss of home and land. May he pay you for the burden you carry these four hundred years and reinstall the idol at Thalakadu. Then from the eighteenth generation the Odeystan's family will be free of my curse and shall begin their rise to another epoch of glory and power in a new world."

The series of events following this utterance caught Sankaran Namboothiri completely by surprise.

First Queen Alemelamma bowed and held her belly in pain and seemed to go into labour. She then requested a midwife to accompany her as she walked along the forest path that led to an overhanging rock that overlooked the river. Sankaran was disinclined to follow her feeling it would be the midwife that she would need at this moment rather than a teacher. Suddenly from the forest behind them emerged more than a dozen soldiers of Srirangapatna. The guards seized Sankaran, the young priest in his company and the servants of Alamelamma. But for Alamelamma and her midwife who witnessed their arrest from the overhanging rock, all of them were held in restrain firmly by the soldiers.

Instantly Alamelamma shouted out to the soldiers to stop in their tracks or else she would leap into the river, some twenty feet below. Some Mayilangi inhabitants accompanying the soldiers taunted her disrespectfully at which the captain of the guard admonished them to silence with a drawn sword. He turned to Sankaran and pleaded him to talk to Alemelamma. But Sankaran was tongue-tied and grief stricken for he knew the end had come. He had heard the utterances of the Devi and not Alemelamma. And the Devi still possessed her. He wept silently. By now the captain of the guard was on his knees, hands folded and beseeching Alamelamma not to take that extreme step. Alamelamma's only answer to all his pleas was –"Can you show me my father? Where is he?"

To which the captain of the guard answered, revealing a secret that was kept from Alamelamma for fear of her life and health by even Queen Lakshmi Chellamma, "That was not the Odeystan's fault. Your father was killed on his way back to Mayilangi by some adversaries here at Thalakadu who did not wish him back."

The captain of the guard then realized his folly in revealing this tragic information at so inappropriate a moment. He now tried to take a few steps forward but Alamelamma moved further to the edge of the slippery rock, her clothes being resolutely held by her midwife who was terrified by the imminent tragedy. Crying aloud she kept reminding her queen of the baby in her womb.

By now several more people and Srirangapatna's soldiers had gathered on the banks of the river. The queen held up the silver chest in her hands. "I have never worn or desired these ornaments," she shouted at the captain. "They belong to Ranganayaki. I shall hand them over to her when I meet her in heaven. But I shall ask her why these ornaments that I willingly gifted her became more important than my father, my husband, my kingdom and my child. Would any of you let me live in peace if I were to drop this chest into the Kaveri?"

The silence of the captain and the teeming residents of Mayilangi seemed to confirm to Queen Alamelamma what she wished to know. She wrested herself free of her midwife and sat down on the rock, her legs dangling over the edge of the rock and the silver chest placed precariously on her swollen belly.

"We can retrieve the jewel box but we may not be able to save your life on time," shouted the captain of the guard in one last effort to compel her to desist from jumping into the river.

Alamelamma shouted back, "It is to pathaala that I dive. Your Odeystan will never lay eyes on Ranganayaki's ornaments again for this section of the Kaveri shall forever be a whirlpool. May what I uttered today never be forgotten. May the pride and wealth of the priests of Talakadu be sand, May Mayilangi become a whirlpool as it receives me, and may every Odeystan's joy of progeny be interrupted by afflictions and disease for four hundred years."

A loud exclamation of alarm rang through the crowd as she slipped off the rock holding the silver chest to her stomach. The midwife tried to grab the queen by her hair but was left with a clump of strands in her fist. Alamelamma had disappeared into the swirling waters and the whirlpool that she spoke of was there for all to see. Sankaran fell on his knees and wept bitterly. None dared to dive into the river after her. The soldiers seized the midwife and all of them were marched to Mayilangi to the commander stationed there. All that the captain was able to show the commander on their arrival was the strands of Alamelamma's hair that was wrapped in a cloth to hand over to the Odeystan at Srirangapatna.

Sankaran Namboothiri further states that he was immediately released by the commander's orders. He was not harassed by the commander or any of the soldiers as he was seen to have been a devoted teacher and a Brahmin priest doing his ordained duty to a royal family.

Following Alamelamma's death he decided to return to Srirangapatna as he did not wish to involve himself with the priests of Thalakadu. He bade farewell to the surviving queen, Lakshmi Chellamma, for the last time knowing quite well that he did not intend to return to Mayilangi where too many tragic memories haunted him. And as far as Sankaran could tell Chellamma never left Mayilangi again.

The portion of the ola containing the narrative of Sankaran Namboothiri's return to Srirangapatna was severely damaged by the fire and water at Jacob de Jong's villa at Batavia following the Japanese bombardment. In O. Kannan's next translated page of the ola there is a mention of Sankaran's disappointment on arrival at Srirangapatna to see that a portion of his lands had been converted into a graveyard and his house looted and even missing its doors.

Following several ola leaves that were missing or damaged, the narrative suddenly indicates that Sankaran was now a priest at the Cheluvanarayana Swamy Temple at Thirunarayanapuram deep in the Mahishuru kingdom. What prompted him to travel there is not known but he states in great detail that he was being visited frequently by the Raja Odeystan whom he had grown to respect despite what had befallen Alamelamma at Mayilangi. Sankaran had apprised the Raja Odeystan of the curse of Alamelamma and the King was often very depressed by the turn of events. The king firmly believed that a series of misunderstandings as well as unfounded suspicion was what led to the tragedy at Mayilangi, something he had not anticipated but felt fully responsible for. For several months the Raja Odeystan received instructions in the Vaishnava Dharma from Sankaran and two other Malabar Brahmins.

Following the Navaratri of the year 1616, the Raja Odeystan fell ill and suffered for several months. Sankaran Namboothiri travelled to Malabar to fetch vital herbs and medicines as well as physicians for the king. The Odeystan recovered, but in the following year, weak and emaciated, he stated privately that he wished to hand over the reins of his kingdom to his successor and live as an ascetic peacefully serving the lord someplace else. This was not easily accomplished.

But one night, following a bout of fever, he left instructions to his successor and arrived at the Garbagriha (sanctum sanctorum) of the Cheluvanarayana Swamy Temple where a few hand-picked priests awaited him. He stepped into the sanctum sanctorum closing the door behind him. Sankaran Namboothiri and two other priests from Malabar awaited him there. Placing his crown, royal robes as well as all his ornaments at the feet of the deity, he followed Sankaran through another door and unseen by anyone, left the premises of the temple in the guise of a poor Brahmin and headed for Malabar, never to return to Mahishuru again. Details of the hazardous journey through the Western Ghats, as narrated by Sankaran, makes interesting reading.

More damaged ola texts later, O Kannan translates that Sankaran Namboothiri was now in the service of Sri Guruvayurappan at South Malabar with the Odeystan as his humble assistant in matters of temple maintenance and architecture. In a final act of devotion, the aging king of Mahishuru, now living a simple Brahmin's life resolved to rebuild the central shrine. The work was commenced after the monsoons receded in 1637 and completed in1638.

It was about this time that Sankaran Namboothiri received the first offer to preside as melsanthi (chief priest) of the Guruvayur temple. There is a mention of a visit by Raja Odeystan to Tirunavaya to meet Shri Narayana Bhattathiri another scholar of the Namboothiri clan. It was on his return journey from this visit that Raja Odeystan died peacefully in his sleep on the 12th day of Kartika,1560 saka (3rd November 1638) within weeks of the completion of the Sri Guruvayurappan shrine, and was cremated on the bank of the Peraar River following a simple ceremony. Keeping to his wish, his passing was never communicated to his family at Mahishuru.

Otheyoth Kannan's translation of Sankaran Namboothiri's ola narrative ends abruptly following the story of Raja Odeystan's death. In 1957 a newspaper article in Borneo carried a small story about Jacob de Jong's manuscript collection that had been destroyed by the Japanese with some reference to the Mysore Dynasty. Again in 1961 a more detailed account was carried in a Malayalam publication perhaps released by O Kannan.

However, in 1962 O Kannan wrote to His Highness Jayachamarajendra Wadiyar along with an introductory letter from William Codrington Goode, governor of Borneo, informing the former of his curious discovery of the de Jong ola manuscripts. He did not receive a reply. In 1971 O Kannan again wrote a letter to the Maharaja specifically requesting audience with him but did not receive a reply or an appointment in return. In 1972 he travelled to India (Bangalore) and after much effort managed an hour's audience with the Maharaja. What transpired between them and what happened to the ola he presented the Maharaja is not fully known. O Kannan died in 1984 at the age of 70 in Jakarta, Indonesia. Only a few months before he died, he revealed to his family what H H Jayachamarajendra Wadiyar had said to him on his visit to India.

"Very impressive Mr. Kannan, but you've come 38 years too early. The four hundredth year the manuscript speaks of falls in the next century in 2010, many years from now. By then I wonder if anything of the Dynasty will remain even in Mysore. At the moment royalty in India is more worried about that Congress "devi" in New Delhi who is determined to destroy our heritage with her pickle of socialism and democracy. Even Her Highness, Devi Alamelamma could not have predicted this state of affairs when she cursed our forefathers."

Thus ends Sankaran Namboothir's strange account, written nearly 400 years ago, about a living dynasty of our times, inscribed on coconut palm leaves, for posterity.

FATHER, SON & THE HOLY GHOST

I t was on a stormy day in the year of our lord 1652 that Sankaran, then a boy of seventeen, riding along with his father, found themselves in the guise of Roman Catholics, on a dark and lonely road, entering the grim gates of the fortifications of a place that had been, Sankaran believed, even abandoned by God. The once powerful city of the Bijapur Sultan, Ismail Adil Shah, with its ruined mosques and temples, run over by the Portuguese and administered in the only way these foreign devotees of our lord knew. By Holy Inquisition. At dusk, as they slowly urged their ponies forward towards the ramparts of the city, evidence of such inquisition could be seen winding down the dark slope in the shape of a slow procession of hooded Franciscan monks and black cassocked Jesuit priests, crucifixes and flaming torches held high, leading innumerable groups of pall-bearers towards a mass funeral beyond the moat outside the battlements. Their low-voiced Latin chants and hymns grew more ominous than the whistling of the wind as a storm slowly gathered momentum from the Arabian Sea. The squall picked up and howled like a banshee as father and son stood on that dusky evening at the entrance of the city called Aguada, beside the Mandovi in Goa province on the western coast of the great peninsula, respectfully waiting for the gruesome parade to exit the gates before they could enter.

His father, a Nair gem trader, dismounted and stood by his pony. Sankaran did likewise, wondering what this strange pageant he witnessed at the gates of this city was all about. His father was a well-built, long-haired man of forty-seven years who had been a soldier for some years under the Raja of Kochi until the trading community of Malabar showed him the road to prosperity. His beard was still largely black and he wielded his weapons with rare agility.

In the diminishing light and the gathering storm, Sankaran beheld the dismal spectacle at the city gates with a sinking heart as it dawned on him that some catastrophic event had to have occurred within the walls of their foreboding destination for so many dead to have to exit the gates in a single procession.

"I don't like this place," he tried to whisper to his father, barely audible in the screaming wind that tore at their garments and made their animals ill at ease. "Can't we leave and go elsewhere for tonight and perhaps enter the city tomorrow in the light of day?"

"We have someone within these walls anxiously awaiting our arrival," his father whispered hoarsely in reply. "Wait and be patient. We have come all the way from Malabar, travelling many weeks to reach here. Our arrival is already delayed by several days. It is now hardly a matter of hours. Don't let such sights make you lose your courage, son." He tried to put an arm around Sankaran which he resented.

"What sort of people live within these walls?" he remembered asking, to which his father maintained a stoical silence.

The last of the grim minstrels trailed out of the gates before his father nudged him forward. They pushed and dragged their reluctant mounts over the creaking timber that bridged the moat. At least a dozen fourteen feet long *makara* crocodiles launched themselves noisily into the dark waters as they led the tired and edgy ponies over the conduit. They walked slowly towards the guards, some twenty of them who, from their vigilant demeanours, were clearly observing their arrival over the concourse to the fort with measured caution. They wore armour and chainmail and carried *arcabuz* firearms. Their extreme sensitivity to visitors could be seen in the instant lighting of their matches cords, that could instantly ignite and detonate their loaded matchlocks, if the approach of the two strangers had been anything more than a slow saunter. The duo made sure their hands as well as the swords they wore were visible as they neared the menacing militia. Three black-bearded soldiers armed themselves with their famed six-foot *alabarda* spike-and-axe infantry weapon, a dozen of which leaned against the inner walls inside the gateway. Men with crossbows were suddenly visible above the battlements moving among the muzzles of cannons that protruded from every bastion. A stranger did not enter Portuguese Goa easily.

Five Estrela mountain dogs straining on their leashes barked rapaciously at them, occasionally panting to catch their breath in the humid tropical air they were unaccustomed to. They bared their fangs and frothed in the mouth due to the incessant barking.

"Halt and identify yourselves!" The terse order was in Marathi and repeated again in Portuguese of which only the latter was understood by his father owing to the presence of these foreigners at home in Kochi and Malabar for the last 150 years. They were now within musket range and the darkness caused by the impending squall was making visibility difficult.

"Eu sao José. Não podemos entrar em paz," (I am Joseph. We come in peace.) his father responded with well-rehearsed diction.

They halted a few yards before the gateway.

"Ele é meu filho Matheus," (This is my son Mathew) his father spoke again waving his hand in Sankaran's direction. Sankaran instinctively felt his chest for the string with the wooden crucifix they had uncomfortably thrown about their necks a few miles earlier when the fortress was first sighted.

"Where do you come from?" queried the guard again.

"From Malabar. From the kingdom of Kochi."

"State your purpose."

"We carry a message for Camilo O Rei."

Sankaran breathed a sigh of relief at the instant recognition of the name his father uttered, for the sky had just broken, belching out its first torrent accompanied by successive bolts of lightning and thunder. Sankaran wondered about the funeral procession that had just made its way out towards the river, their strange chant now drowned by the uproar of the pounding deluge. The sound of the reverberating thunder and howling wind momentarily silenced the dogs but set the ponies neighing and stomping about in agitation prompting a couple of guards to grab their reins to control the animals while Sankaran and his father were searched. The night was now well upon them.

They were immediately ushered in and divested of their swords. As torches were lit, they were searched for firearms, gunpowder, Hindu or Islamic articles, inscriptions, manuscripts and books. They were queried if they possessed native symbols or any kind of talisman, even whether they carried *tulsi* plant leaves, betel or areca nuts, none of which were found on their person. Had they any, they remained at home in Kannur in the face of the holy inquisition they were well warned about before commencement of their furtive journey to Goa. Save the crucifixes that they wore around their necks and a sealed message his father carried in a bamboo case, even the gold coins they carried were counted, weighed and deposited with the guards deployed to escort them into the city.

Having undergone the formalities of reception, they were led into the streets of a city in darkness. Two tall soldiers marched them through a maze of passages and barracks that led from the outer walls into the city. They were met with curious and hostile gazes by the denizens of the garrison they passed. But for the guards escorting them, it appeared they would have been run through by the blade of many a drunken soldier before they even cast eyes on the inner city.

"Ah-ha! rice Christians!" jeered a one-eyed soldier of some rank, holding a large metal cup, standing outside a doorway from which emanated the odour of stale liquor. The guards saluted him.

"From Malabar. Carries a message for Camilo O Rei," explained their escort.

The soldier of rank stepped out on to their path despite the rain and his singular eye regarded their riding pantaloons and thick black tunics with suspicion. The other eye was a grotesque welt he displayed with pride. Sankaran's father stopped and looked him in that one eye in a fashion he had seen his father do all his life whenever confronted by a stranger. It was a haughty attitude he had acquired under the Kochi army, a demeanour that exhibited innocence, honesty and fearlessness but which had also on many occasions preceded an avoidable duel.

The one-eyed captain relaxed and let them pass, but not without another scornful taunt of "rice Christians!" His father's only reaction was a clenched jaw as they ambled along. Bereft of their swords, Sankaran felt a sense of relief. But he also knew his father would not have let the captain's affront bother him at the expense of the secret mission he held more important and which was now hopefully nearing its end.

Sankaran recalled the sense of some terrible premonition as they walked into paved alleyways now gushing with rain water and dirt. Even the pungent urban air they inhaled carried an ominous stench that he could not ever forget. An occasional whiff alternating between sea-salt, sweat, burnt flesh and blood. A slaughter house, a meat-curing shed or even a tannery back home did not presage a sense of such horrific apprehension with its odours as did the torpid air in these alleyways. They walked perhaps a quarter of a mile in silence before the streets grew broader, the air smelled cleaner and a few trees came into view.

Sankaran wondered about his father. Strange was the mission of this man who could trust and convince only his own begotten son to accompany him, much against the wishes of his mother. He tried not to think of her. Her memory seemed terribly misplaced in the situation in which they treaded.

Drenched to their skin, they finally halted outside a gated courtyard within which stood a large, rambling stone house whose grey façade matched the weather and the sombre mood they were in. Their escort knocked at the door. It opened almost immediately. A short conversation ensued following which they were ushered in without ceremony by a swarthy Marathi youth in foreign clothes. Sankaran and his father found themselves inside a large hall lit by innumerable candles that appeared to be positioned to dissolve every shadow in the room. In the centre of the hall sat a regal gentleman in a long, well-fitted coat and shoes that tapered at the toes. The embroidered ends of a fine muslin scarf covered his throat. He had a high brow, well-shaped moustache and the trace of a carefully trimmed beard at his chin.

Trickling pools of water from their drenched garments they hesitated to step further than the threshold, a polished wooden floor covered by an exquisite carpet. Seeing their indecision, the man suddenly stood up and walked towards them addressing the two armed soldiers over his father's shoulder. "You two may get back to your guard. I have identified my guests. There is no cause for concern anymore." The soldiers retreated obediently. "And restore my guests their possessions, horses and their weapons immediately." He spoke with authority as he waved at the Marathi youth who immediately joined the departing guard. "Bring their horses to the back where I have my stables." As he waved the youth away, he shut the door behind them.

"Sekharan, how are you my good man?" he hugged Sankaran's father's wet torso. For the first time since their arrival at Goa he saw his father smile, perhaps at being addressed by his real name. Grim and wry, but a smile nonetheless, something that could not have manifested unless his mind was at ease.

"You appear to have sprung some deep roots here, Your Highness," his father responded in Portuguese. "This is Camilo O Rei," his father explained in Malayalam, turning to signal a discrete eyewink in his direction. "King of the whole island of Lanka. Your Highness, meet my son Sankaran, now Matheus for convenience."

Sankaran looked quizzically at both of them as Camilo laughed at the introduction. Then they exchanged banter in chaste Portuguese interspersed by whispers, chuckles and natter like childhood friends. They went on in that manner for quite a while till Sankaran was convinced that both his father and Camilo O Rei shared a cherished past he knew nothing of. He ignored them for the moment. The warmth from the numerous candles was causing vapours to rise from his damp clothes as he gazed at the unusual room they occupied. Curious and exquisite pictures adorned the walls alongside weapons and candle-stands. The walls were washed white and the tapestry that adorned them were beautiful and delicate.

The monsoon storm raged outside. The wind whistled and the torrent battered the roof under which they stood. But not a flame flickered within.

In due course his father beckoned him, speaking in Malayalam. "Come let us refresh ourselves. His Highness must depart now. We must respect his hospitality and conduct ourselves as required by our present circumstances." They bowed respectfully at the impeccably dressed gentleman as he departed with an approving smile in their direction.

Camilo O Rei the king of all Lanka left them almost as quickly as a horde of Marathi and Konkani servants and assorted retainers arrived to divest them of their wet clothes. They were led into separate quarters within the premises of the large house where they were sanctioned a hot bath and presented with some unusual but very comfortable Portuguese attire. They emerged from their ablutions resembling some burlesque conquistadores, for once able to smile at each other in rare hilarity at their transformation after a long and distressing journey.

"They don't have shoes my size," complained his father in mock annoyance as he met Sankaran bare-footed once again in the candle-lit hall. "They don't have *camisa* my size," Sankaran alternated in good humour flapping about to exhibit the oversized shirt he was provided to wear. "I'll be the gladdest to see my own tunic back once they have washed the Mahishūru dust and the Maratha grime off it."

They heard the sound of hooves, the nickering and snorting, as their ponies were brought to the rear of the house. The Maratha youth came into the hall a few moments later and respectfully returned their swords, money and other possessions. When the servant had departed a serious look came over his father. "Son, the time has come to tell you of the grim nature of the mission we have undertaken, a mission of extremely dire consequences were its purpose known to the Portuguese authorities. Only then will you understand the importance of this arduous journey we have made and why we are here today. We shall be resting here for a few days. But while we do that, let me tell you the story." With that his father commenced the narration of a most astounding tale:

"Sankara, as you know, we have many friends among the community called the Saint Thomas Christians at home in Malabar. You have heard them referred to as the Syrian Christians or the Nasranis. They have thrived alongside us in Kerala in peace and tranquillity for the last one thousand and six hundred years. Even the Knanaya Christian community who arrived on the Malabar coast a few centuries after Thomas the Apostle, integrated into the Saint Thomas Christian community and called themselves Nasranis. And all these people have remained in communion with their chief priests or patriarchs in what is called the Church of the East, somewhere in the Syrian region. I have met merchants who have been to this great church in a place called Seleucia on the coast of the Syrian kingdom.

"Now in recent years, since the Portuguese arrived and took control of some of our coastal regions, their attention was drawn to the great number of Christians already in existence here, tracing their ancestry and religious traditions to Thomas, the Apostle of Christ."

"In fact, that was a bitter pill for the Portuguese to swallow," remarked Sankaran, "as an older and, shall we say, a more original form of worship, as preached by an apostle of Christ himself was already thriving in our lands."

His father continued. "The religious politics of Europe really hit our Christian brothers here about 50 years ago. You see the church in Europe was itself divided into the Latinized or Roman Catholics on the one hand and the Orthodox Church of the East on the other. Now, as I mentioned, our Christians still preached in the ancient Marthoma tradition, that is in Syriac form in which their scriptures existed, of which Aramaic, the language used by Christ, was a dialect. They drew their liturgy from the church of the east."

"Until the Portuguese arrived," Sankaran remarked. "Yes, I know about this."

"Yes, you must have also noticed, Sankara, since the last 52 years or so, with further colonization and using Goa as their headquarters the Portuguese have been bringing Roman Catholic priests headed by an Arch Bishop to our lands to take over the religious leadership and supremacy from the Christians of Malabar. The Jesuits of the Society of Jesus in particular have been attempting to Latinise the Thomas Christians under the jurisdiction of the Portuguese padroado and into the Latin Rite of the Catholics."

"They have succeeded to some extent," observed Sankaran.

"Not without resistance and resentment," reminded his father. "Now the Nasrani Christians of Malankara are well established and have been following the Marthoma tradition of this land, just as Thomas had preached to them. The Portuguese tried for a long time to lure the Nasrani's with both money and positions to come under the reign of the Roman Catholic Church, but the Nasranis would not be tempted.

"Finally, one Shakuni-type character, an extremely intelligent but devious man, an Arch Bishop of Goa named Alexio Da Menezes tried to influence and force the Malankara Church-head Arch-Deacon Geevarghese of the respected Pakalomattom family to bring the Malankara Church under the control of the Roman Catholic Church of Goa. All the Malankara church representatives including Arch-Deacon Geevarughese unanimously refused to entertain such a proposal. The wily Arch Bishop Menezes then used his influence with the Raja of Cochin and summoned a meeting of all the representatives of the Church at Udayamperur."

"When was that?" enquired Sankaran.

"Half a century ago," replied his father. "How this man must have induced the Hindu king, I fail to understand, Sankara, but the Raja threatened that absentees to the meeting would end up having their properties confiscated by the state and lose all existing privileges they enjoyed in the kingdom. Thus the historically significant Udayamperur Synod took place about 52 years ago, led by this Bishop Menezes, the Portuguese governor, higher Government officials, and armed Portuguese soldiers with the full support of the Raja of Cochin.

"Oh, is that how they ended up under the Roman Catholic Portuguese?" Sankaran exclaimed.

"The sad and hapless Arch Deacon Geevarghese along with 133 priests, 10 deacons and 660 laymen attended." Sankaran's father's voice took a sad note. "The meeting enforced decrees upon our Christians to accept the faith and traditions of the Roman Catholic Church and the authority of the Pope. The Malankara Nasrani Syrian Christians reluctantly signed the decrees, as they were afraid of the Portuguese opposition and the wrath of their own King."

"But they must have accepted the Roman authority with dissent," Sankaran observed. "The Portuguese were triumphant only because the St. Thomas Christian's east Syrian traditions and liturgy, which they had been following since the time of Christ, was finally replaced by Latin Liturgy and traditions of the Roman Catholic Church. So, what you are saying is that the Synod of Udayamperur finally brought the Saint Thomas Christians fully under the authority of the Latin Archdiocese of Goa. Well, well. So that's how it all happened? I always wondered."

"Archbishop Menezes high-handedness and arrogance, together with the stupidity or perhaps ignorance of the Raja, crushed the independence of the ancient Church of Malankara, one of the principal churches of the Saint Thomas Nasranis," explained his father. "Till then, religion by force was unknown in our land."

His father continued the narration. "The feeling of resentment at the Portuguese hegemony over their ancient religion has been fermenting among the Nasranis for half a century now. Lately, their need to regain independence has become even stronger as they witness the corruption and injustices under the Papal yoke the Portuguese had placed upon them. To realign themselves once again with the Church of the East, they knew they required a Bishop from the Eastern Church for their rescue. The fact is that many letters were written by the Nasranis to their parent church in Seleucia, but replies seldom make it back to Malabar. The Portuguese who now control the sea intercept their letters of appeal for Syrian prelates. I have heard from merchants that there were occasions when attempts of Eastern clergy to come to Malankara were physically thwarted even as they boarded at Hormuz. The Portuguese mercilessly kidnapped and even murdered some of the Syrian and Persian Bishops, completely discouraging the arrival of any new eastern Bishops to this region."

"That does not explain our purpose here," Sankaran countered. "What are we doing in Goa? This place smells evil and sacrilegious in ways I cannot explain. I have no doubt that horrible things are happening here."

His father looked upon him with a solemn gaze. "I would not want any danger to visit us. I promised your mother that. But I hope you are able to wield your sword with the same calmness and ruthlessness that I have trained you to."

Sankaran was silent. His father continued. "I could not trust anyone else for the task at hand," he was silent again for a brief moment. "Well Sankara, the sooner I speak of it, the more prepared your mind will become. This is why we are here. Even as I speak, somewhere in the labyrinths of this fort hides a man who is a Bishop of the East, a man who with great care, disembarked at Surat. In the guise of a jewel merchant he has dared to arrive at Goa. The route further to Malabar by sea is too risky. Every human being is scrutinized very closely by the Portuguese. However, through a Nair Malayalee he met at Hormuz some months ago, he was able to send a message to Archdeacon Thomas of Malankara of his possible arrival at Surat and the manner in which he would communicate from Goa in the guise of a jewel merchant. A week before we started our journey from Malabar, a business proposal was received from a rich merchant presently stationed at Goa, a man named Alexis, enquiring if the Malankara church required new embellishments of gold, silver or precious stones for their altar. This was the cue Archdeacon Thomas was waiting for. We have now to safely escort him out of Goa."

"And what part does Camilo O Rei, the king of Lanka, whom we just met, play in all this?" Sankaran enquired.

"Camilo O Rei the king of Lanka, is a descendant of Dona Catherina, or Kusumasana Devi, her name before she converted to Catholicism. She ruled the Kingdom of Kandy which is roughly the eastern half of Lanka. She was a child survivor of a smallpox epidemic which effectively wiped out her entire family, the royal family of king Karaliyadde Bandara. As an orphan she was brought up by the nuns of the convent in Mannar. Hers is a short and sad story, a pawn in the devious machinations of managing state affairs between the marauding Portuguese invaders and the local royals. She was dead by the age of 35 having borne six children for the royal lineage serving two kings. Camilo O Rei is one of her descendants and could become king of Lanka if the Portuguese succeed in recreating their stronghold there. He remains in a sort of protected exile in Goa for now. But his lineage and obvious status is what I hope to put to our use. He is also a good friend of Manuel Mascarenhas Homem the present governor of the small portion of Lanka that the Portuguese still hold. In his youthful days Camilo led a rather lonely life. I was his only friend. For some years while he was at Kozhikode and Fort St. Angelo at Kannur, we rode, fenced, hunted and ate together. I once saved his life, many years ago, when he was surrounded by some Moors and Mappilas at the Mappila bay, who for some reason were out to kill him. He owes me that one. As we planned this journey here to Goa, I thought it wise to have him know in advance of our arrival and use the leverage he could provide to accomplish our task."

"Does he know the identity of our jewel merchant?" Sankaran enquired.

His father shook his head. "Camilo knows nothing of our purpose here. He believes the gentleman from Surat is a jewel merchant. I cannot risk revealing the truth to anybody with Portuguese interests, not even my childhood friend Camilo. But at least we can exit the fort with a letter that certifies the man as an authentic jewel merchant. Camilo will do that much for me, when I request him. I am sure of that. That is all I need."

Even in the comfortable quarters provided to them by virtue of being Camilo O Rei's guests, the goings on within the fort could not be avoided or ignored. The mood was sombre as the Inquisition of Goa was painfully visible and disturbingly audible as more dead bodies were evacuated from the city following cries of agony and the odour of burning flesh that reached their nostrils even up to the great distance where they were quartered. Hindus and Muslims died in great numbers as well as recently converted Christians who were suspected of not being quite faithful to the Catholic way of life, or suspected to have converted only to remain alive. Rice Christians!

Sankaran and his father remained in the Portuguese ward for the first night and the following morning, avoiding being seen too often outside their quarters. This wasn't difficult as the heavy rain had not quite stopped even by midday. The afternoon passed by in a slow drizzle and Sankaran could sense an uneasiness in his father's otherwise calm and alert composure. When they stepped out of their quarters after a late supper to check on their ponies, it had stopped raining and for the first time that day, they heard voices.

With a flaming torch held high, Camilo O Rei could be seen walking with a distinguished and elderly looking gentleman in a grey beard, shirt and black sleeveless tunic, wearing a broad belt over baggy trousers typical of merchants elsewhere in the region. He looked strong and athletic despite his age and wore a sword as if he knew how to use it. As they approached, Sankaran had no doubt as to who the gentleman with Camilo was.

His father greeted Camilo and the elderly gentleman with a bow. Sankaran did likewise.

"Here is Alexis! Come from Surat to meet your needs!" introduced Camilo with a wave of his hand. "Gentlemen, stay indoors and discuss everything you wish to. The weather promises to be as foul as yesterday. I have other matters to attend to. Jewels are not my priority yet. Not yet! Repeat Mappila Bay!" He laughed condescendingly as if some joke was meant by his last words. Sankaran's father forced a laugh as if he detected some obscure humour.

Once inside, his father hurriedly ordered him to close and fastened the heavy wooden door. Sankaran obeyed. The elderly man sat down on a chair he was shown by Sankaran's father. The old man looked grim and anxious as he extended a hand upon which he had just slipped on a bright-stoned gold ring.

"That will not be necessary. Put it away," his father addressed the elderly man. "We will not be kissing your ring. We are not your Catholic or Saint Thomas Christians. We are Hindus. Nairs from Malabar, sent to escort you out of Goa and protect you on your journey.

But do accept our salute and our deep appreciation for the risk you are taking for our Christian brothers in Malabar."

"Not Christians, eh?" the old man repeated, a sneer appearing through his grey beard. "I am not Alexis your jeweller either. I am an Inquisitor of the Holy Order of the Society of Jesus on behalf of His Holiness, Pope Innocent the tenth. You two have just sounded your death-knell! Good Camilo has gone to alert the guards who will be here shortly." His hand gripped the hilt of his sword.

It was then that his father struck. In less time than Sankaran could blink his father struck the man across his temple with his bare hand, putting him into an instant state of sleep. The man nearly pitched forward from his seated position in the chair but his father instantly pushed him back against it. His twitching arm released the sword, still in its scabbard, and fell limp by his side. His father then removed the ring from the unresisting finger.

Almost immediately, there was a soft tap on the door. "Are you done, Sekhara?" It was Camilo O Rei.

"Go on, open the door," his father ordered. Sankaran carried out his instruction immediately. Camilo burst into the room, closing the door behind him. He was wearing his sword. "We have very little time, Sekhara! How long will he remain asleep?"

"For about half an hour, I should think," Sekharan replied.

"We will have to be rid of him first," Camilo declared in earnest. "Come, help me carry him out of here. We'll have to throw him over the ramparts. There is an unguarded portion of the fortifications I will lead you to. Hurry!"

It all happened in an instant of intense furtiveness. The sleeping inquisitor was heaved upon Sankaran and his father's shoulders while Camilo led the way at a quickstep that was only short of a sprint. They panted up many stone steps, around bulwarks and battlements before reaching a point where an embrasure indicated by Camilo showed just about enough gap to drop a human body through. It was done, the inquisitor remaining wedged and suspended in the masonry for just a moment before falling away and disappearing into the waters below with an audible splash. Sankaran shuddered as he heard more splashes. Crocodiles were launching themselves towards an unexpected dinner. All three were winded by the pace at which things happened.

"Get back to your quarters and wait for me," Camilo ordered in a hissing whisper as he broke away from them. "Check your saddles. You will be riding tonight."

With that, the king of Lanka disappeared, while they silently retraced their way back to their quarters.

"Repeat Mappila Bay," muttered Sekharan, breathing heavily upon entering. "That was his forewarning to me. Something must have gone wrong that caused that Portuguese inquisitor to confront Camilo and try and trap us. So far Camilo has proved to be reliable. But let us wear our swords now and stand by our ponies at the rear. We can watch anyone who might approach our door."

"What happened at Mappila Bay?" enquired Sankaran in a whisper as they buckled their belts and slipped their scabbards on to them.

"To put it briefly, I once long ago utilized the same technique to put a Moor to sleep the moment his hand reached for the hilt of his sword. It was a similar situation. We were young boys then. Camilo's beautiful sister was playing with us on the beach. The Moor, impersonating one of the Raja's officials and, taking us to be some urchins from the local village of Kannur, was trying to carry away the girl by threatening us with arrest for trying to steal a boat. We had simply stepped into one to keep clear of the hundreds of crabs on the sandy beach. Seeing the Moor fall, some more Moors and Mappilas rushed us with swords in hand. One nearly decapitated Camilo as I leapt out of the boat and felled them one by one. The rest of them scattered out of fright."

It was a long wait before Camilo O Rei appeared, once again with a flaming torch held high and accompanied by another elderly man. "Your man, the real Alexis is here, Sekhara," he introduced the stranger. "I had kept him in hiding from the moment he arrived from

Surat. I didn't want someone here think he might be a Bishop from the East," he smiled a mischievous smile at Sankaran and his father. "You can get acquainted properly later. Now get on to your ponies and get out of here. There are a couple more in the stables, ready and saddled. I have stuffed the saddlebags with enough food and water for the three of you for a couple of days. I will accompany you to the gates. I doubt we should run into anyone tonight but the blessed rain, which should pour in torrents any moment. I will deal with the guards at the gate and see you through."

All four mounted their ponies and rode slowly, walking the ponies through the steadily increasing drizzle. This ride through the eerie fort city of Goa in the ever increasing rain would forever remain in Sankaran's memory. It felt like eternity, marching over street after street of cobbled stones, hoping the sound of the rain and wind would keep the noise of their hooves from the ears of the drunken soldiers and guards sheltered in their barracks on either side of the streets. As they approached the outer walls the torrential downpour was now interrupted by bolts of lightning and loud claps of thunder.

The guards at the gates appeared to have been expecting them. They saluted Camilo in immediate recognition, silently opening the gates for them to depart.

"I have my own trusted men at the gates, tonight," Camilo spoke in a low tone. "You have a long way to go. I will not delay you any longer. It was a pleasure to do this bit for your Christian brothers back home. And a fine Christian you'll make too, Sekhara!"

"I'll never become a Christian," Sankaran's father confessed looking disdainfully at the dismal fortress he was exiting.

"And I'll never become a king," confessed Camilo O Rei, the de facto king of Lanka.

Sekharan turned to his friend Camilo and placed a hand on his shoulder. "You always were one, Your Highness! I am thankful. Very thankful for the kindness you have shown me and my son. And also for taking care of and handing me my guest."

"I wish you a safe journey home, Sekhara," the king of Lanka proclaimed in reply as they crossed the creaking timbers that bridged the moat. "Farewell. Once out of the city gates you're on your own. Be gone before the dawn lights up the horizon and someone from the ramparts notices the father, the son and the holy ghost."

They rode away smiling, knowing the mischievous face of the king of Lanka was watching them from the gates of Goa as they disappeared into the night.

It was many miles away from Portuguese territory that they finally decided to stop and eat. It had stopped raining as they rode further inland from the coast. The rising sun was already hot, as early as it had begun to glimmer through the eastern sky, shining like needles of light through the forest foliage. They chose a large banyan tree that shaded them from the sun before the saddlebags were opened for food.

Father and son now gazed at the stranger who had not spoken a word through their entire ride. He was an older and much frailer man than the inquisitor they had fed to the crocodiles the previous night. He appeared exhausted by the night's adventures and appeared to have some difficulty even swallowing the bread, fruit and honey that they sat down to consume.

"We are sorry about the circumstances of your arrival and departure from that infernal city," Sankaran's father spoke to the patriarch. "Do you feel unwell? Is the food not of your liking or are you in need of some rest? I am Sekharan and this is my boy Sankaran."

"I am Mar Ahatalla, and I am dying," came the shocking reply. "I have made several attempts to come to Malabar, over many years. My efforts have constantly been thwarted by the Roman Catholics who await in Melinde, Hormuz and every other port, to guard against the arrival of any bishop sent by the Catholicos of Seleucia, the Eastern Church. I have arrived this far at great risk. I have nobody and nothing to go back to but my church. So I chose to rather march forward as my Lord chooses. At Surat some Indian doctors have diagnosed my disease as a form of carcinoma. I have little time to accomplish what

I have set out to do. If I manage to ride and keep pace with the two of you, how soon would we reach Malabar?"

Sankaran now felt surprised at his father's plan. "I had no intention to take you to Malabar and endanger your life," his father explained. "The Portuguese would make all efforts to arrest and be rid of you. Instead I have another plan in execution already. Ere we left Malabar, I had conspired with the Archdeacon Thomas of Malankara with the plan to escort you to Mylapore, near Madrasapattinam instead of Malabar. Representatives of the Archdeacon will meet you there at an appointed date. We have enough time to travel through the Mahishūru kingdom, through Bednur, Basavapatna and Sira before we move further south through Kolar and Salem. Then it will take another week of riding eastward before we arrive at Mylapore."

It was towards the end of a blazing hot day in late July that the Portuguese guards at Mylapore observed three travel-worn men slowly ride their ponies into the town. There was not much resistance to their entering the region, having explained their identities as small time traders seeking better products in the Portuguese territory. The stifling heat had reduced their countenances to a tawny hue. They finally found shelter only in the paddy-threshing yard of a Muslim businessman, who listened with great interest to the fictitious story of their business interests in Hyderabad, the kingdom of Muhammad Quli Qutb Shah.

"The paddy is not due for harvest yet and so these rooms will remain empty for two months," the Muslim farmer explained. Then having extracted an unjustifiably large sum as advance for accommodation and food, he left them alone in a large barn with a deep well beside it for their water requirements. Sankaran's father decided to let the ponies feed and rest for some days before selling them.

The appointed day arrived and Sankaran accompanied his father to a foreordained spot near the Nossa Senhora da Luz, an old church. As expected, two men assigned by Archdeacon Thomas from Malankara, disguised as local traders awaited them. Without much ado they were led to the barn, where after many years of patient waiting, two Saint Thomas Christians of Malankara finally set eyes on a Bishop of the East.

Mar Ahatalla feebly rose to greet them. To his amazement, Sankaran's father handed him a gold ring embellished with a bright stone which he instantly recognized and slipped on to the middle finger of his right hand. The two Syrian Christian deacons Chengannur ltty and Kuravilangad Kurien from Malankara knelt before the Bishop and kissed the ring, with tears of joy streaming down their faces.

"I have prepared letters for you to carry to Malankara," Mar Ahatalla addressed the two deacons," handing them a small package he had been carefully hiding in his person since leaving Surat. "It carries my insignia and the necessary seals."

"And what of Your Holiness?" enquired Kurien, still teary-eyed and on his knees.

"I cannot travel to Malabar until it is safe. Not until I receive word of the repercussions that will follow the pronouncement of my letters to our people there. You would have done your duty in delivering these letters to Archdeacon Thomas. Now only God will dictate the course events must take."

Sankaran and his father stepped outside the barn to allow the clergymen to converse, congregate and pray.

"What is to happen now?" Sankaran enquired of his father, wondering if Bishop Mar Ahatalla would ever find it safe to travel to Malabar.

"He is dying of some incurable disease," responded his father. "He can do little. At his age, he should go home to some place where he may die peacefully. The Portuguese would torture him and subject him to much humiliation if he presents himself in person. His letters are a much better tool to foment the kind of rebellion the Saint Thomas Christians need."

"He is a stranger in a strange land," observed Sankaran. "Once the two deacons leave for Malabar, we cannot abandon him here. Mylapore is still Portuguese territory."

His observation left his father in deep thought. The two of them strolled casually outside, going around the barn many times in silence.

"Son," his father addressed him eventually. "What would you consider a success for our brothers, the Nasranis? What would best serve the Thomas Christians of Malabar?"

Sankaran pondered over his father's question for a while. "Well, for the Nasranis, what I would consider a triumph would be freedom from the Roman Catholic hegemony, freedom from the Papal yoke that these Jesuits of Goa have placed them under. Freedom to pursue their own way of worship without the dictate of the Portuguese. To follow a tradition they were accustomed to for over a thousand and six hundred years. Free from the Latinization they have been enduring these last fifty-two years."

"Well-spoken Shankara," his father complimented. "Now tell me, what would you consider a success for Bishop Mar Ahatalla?"

Sankaran was prompt. "To see his people, the Saint Thomas Christians revert to the Church of the East and pursue the liturgy of their choice. I cannot think of any other ambition he could have. He is a dying man. I doubt he seeks any official position in the hierarchy of the church but to see their autonomy restored."

"True," his father approved. "And what do you and I want?"

Sankaran smiled. "To be done with this business and be home. I miss those coconut trees swaying in the breeze."

His father halted and looked at Sankaran astutely for some time.

"Then, my son," he spoke, gazing at the door of the barn inside which the Bishop of the east held communion with his two principal deacons from Malankara. "Are you prepared to perform a bit of mischief for the benefit of us all?"

Sankaran nodded.

When the deacons from Malabar emerged from the barn, Sekharan had only one advice to give them. "Hurry. Depart for Malabar immediately. Deliver the letters to your people. I will guard and serve your holy father's needs as best as I can."

As they departed, Kurien the older deacon blessed Sankaran's father. "You Sekhara, will make a good Christian!"

Sankaran felt his father shudder. "Have you ever been to Goa?" he enquired in abrupt response.

When the two deacons had departed, Sankaran's father entered the barn. Sankaran followed him inside. Bishop Mar Ahatalla sat on a heap of hay looking pale, but peaceful. Sankaran wondered what unspoken pains the old man must have endured through his entire journey. For a dying man he never complained of anything. He was able to sit with an admirable composure of silence and equanimity.

"I have a plan, Your Holiness," began his father squatting respectfully on the floor of the barn before the Bishop. "I request you to write one more letter."

Three weeks would pass before Sankaran and his father arrived at Malabar. They stood respectfully before a shocked and anguished Archdeacon Thomas, head of the Malankara Church.

"He says he has been taken prisoner, Sekhara, how did this happen?"

"His Holiness could not be moved out of Mylapore easily," explained Sekharan. "Within a few days of our arrival there, rumours were rife about our arrival. The Portuguese were looking for two Malabarees and a foreigner. Every road and river crossing was heavily guarded. It was with difficulty that we arranged the meeting of your deacons with him. But having achieved that we were soon on the run again to avoid the Portuguese. We travelled mostly under cover of darkness, but their pursuit was relentless. Our progress was slowed, as His Holiness was travelling in poor health and fragility, requiring rest and shelter very frequently. Finally when we were located and surrounded by the Portuguese militia, my son and I had no choice but to collect this last letter from His Holiness and depart under cover of a lucky thunder storm that struck the region that night."

"He believes he will be taken to Goa to face the Inquisition and has requested us to rescue him," the Archdeacon announced. "We need to send spies to keep us informed of all the Portuguese vessels that depart from the East Coast. From Madrasapattinam and every other port. Every single vessel will require to berth at Cochin or Kozhikode once they circumnavigate the peninsula for supplies. We will conduct a rescue mission before they leave our harbours for Goa. Moreover, I will inform our people of these developments and we will commence our protests with the Portuguese immediately."

Meanwhile, Bishop Mar Ahatalla lay dying in a secret hideout in Malabar despite the best medicines Sankaran and his father could procure. "I do not wish my people to see me like this," His Holiness begged. "It will break their spirit. Your idea was good. Let them believe your story, Sekhara and revolt as they should have done fifty years ago. The anguish they feel at not being able to see me will cement their ties to the Eastern church far better."

When the Saint Thomas Christians heard of the arrival of the suspect ship at Cochin three weeks later, they marched 25,000 strong onto the harbour demanding the immediate release of their Bishop. The confounded Portuguese could not accede to their demand as they held no such prisoner. Finally, in order to prevent any attack on their officials and ships, they spread what they believed would serve as a more palatable story, that the unfortunate Bishop Mar Ahatalla had been accidentally drowned. It only made matters worse. Nobody believed their story. The Nasranis suspected foul-play. The summary disposal of their Bishop shocked the Christian community and wounded their feelings beyond repair. They refused to believe that Mar Ahatalla had drowned accidently. Within weeks, anger against the imperious Portuguese and their arbitrary actions effervesced into a mass upsurge which heralded their severing all connections with the Goan Church. As Sankaran's father had well foreseen, the incident of

Mar Ahatalla presented an occasion for the St. Thomas Christians to retaliate with a spirit, unity and moral ground they did not have fifty-two years ago.

Their determination finally culminated on January 3, 1653, when under the leadership of Archeadeacon Thomas, an assembly of about 25,000 Nasrani Christians assembled at the Church of Our Lady in Mattanchery near Cochin to take a historic oath. Their priests, leaders and the people congregated near a large granite cross that stood in the grounds of the church. Crowds of onlookers also gathered outside the church compound.

Under a discreet shade of a large mango tree, outside the compound of the bustling church, two men carried a veiled palanquin. The frail figure reclining within the palanquin breathed heavily as he watched the proceedings in secret. The two bearers of the palanquin were a father and son.

Since all the people could not touch the cross simultaneously for the purpose of taking the oath, they held onto ropes that were fastened to the cross in all directions, causing the cross to bend to their collective force. Then in one voice they took the solemn oath of freedom from the clutches of the Roman Catholic supremacy and the pledge to follow only the Malankara Nazrani traditions. The *Koonan Kurishu Satyam* (Oath of the Bent Cross) was now a history of the land.

As the ceremony of the oath was completed and cheering broke out among the crowd, the veiled palanquin silently moved away from the shadow under the mango tree outside the church, unseen and unnoticed by anyone. Only the man and his son were aware they were no longer bearers of a palanquin. They were now pall bearers.

A Fort Is Breached

"Savithri, make sure that Sankaran cuts down at least fifty of them. And he is not to leave this place till they are de-husked and placed in a basket in the courtyard for purification." The order was terse and with a finality that was emphasised by the slamming of a door. Her aging husband had arrived home after his morning visit to the temple, in his usual fluster of mild rage.

The pitiable sight of the young Savithri standing at the edge of the courtyard overlooking the coconut grove, wrapped in bundles of cotton cloth called a *vesti*, that was her customary clothing, holding an oversized *marakuda* or cadjan parasol to shade her from the sun and from strange men, would forever be etched in Sankaran's mind.

Her husband could still be heard shouting orders and assigning chores to other members inside the sprawling *illum*, the Namboothiri Brahmin family mansion, punctuated by sounds of slamming and banging that the family was growing accustomed to. It was his way of venting frustration. Frustration at his disease for which the local *vaidyan*, the village's Ayurvedic physician, had stopped giving him hope. At the age of sixty, his manhood was under siege by a condition that he refused to accept. A case of impotency that was the combined result of poor diet, a severely fluctuating blood pressure, addiction to chewing tobacco and the recently acquired habits of smoking strong pungent English cheroots and downing cantonment whisky.

Health issues were well underway even as Chemmanthatta Kuriyedathu Raman Namboothiri, Raman to his people, entered his forty-fifth birthday. His first wife had died a year before of an unknown and undisclosed disease which only the village *vaidyan* knew of, along with the fact that it had been brought home by Raman's promiscuous forays. Following a prolonged period of ill-health, he thought he had recovered sufficiently to marry again. He was not to know that the *vaidyan's* medication had not overhauled his loins to the virility his mind and fertile imagination had him believe.

Raman was left with more doubt than scruples and would continue on nocturnal expeditions to try and revive his now flagging métier, but to no avail. He was laughed out of most places ere he entered and the regulars who pitied him tried bizarre methods to have him perform, but mostly with the motive of draining his wealth more than his energy. It became apparent to him that even experienced hands and bodies could no longer stir the comatose object of his obsession. Fervent prayers in the morning at the local temple and ardent vices in the night in places of ill repute constituted Chemmanthatta Kuriyedathu Raman Namboothiri's life.

It was again the village *vaidyan*, with all good intentions of bringing the wayward Namboothiri Brahmin back on to the good road of virtuousness, who planted the idea of remarriage in Raman's head. He even qualified his suggestion: Perhaps marrying a very young and extremely beautiful girl might just reinstate his libido to the indefatigability it once enjoyed. Being a Namboothiri himself, the *vaidyan* even knew enough families in the district to also suggest who a possible bride might be. Savithri, daughter of Kalpakasseri Ashtamoorthi Namboothiri of Mukundapuram Taluk. A girl who could read and write.

The girl was then nine years old, having just been burdened with the misfortune of an unusually early puberty. The marriage to the sixty-year-old man which followed shortly would be as much a shock for her as the sight of menstrual blood oozing out from between her legs only a few months prior to it. That year was 1893.

The unsuspecting *vaidyan* had no idea that his innocent therapeutic prescription had set into motion something that would shake the very pillars of the caste and feudal system of the land and unleash tremors that would rock even the foundations of the kingdom in the days to come.

In the same year that he married Savithri, eleven-year-old Sankaran was hired by Raman, not just for his trustworthiness but also for being an active and obliging boy who found time after school to earn some money. Raman also believed the young Sankaran was the village's proverbial idiot who could do no harm even if allowed into the Namboothiri's sacrosanct compound. He was clean, obedient, submissive and spoke very rarely. He went about his given task with care and appeared grateful with the wages paid. There was enough work to do in the compound for two whole seasons and the sight of Sankaran on the top of one of his coconut palms gave the Namboothiri *illum* a sense of security and satisfaction.

There was another reason why he employed Sankaran. Sankaran's oldest sister Madhavi was his young wife Savithri's *thozhi*, an escort, chaperone and attendant. A hired one, but nevertheless her nursemaid and protectress. This was a strict custom in the Namboothiri caste and household. None of their women would be seen without such a *thozhi* or governess in tow at all times. The *thozhi* was also a witness and proof of the noble Namboothiri woman's chastity.

Sankaran worked in the orchards and plantations around the large Namboothiri mansion, which sat on a ten-acre compound, bordered on all sides by a thick wall of loosely piled laterite rocks serving as a boundary. This was their high ground that overlooked another thirty acres of low-lying and often flooded paddy-land that belonged to the

Namboothiri household. The caste of labourers that worked in the paddy-fields were prohibited from entering the high-ground.

About a hundred meters from the mansion, within the compound's perimeter and much closer to the coconut grove, was another structure, the family referred to as a *pora*, a much smaller house consisting of about three bedrooms and a kitchen. This thatched-roofed structure served as a quarantine exclusively for women, who were required to retire there during the period of their menstruation and take a ritual bath thereafter before being allowed back into the mansion. The *pora* mostly lay in disuse as only Savithri was now required to retire there for three or four days in a month, the other older women having aged well past their menopause. Of course she would be accompanied by Madhavi who would herself be experiencing menses due to the menstrual synchrony of both women caused by close association over a considerable length of time. The men of the house stayed far away from the *pora* to avoid pollution.

The coconuts felled, Sankaran paused to wipe beads of sweat off his face and slid down the last palm tree, ready to carry the harvest into the courtyard to dehusk them. Savithri, observing this, moved back a "safe" distance away from him. The Namboothiri community caste laws that she was required to observe meticulously ensured that she positioned herself twenty paces away from any man, however high his caste. As Sankaran deposited the coconuts in the courtyard, she found she had retreated to the threshold of the door her husband had just slammed.

The door opened. It was Madhavi, carrying a cane *mooda* for her mistress to sit on.

"Oh, please do supervise my brother's task with great care," she advised Savithri in mock seriousness. "Just in case he's forgotten to count up to fifty."

Savithri sat down on the *mooda* still holding the cadjan parasol. Her beautiful and dignified countenance did not betray her inner turmoil even to her maid. She sat silently, her eyes fixed on the business of gathering and dehusking the coconuts as her husband had ordered.

"Madam, there are only coconuts in this grove and only one method by which to cut them down," Madhvi continued in the same mocking tone. "There is only one way to dehusk them and only one courtyard that Sankaran, my brother, has been gathering them in, for the last many years. And you know what Madam, he does know how to count to fifty."

This finally made Savithri laugh. "You dare tease me, Madhvi!" she countered in a whisper at her maid. "Did you not hear my husband give me those orders. Do you think I want to disobey him?"

Madhvi raised her eyebrows, "Oh don't you? Well that's a change. In which case I do have a few programs to cancel, don't I?"

Savithri tilted her parasol to shield her face from Sankaran and made a face of mock annoyance at her maid. "Nobody changes my program. Not even my husband. That is one area of my life I and I alone control," then assuming an air of her real status, she frowned at her maid and pointed at Sankaran who was now fumbling about among the heap of coconuts.

"What's wrong Sankara?" his sister called out. "What are you groping about? When are you going to dehusk the coconuts?"

Sankaran's curved Malabar chopper had been misplaced and he was rummaging about the fifty coconuts which lay gathered on the yard. "My chopper! I just had it with me. Where has it disappeared to all of a sudden?"

"Oh no! It's already getting to be dusk," Madhvi reminded him. "You'll end up dehusking them in the dark. Where could you have dropped it all of a sudden? You had it in your hand a moment ago when you hacked down the coconuts."

Sankaran looked perplexed. "Where could I have dropped it?" he felt a little infuriated as he walked through the grove to locate where he might have left it. He searched around the grounds where he had picked up the last of the coconuts from but could not locate it.

"I better go look for another chopper in the kitchen," Madhvi decided. "Otherwise this business is not going to end even after sundown." Then in a low conspiratorial whisper she took a final dig at her charge. "Looks like my brother's delay is putting paid to your nocturnal program, madam!"

"Oh, just shut up and look for a chopper!" Savithri flushed slightly as she shooed her maid away. "Now can you see why this kind of work needs supervision?"

As Madhvi disappeared into the house, Savithri beckoned Sankaran with her forefinger. A little startled at the unusual gesture, Sankaran walked towards her slowly, his body assuming a reverential bow as he approached the lady, stopping at a point he assumed was about the statutory twenty paces from her person. But to his discomfiture, she cast the parasol aside, exposing her face in the most uncharacteristic manner as she continued to indicate with her forefinger to him to come closer. Sankaran swallowed in nervousness at the disparate situation he was being put into. It was like murder. A social taboo he was being asked to breach. Her finger would not stop moving as she continued to indicate he was not close enough to her satisfaction. At about ten paces from the venerable lady his trembling legs refused to function or support him. He squatted on the courtyard floor like a half-trained and nervous pup refusing to comply to any obedience drill.

His mouth went dry as he gazed upon her face. It was the most beautiful face he had seen. Fair, oval and flawless. Doe-like eyes that appeared as if they were smiling on their own. Perfectly formed lips that curved ever so slightly at the corners, displaying an expression of sarcasm even as she boldly looked into his eyes. Over the shock of beholding her beauty he also realized for the first time that she was just an adolescent.

"Whether you finish dehusking the coconuts or not, you will leave the *illum* before sunset, do you understand me?" she ordered in a low voice just sufficient for him to hear. She glanced furtively at the door through which Madhvi had disappeared. "Make whatever excuse you need to. Broke your chopper, hurt your arm or whatever you think fit. But be away by sunset," she now lifted the same forefinger, wagging it as a sign of warning of some dire consequences if he disobeyed her.

"But the master ordered me…" Sankaran began to plead, but he was immediately silenced by the icy tone her voice took. "Forget the master for once and listen to me! The kitchen does not require fifty dehusked coconuts first thing in the morning. Ten will do. You can come back tomorrow and dehusk the rest. The master will hardly pay attention to a little slackness on your part. I'm sure you are more valuable to him than that, are you not, Sankara? Now step away before anyone comes by."

Sankaran had barely retreated to the permissible distance from the mistress before Madhvi appeared at the doorway with a chopper. "Sankara, try this," she addressed her younger brother, "It hasn't been used for a while, but I cannot find any other sharper than this in the house." As she handed Sankaran the chopper she did not fail to notice that her mistress, in a quick motion, had only just covered herself with the parasol and also that her otherwise quiet and composed brother was mildly distraught and shaking like a leaf.

Back home that night, Sankaran had difficulty sleeping, wondering at the loss of his chopper and the strange behaviour of his mistress. Sankaran admired women. More than that he respected them. He was deeply aware of the inconsistencies of his society that created a Savithri. How old could she be? Eighteen? Twenty? The wife of a sixty-year-old, ill-tempered and dishevelled old man? Unbelievable. Above all he had heard many unconfirmed stories and rumours about the man's conduct as well as his health. But the most bewildering moment of the day had been the beautiful lady's mysterious conduct.

Next he wondered about his chopper. How in heavens had it vanished? It was not easy even to dehusk ten coconuts with the blunt and under-weighted chopper his sister had handed him. And boy! Did the sun set fast this evening? He had sensed his sister would have a few awkward questions to ask him. He had somehow managed to melt into the shadows of the grove while Madhvi was preoccupied with her mistress. Then he had rushed home, washed up, wiped his face and hands...wait a minute! He suddenly remembered where his chopper was! Good God! Why had it not occurred to him earlier?

Lying on his bed, it dawned on him that while he was still aloft the last palm tree, he had struck the hooked end of his Malabar chopper into the tree-trunk to free his hands for the purpose of removing his turban and wiping the sweat off his face. He had slid down and commenced collecting the coconuts from all over the ground, quite forgetting where he had left the chopper.

There was only one thing to do about it. He would have to wake up an hour earlier than usual and make it back to the *illum*. Once he retrieved the chopper from the tree he could work on the remaining forty coconuts even before the old Namboothiri discovered that he had not finished his task. He hated the thought of listening to an angry rant from his master first thing in the morning. Sleep finally came to Sankaran as a sense of relief calmed his mind.

When an important purpose was at hand, it was not like Sankaran to oversleep. Habit had tuned his sleep cycle to obey his mind. And his biological need to rest was satisfied on such occasions by the rare ability to sleep a deeper sleep in compensation for the shorter period that he lay in bed. He woke up more than an hour before he had planned, quickly freshened himself and headed to the *illum* in the moonlight. He used a small side gate to enter the compound and reached the grove with ease. Even as he began to climb the palm that he remembered driving his chopper into, he could see its curved blade glinting in the moonlight high up on the tree.

Sankaran had barely reached his chopper when his attention was suddenly drawn by a movement in the direction of the *pora*, the outhouse that functioned as a ladies' quarantine a few yards from the grove. It startled him sufficiently to have him freeze into a state of immobility on the tree immediately thereafter. There was a subdued murmur of conversation after which a door of the quarantine house opened and a lady wrapped in white cotton emerged from it. The ghostly figure held an oversized *marakuda* or cadjan parasol under the moonlit night, stealthily making its way to the mansion. Sankaran was in no doubt as to who was under the parasol. And the spinning of the parasol several times in her hand betrayed her action of looking over her shoulder at the *pora*. She even paused for a moment below the tree he was perched on. Fortunately for Sankaran, she did not think of looking up. For at one point he was so directly above her that he might have lost his grip and landed on the *marakuda* as she furtively made her way towards the main house. Soon a door of the *illum* opened and she disappeared into the shadows of its interiors.

Sankaran now pondered over whether it was wise to walk into the courtyard to dehusk the remaining coconuts. He was aware of the purpose the *pora* served in the Namboothiri's household. But the murmur of conversation that he had heard, followed by the unusual hour of the parasol bearing figure's departure from the outhouse, unaccompanied and unescorted by his sister, her hasty and sneaky disappearance into the *illum* didn't all quite add up or make any sense to him. At any moment now, he expected Madhvi his sister to also emerge from the *pora*, whatever her cause for delay might be and head in her mistresses' footsteps into the *illum*. He was not interested to know what their business in the *pora* that night might have been.

Still in mild confusion over what he had witnessed, he slid up the palm further to retrieve his chopper from the tree. He had barely detached it from the bark where it was wedged when he once again detected a movement at the very door from which the parasol bearing figure had first emerged from the *pora*. God! Now he would have to do all kinds of explaining to Madhvi, for she would in most likelihood notice him atop the tree and wonder why he was at the *illum* so early. But even before he could think of a reasonable answer his eyes beheld something that startled him so much that he nearly lost grip of his perch.

It was not his sister, Madhvi, who emerged from the *pora*, but what looked like a young Nair gentleman, well built and wearing gold jewellery that dazzled in the moonlight. His sweat-glistening torso was uncovered, except for a white mundu that was neatly wrapped around his waist. His long hair lay untied and as he silently walked under where Sankaran sat perched like a shocked night owl. The man's heavy breathing betrayed his exertions of the night as he let himself out of the little side gate through which Sankaran had entered. Once outside the *illum* compound and well into the paddy fields, he could hear the man begin to whistle a blissful tune, fearlessly and as casually as if he were welcoming the morning sun.

"Oh, my God," thought Sankaran. "The beautiful mistress of the *illum* has a secret lover! That too below her caste! Good God! Think of the pollution and the scandal if this were to be found out by someone! How long must this have been going on? Does Madhvi my sister, her *thozhi*, even have a clue?"

Before his master, Raman Namboothiri, returned from his daily morning duties in the neighbouring temple, Sankaran ensured that all the coconuts were neatly stacked in a basket in the courtyard. While he awaited the day's instructions at a respectable distance, his master set about purifying the contents of the basket amidst chanting of prayers and the sprinkling of holy water that made the coconuts sufficiently clean and sacrosanct for use in the Namboothiri kitchen.

"Don't you touch them once I'm done," he warned in his usual malicious manner. "I have never allowed a single impure article into the *illum*," he proclaimed with a final splatter of holy water.

This morning the irony was not lost on Sankaran. His mind began comparing the flawlessly beautiful figure of the young mistress of the *illum* with the gangly looks of her puritan husband, a grey, balding individual with a permanent scowl on his face and bags under his eyes. His shoulders were stooped and wrinkles that had long etched his face now invaded his neck and chest. Even his voice was a forced rasp from too much chanting in the temple.

"I have work to attend to at the temple," he added. "You will sweep this courtyard and take the day off."

Sankaran nodded in acquiescence, not able to look at the man in the eye. The bejewelled Nair's image in the moonlight kept popping up in his mind.

"Today is Thursday and also an auspicious day. Many weddings will be performed at the temple. Inform your sister that I am off," he rasped, placing an umbrella under one arm and holding the end of his yellow silk mundu in his hand. Sankaran thought he looked pathetic as he shuffled down the front path on his way to the temple. Broom in hand, Sankaran watched the slouched figure disappear down a mud track in the paddy fields.

"Weddings, weddings and more weddings!" the familiar voice that mocked the departed man startled Sankaran and made him spin around. The freshly bathed figure of Savithri, ash and sandal-paste anointed on her forehead and wrapped in a starched, sparkling white *vesti*, emerged from the *illum* doorway.

She stood on the wooden threshold looking at him quizzically before he could regain his composure and resume sweeping the courtyard.

"Do you know how to write or read?" she tilted her slender neck as if to look him in the eye despite his downcast head. Before he could answer, she interposed "Are you upset about something?" her sharp instincts seemed to have picked up something in Sankaran's demeanour.

"I could not complete college," he straightened up and replied as if to help unbend the tilt of her head. She smiled, revealing a perfect set of teeth with a hint of dimples on both her cheeks. "Oh, that's not so bad. You have completed your matriculation, haven't you? You are not a school-boy anymore."

He began backing off, aware that their distance had to be maintained.

"Wait," she raised a hand that made him stop. "You know, a year before I married your master, a very important man visited our neighbourhood. I remember listening to him through an interpreter. So many years since, everything he said makes perfect sense. But at that time even my father was perturbed by the man's obnoxious statements against us Namboothiris and all our communities in Malabar."

Sankaran worried whether he was still within the tabooed distance from her. But she appeared unconcerned and continued. "The man spoke Sanskrit, English and Hindi. But I was told he was a Bengali from Calcutta. He called Malabar a madhouse of casteism, a lunatic asylum of inequality that oppressed the poor and the landless. He was severe in his criticism of our Namboothiri ways and the hegemony exercised by our men against everyone including their own women."

Sankaran was sure the forbidden distance had been breached. He decided to distance himself from her by the act of sweeping.

"His name was Yogi Vivekanandan," she continued. "He was contemptuous of our practice of untouchability and the economic disparity." She stopped. "Are you listening to me?"

He stopped sweeping because she sounded annoyed. "But Mahayogi Vivekanandan, for all that he spoke against the Namboothiris couldn't make a dent in our age old system. He could not change a thing. Do you know why, Sankara?"

Sankaran shook his head.

"Because," she began with a strange smile that made her look older than her twenty-two years. "Because, as the great Chanakya, the Kautilya Brahmin who overthrew the Nandas once said, -the best way to breach a fort is from the inside!"

Sankaran stood still trying to understand what was going through the noble young woman's mind. Had this something to do with her visitor of the night?

Almost in answer to his thoughts, she added. "And the fort has been breached long ago, Sankara! Now we have only to wait and see how many heads roll. Ah! I see you have your slippers on, Sankara. But did you go home without them yesterday?"

Confused and a little taken aback by that sudden query, Sankaran blurted, "No. I had them on when I went home yesterday."

"Then your slippers must have a life of their own," she looked him straight in the eye. "What were they doing at the base of a coconut tree near the *pora* an hour before dawn this morning?"

Sankaran began to tremble. "My chopper. I had to get my chopper," he began but it was useless. He knew that she knew what he knew.

"Don't worry Sankara," her voice took a condescending note. "I will not set that Nair gentleman on you. We were talking about Mahayogi Vivekanandan weren't we? Do you think we live in a fair society? Do you? Sankara, you are educated. Say something! We suffered in the hands of Hyder and Tipu because of this. We still haven't learnt from our stupidity. Sankara, say something. Don't you have even an opinion to express?"

Sankaran wished he was atop some coconut tree, far from this strange woman. He resumed sweeping wondering where on earth his sister Madhvi was. The lady would not take such liberties with him when a third person was around. Oh, like a prayer answered! He heard Madhvi's voice as she appeared at the doorway from somewhere inside the house, *marakuda* in hand.

"Oh Madam, there you are. I was looking all over for you." She turned to Sankaran. "Are you not done yet? Don't you have more work to do?"

"Master has given me the day off," Sankaran found his voice. "I'm almost done."

It was with a sense of relief that he left the *illum* that morning.

It was only on Saturday that Madhvi got a few hours off and was able to return to her own home that she shared with Sankaran and the rest of her family. Sankaran was waiting for her at the well to accost her before she entered their house.

Sankaran narrated the story of his previous night's adventure to her, how he had retrieved the lost chopper and finally the – he wondered if she would believe him – she must – it was not a dream – not a ghost – he hadn't been drinking – a tall, well-built, long haired, bare-chested man bejewelled and with the confident gait of a Nair...

"Sssh!" Madhvi lunged towards him, her palm clamping over his mouth. "Don't! Don't speak! Not a word more! Oh, Sankara, I had hoped you would never ever witness this." Tears flowed down her face. "You can guess what fate awaits me. You can guess how this will go against me. I have been her *thozhi*, her supposed protectress for eleven years! I have not been able to stop these men! Not once, Sankara!"

"Men! You mean there are..were..others? Different men?"

"It was always different men," Madhvi wept. "You don't know Savithri, my mistress, brother. You don't have any idea of the life I'm living all these years, brother. She is the most sought-after and expensive prostitute in the whole of Kochi. A prostitute who goes by the pseudonym Tathri."

"What? What are you saying, sister?" Sankaran could hardly believe what he was hearing. He had heard rumours of such a woman. "Tathri, Lady of the Night, Tathri, The Cuddliest Courtesan, Tathri, Fallen Woman Worth Falling For, Tathri, Next Thing To Heaven…" Sankaran began rattling out a name he had heard whispered around Kochi for years. He even believed, as most less powerful men and those who did not enjoy the privilege believed, that Tathri was a myth.

"What about her husband, Raman Namboothiri?"

"His cannon has no ammunition!" She hoped Sankaran understood. "What?"

"The cobra has no strength to raise its head. No teeth. No venom. It is as good as a banana peel!"

At this Sankaran broke into a laugh. Then laughed uncontrollably till he couldn't stand any longer. He plopped down on the stone plinth that surrounded the well and leaned against its wall holding his belly.

Madhvi sat beside him barely smiling. "It is a disease, for God's sake, Sankara! He has been that way from the time he married her. It was as if he married her deliberately to waste her life."

"But he'll definitely murder her the day he discovers this affair," Sankaran stopped laughing. "This happening in a Namboothiri family!" Sankaran shook his head in a gesture of disbelief.

"I doubt if he can do anything but pray," Madhvi's response perturbed Sankaran. "Some of the men whom she entertains derive their pleasure from the fact that she has the strength of a wild animal. Others who have tried to abuse her or disappoint her in any way have been shown the door with bruises that could only have been received in battle. Her husband would not dare touch her."

"What is she?" Sankaran began seeing a larger than life image in his mind.

"She is just a simple Namboothiri girl, Sankara. I have known her when she entered the *illum* as a child bride." Madhvi's tears flowed down again. "But circumstances, some unusual situations and unspeakable events have turned her into what she has become today. Apart from her strength, she has enough wealth accumulated to buy the illum as well as all its related lands five times over. Let me tell you the story of Savithri, daughter of Kalpakasseri Ashtamoorthi Namboothiri of Mukundapuram Taluk.

"I have heard her father Ashtamoorthi say that Savithri was an exceptionally bright child but that from about the age of five she had begun to question everything that she saw and experienced in the Namboothiri community to which she belonged. She questioned their customs, traditions, rituals and beliefs. Initially her questions were taken lightly in the belief that it was nothing but a child's curiosity. But within a year or two, her behaviour began to be seen as some kind of obsession. She was never satisfied with the explanations provided. She even criticized and rebelled on occasions. She was once taken aside and whipped severely by Ashtamoorthi when she ridiculed some of the rules, rites, norms and ceremonies before prominent members of the community. On another occasion, her father was taken aback when she challenged a senior Namboothiri of the community to a debate. She insisted she would prove that as a Hindu Brahmin sect, the Namboothiris had twisted and misinterpreted the vedas to suit themselves. For fear of being beaten at the debate, the elderly priest rather advised an exorcism claiming that he wished to identify the *yakshi*, or witch that resided in the girl first before preparing his strategy to defeat her. This debate fortunately did not materialize for the elderly priest died following a stroke. The unexpected death of the elderly Namboothiri priest only vilified her chances of securing a young, decent and eligible bridegroom.

"Matters came to a head when the poor girl attained early puberty, another sign of the *yakshi* residing in her! Her education was immediately stopped and she was confined within her home. When Raman Namboothiri approached her family, the prospects of a fatherly old man offering to marry the cursed girl came as some kind of twisted blessing.

"The worst was yet to come. On her wedding night she was raped by the younger brother of an intoxicated Raman Namboothiri who lay in a drunken stupor while the crime was being perpetrated. This was done with the full knowledge of some other elders of the family purportedly to "purify" her and drive the *yakshi* out of the girl. You see Sankara, Raman is the eldest and his life was more valuable to the family than any of his younger brothers, as according to Namboothiri custom, all property was held in his name. Her brother-in-law's death shortly after "confirmed" their suspicions and the belief that a *yakshi* had indeed been residing inside the girl and that with the brother-in-law's demise the *yakshi* had finally been vanquished and had departed for good."

"My God, sister Madhvi! Do you believe some *yakshi* actually resided in Savithri's person?" Sankaran sat numbed by the narrative.

"That night Sankara, I believe that very night that she was raped, a *yakshi* actually began to reside in her. Never before that. That *yakshi* resides in her now even as we speak. The *yakshi* is Tathri. The untold truth is that Raman Namboothiri was never able to hold his ladle up in her presence. Every time he entered her bedchamber, he felt subservient, depressed and his dipper deflated with some kind of unknown fear. You can imagine the frustration of a man who has never had the opportunity to love a wife as beautiful as Savithri. He ended up sleeping separately in another part of the house which he could enter even if he was drunk, a room where he could freely sit and drink and smoke his evil-smelling cheroots.

"The turning point came one Saturday following her sixteenth birthday. Like today I had a few hours off. Five to six hours that I come home here as usual to spend time with all of you. Except that on that fateful Saturday I inadvertently chose to get back to the *illum* a couple of hours earlier than usual. Her bed-ridden mother-in-law, her two old aunts - one near blind and the other quite deaf - were all in their respective rooms preoccupied with whatever their poor souls found to pass the time. But I could not find Savithri anywhere. Not in her bedroom, her washroom, the kitchen, courtyards or the grounds. Which made me search the one other place only she and I frequent. The *pora*.

"Sankara, I cannot speak of all that I heard and saw that day, but it is suffice to say that I was not sure whether to stay there or run. Even today I am unsure of what I should have done. For they had seen me enter. While they stared at me, she over his shoulder and he through a mirror that was on the opposite wall, with not a shred of clothing or a scintilla of shame, I nearly passed out. I ended up spinning around, covering my eyes with both hands and collapsing on to the floor trembling all over. And there I remained squatted till her visitor had departed. Today I don't even remember who he was, but my relationship, my very equation with my mistress changed from that day."

Sankaran looked at his sister with a feeling of pity. He wondered what else she had endured that she chose not to speak of.

"She did not have a word of regret or apology to utter," Madhvi continued. "It became a kind of unspoken understanding between us. An undiscussed pact. Her haughty, icy and unrepentant expression forewarned in clear terms that if this matter were to ever get out, it was not her but *my* reputation, as her *thozhi,* that would suffer. She was my charge. Whatever befell her would be pinned down as my negligence. Worse, it could easily be construed that I even taught her these deviant ways. You see Sankara, she had my complete silence, loyalty and cooperation without uttering a word.

"It took me a long time to understand Savithri and why she became the way she is." Continued Madhvi. "Today I see the path much more clearly. It began with a deep conflict within her. Unanswered questions. Severe pain, abuse and ignominy despite being born into the highest caste of the land. Observing and experiencing the despicable acts and deeds of those who were supposedly in direct communion with God. The contradictions, the hypocrisy and the injustice around her. Unlike many of the Namboothiri women, Savithri could read and she was a voracious reader. The plight of the underprivileged, the untouchables and the women in particular left an adverse and unresolved problem in her rapidly maturing mind. Sankara, as frightened as I am, I have begun to admire her. As morbid and nasty as it all sounds, I intend to protect her in whatever way I can. In the best way I can. She has made me more conscientious of my duty than I ever was. Despite Tathri, I have to find a way to save Savithri" Her tears again flowed down helplessly.

"But to what end?" wondered Sankaran aloud. "To what end is this secret rebellion of hers directed? Something of this nature cannot be hid long. And if word ever gets around that this woman of ill repute Tathri is the same Savithri of this *illum,* I cannot imagine the upheaval that it will cause, a storm of unfathomable proportions. We will all be swept away by it."

"Yes, it is only a matter of time, I fear," echoed his sister.

"She tried to tell me something about breaching a fort from the inside," Sankaran tried to recall. "I was too nervous to understand what she was going on about."

Madhvi placed her hand on Sankaran's shoulders. "Brace yourself, brother. Hard times are coming. I can only speak to Savithri. She and I can have a conversation. But Tathri is a total stranger. What she will do next is unpredictable. I have seen Tathri momentarily manifest herself when you are in the courtyard. While Savithri is demure and conforming, Tathri is bold, talks a lot and refuses to hide behind the parasol. Tathri will go to places and do things Savithri would never dream of. Dear brother, I fear for you whenever you step on to that courtyard. Please do not, for God's sake, become bewitched or fall for the feminine ruse and lure of Tathri. No man I can think of has ever had enough will power or fortitude to resist Tathri once she has designs on his person. Such is her magnetism."

Sankaran shivered. That was the year 1904.

As the year 1905 came around, Sankaran had a number of opportunities to observe men of all stations submit to the will of Tathri. He deliberately begged for information from his sister Madhvi, only to satisfy his curiosity on the nature and status of these distinguished men. He often unashamedly perched himself aloft a convenient palm tree close to the *pora* just to see and confirm for himself if what he was told was actually happening. He was never disappointed.

One day he was informed by Madhvi that Tathri was expecting an old friend as companion for the night. Someone Tathri had been yearning for since a long time. No other details about this new stranger was available.

An old friend? Was that to mean, an old customer? Then certainly this time it was someone Sankaran had never seen before. Perhaps someone who was a regular visitor before Sankaran's discovery of Savithri's nocturnal occupation.

A little bored with the nightly routine and as a result, a little reluctant, he climbed one of the ubiquitous palm trees overlooking the *pora* awaiting the arrival of the gentleman in question. Half an hour would pass before he would see any movement. He had just begun to yawn but stifled it as he saw the familiar figure of wrapped white cloth with a large parasol gracefully and unhurriedly making its way out of the *illum*. It would not be long before she settled into the *pora* and Sankaran would have to focus his attention towards the side gate. The moon was late, but he hoped there would be enough light to see the visitor's face.

However, Tathri's designs tonight consisted of an unexpected subterfuge. Especially in informing her *thozhi* that she was expecting an "old friend". She had not lied. It was indeed an old friend. It was Sankaran.

Before he could take stock of the situation, the young lady had suddenly changed directions and had arrived at the base of the palm he sat crouched upon. "Come down here, Sankara," she whispered aloud, the familiar forefinger hooked and beckoning.

Sankaran gazed down from under his elbow, his heart in his mouth, wondering whether he was dealing with Savithri or Tathri. Knowing the difference now made it ever so daunting. Beads of perspiration streamed down Sankaran's forehead. His wet palms threatened to slip.

It came as a mild relief that she now appeared to be pacing back slowly behind him. Twenty paces, to allow him to descend. The parasol was in place. Perhaps Savithri wanted to talk to him. As she did sometimes in the courtyard. But then again, was that Savithri or was it Tathri who so often spoke to him in the courtyard?

He tried to think coherently. Logically. It struck him that the worst thing to do at a moment like this would be to dangle stupidly up on the tree in such an undecided manner when his master's wife was calling him. It was the behaviour of a thief. He had done nothing wrong. And what he was doing here at all, well, she certainly knew. She could at most chide him for his intrusion into her afairs. He decided to slide down even if it meant running into her latest beau.

When Sankaran's feet finally touched the ground, he had expected her to begin conversation, but a hand on his shoulder startled him and made him spin around, leaning horror-struck against the palm tree he had just descended. Her face was six inches to his. Her magnetic eyes looking into his. He had not even heard a footfall behind him when she glided twenty paces back towards him to now stand breathing in his face. Her fragrance made his head spin, his legs weak. As she leaned against him, Tathri seemed to have taken total control over his faculties.

He heard her say, "Sankara, you are my last bastion. For tomorrow night, I breach the fort. And I will bid Savithri goodbye forever."

With a final ounce of strength, he didn't think he possessed, he shook her off, clutching his own head with both hands in utter incomprehension and fear, wishing he could cry out loud. She stepped away from him, her brilliant smile looking captivating in the late rising moon. She did not appear flustered or worried. She pivoted around to gracefully unwrap her *vesti*, slowly revealing a slim, perfectly curvaceous figure in a short white blouse, that appeared tight and threatening to explode. In a quick motion she unfastened her long hair, shaking her head to allow the wavy tresses to fall wildly over her shoulders. Then hitching her elegantly laced petticoat high up in a deliberately slow motion, she reveal a flawless calf and thigh, taunting him towards her once again with her hooked index finger.

Something snapped inside Sankaran. He dropped his hands and walked purposefully towards her with a clenched jaw. He met her eyes without blinking and spoke slowly to her. "Tathri, the game is up. I have too much respect for Savithri to even think of touching you. Go breach your fort, shake the ramparts, raise every pillar and plinth from its foundations. Do not think I don't understand what manifested and brought you forth, Tathri. But in the hour of need, in the hour of danger I will stand with Savithri. Your carnal persuasions mean nothing to me."

His words appeared to have had some effect on her. She stopped smiling and began covering herself up, wrapping the *vesti* quickly before tying her hair into a neat knot behind her. She stood still in the moonlight to take a long look at him, her faintly pained face looking ever so beautiful. Then picking up her parasol she walked away without another word towards the *illum* once again looking as demure as Savithri always did.

It was in 1905 that Raman Namboothiri decided to consult his trusted friend, the village *vaidyan* with regard to his failing libido once again.

"As I have told you many times before, your suggestion to me to marry a young girl has not produced the desired results," Raman complained. "She is inexperienced. Even today, twelve years since I've married her, she throws tantrums. She has turned out to be a very violent girl. It is almost as if she is possessed. What is such a girl to know about the needs of a man?"

The *vaidyan* nodded in agreement. "You see, Raman, twelve years ago I scarcely understood your state of mind. I expected an intelligent girl like Ashtamoorthi Namboothiri's daughter to be able to sympathize with your need and eventually adjust her lifestyle for your purpose. Perhaps I was wrong."

"I have not been able to go as far as the door of her chamber before she transforms into a demon. I have tried all the mantras. It appears the Gods have forsaken me!" he wept for a minute. "I need to feel like a man! A real man! Ashtamoorthi Namboothiri's daughter has not been my wife. Ever!"

"You are seventy-two, my dear Raman," the *vaidyan* shook his head watching Raman's tear run horizontally along a wrinkle, like a stream failing to find an outlet. "Is it not time to focus your attention towards yoga and spirituality. You are still drinking that military spirit despite my warning you."

"But I have not received my just dues in the worldly period of my existence," Raman complained unabashedly. "The pleasure of taking a woman. The pleasure of pleasing a woman."

"Oh no! That's not entirely true, Raman," the *vaidyan* consoled. "Have I not known you when you were with your first wife? You went so overboard with your virility that you began to forsake hygiene and decorum."

"Oh for God's sake, don't remind me! That is the past. I have made mistakes. So has everyone. Now tell me what you can do for me?"

The *vaidyan* pondered deeply. "Have you heard of Tathri?"

"Tathri?"

"Tathri, Lady-of-the-Night?"

"No. Who might that be?"

"Tathri! The-Cuddliest-Courtesan?"

"No. But she does sound interesting," Raman wiped his tears and smiled with glee.

"My dear Raman, which world do you live in?" the *vaidyan* sounded incredulous. "The best men in our society are heard whispering about Tathri, Fallen-Woman-Worth-Falling-For.

"Is she expensive?" Raman was eager to know.

"Very. She's not referred to as Tathri, Next-Thing-To-Heaven, for nothing," the *vaidyan* replied. "I was drained of five *pavans* of gold in my two visits to her. But I dare say, I slept like a baby for a week each time she drained me. She's worth her weight in gold."

"Ok. So be it. What are we waiting for?" Raman Namboothiri could almost feel a stirring in his loins.

The night that Tathri breached her "fort" would be remembered by all of Kochi. For that night Raman Namboothiri left the *vaidyan's* premises for a last and final foray to repair his libido.

A loud blood-curdling scream, like the howling of an animal was heard emanating from a local *illum's* outhouse bedroom an hour after midnight. It woke up the neighbourhood and turned out to be the anguished cry of a certain Chemmanthatta Kuriyedathu Raman

Namboothiri, Raman to his people, who had hired a popular, high-class and expensive woman of ill repute, by name Tathri, for his pleasure. After very satisfactory cohabitation with her, presumably in the dark for a few hours, she unveiled herself to reveal to him that she was in fact his wedded wife who had walked into the outhouse from no other place but his own *illum*. Raman's immediate reaction on seeing this, was understood to be the bizarre blood-curdling howl experienced by the neighbours.

His wails and screams attracted a large gathering, especially of men from the Namboothiri community who vacated even the nearby temples to enter Raman's compound in his hour of distress. Raman stood outside the outhouse crying and tearing his hair and for the first few minutes it appeared that he had lost his mind. It took some moments for the men gathered to discern what the nature of the problem was. As Raman calmed down and became more coherent the full import of Raman's statement and the magnitude of the crime hit the community members.

"Oh, I wish I could just behead her," screamed Raman hoping to arouse the already incensed men into a frenzied mob. "This is worse than adultery. This is barefaced prostitution. Pollution! Pollution of our community!"

"Where is the wench?" enquired some of them showing intention to physically assault her.

"Wait a minute," screamed another incredulous voice with some authority. "Let us be reasonable. Raman, you were the one who went to her to seek pleasure. You are her rightful husband. Neither do we see anything unusual in her occupying her own *pora*. If at all we might, by way of curiosity, enquire of you why you entered the *pora* which is reserved for your wife's monthly confinement. It is you who appear to be out of place, not her. This is your compound, your *illum*, your wife and her *pora*. She has not left the compound and no other man but you, her husband, have cohabited with her? How can you have us believe she is a prostitute? What is your evidence? Are you sure you haven't had a simple spat with your wife and in your anger are not simply creating a mountain out of a molehill? Are you drunk?"

"No! No! No!" Raman scrambled about, running among the men gathered in the compound, looking for that one man who could support his statement. But that man was nowhere among them. "Where is the *vaidyan*?" Raman screamed in desperation knowing he was looking dubious and ridiculous in the eyes of the gathered men of his community for not being able to substantiate his accusation.

In exasperation he finally blurted, "Believe me, please! The woman inside the *pora* is Tathri. Have you not all heard of the famous Tathri? Lady-of-the-Night?"

A sudden exclamation of shock reverberated through the crowd. It was obvious that everyone had heard of her. But the authoritative voice once again interrupted him. "Raman, if you have Tathri in there, then you are the one committing adultery, not your wife. I ask you again. Have you been drinking?"

"No! No! Don't any of you understand what I am saying?" sobbed Raman, "Tathri, The-Cuddliest-Courtesan is none other than my wife! She has been seeking and giving pleasure to innumerable men in the neighbourhood. I want justice. Oh I wish I could just set this *pora* on fire and let her roast in it. Tathri is my wife. Do you now understand, all of you?"

Raman's cry to burn the *pora* had a few men step forward in response, but the authoritative voice spoke up once again. "What you have stated just now is shocking to say the least, Raman. But if this is true we still cannot take the law into our own hands and do as we please. Prima facie, there is no evidence against her except your word. Namboothiris that we are, we cannot and will not enter a *pora* as you have done for the purpose of verification. Burning the *pora* with her in there amounts to cold blooded murder. Let us seek the king's permission to hold a *Smaartha Vicharam*, an inquisition, a trial. Those among the public who can recognize Tathri and those among your family who can identify your wife will need to be present. Summon your wife's father. Summon the mistress's *thozhi*. Seek permission of the king to hold an inquisition immediately. Station guards to keep her confined in the *pora*. Let her father not be given the opportunity to accuse us of not being fair to his daughter. Until we receive a reply from the king let us all be patient.

The autobiography of the Raja of Kochi gives us a detailed account of what transpired after that fateful day. The Raja recounts -

In the early part of the year 1905 I found myself occupied in a sensational and sensitive social issue. A 23-year-old Namboothiri woman, Savithri, a.k.a. Tathri was accused of leading an immoral life. As per the prevailing law of the land, a community tribunal is appointed by the Raja to enquire into the misdemeanours of such suspected Namboothiri ladies. The tribunal investigates the accusations and cross-examines the lady as well as the male adulterers who have been accused of illegitimate sexual relations with her, as well as other witnesses in a methodical and ritualistic trial called a *Smaartha Vicharam*. Essentially a trial of chastity.

When this case was referred to me, the *Dasi Vicharam* had been completed by the community. This essentially meant that the community had already questioned the maid servant of the accused and determined the illicit sexual conducts of the accused. All Namboothiri ladies have a maid servant cum companion called a *thozhi*. The interrogation of the maid is known as the *'Dasi Vicharam'*. Based on the information provided by the *thozhi*, a formal request is made to the King for a *Smaartha Vicharam*, with the payment of a nominal deposit. Such was the position of this case.

I was deeply concerned over the ability of the father of the accused to bear the burden of this misfortune that had befallen him because as per the custom of the Namboothiris, during the entire period of the *Smaartha Vicharam* all those connected with the trial are to be accommodated and fed and their other basic necessities met by the accused's father.

If she confesses her lapses before the tribunal, she and the men mentioned by her as being involved are to be excommunicated by me, their Raja. Conventionally, the men were not told what their offence was nor were they given a chance to clear themselves from the one-sided accusation of the woman of ill fame. This curious system, though it offended against the elementary canons of jurisprudence, has the sanction of established usage from time out of mind and was one of the bulwarks of the Namboothiri social system and very jealously preserved by that community.

In the case which cropped up in 1905 a large number of persons belonging to several communities were implicated by the woman in the *Smaartha Vicharam*. The injustice of condemning this motley group without giving the men concerned an opportunity to refute the allegations of the woman was realised by me. In consultation with Sir V. Bhashyam Ayangar eminent lawyer and jurist who served as the first Indian Advocate-General of Madras Province and also as a Judge of the Madras High Court, I framed certain rules for the conduct of *Smaartha Vicharam*. Making a slight deviance so as to establish some fairness to the accused, the persons alleged by the fallen woman to have had illicit intimacy with her were furnished with copies of her allegations and they were called upon to show cause why they should not be dealt with according to the customary law. They were also allowed to cross examine the woman and to cite evidence.

The *Smaartha Vicharam* Tribunal approved by the community, verified and appointed by me consisted of highly capable men of great standing and experience. They consisted of four persons. Jathavedan Namboothiri from Perumannan village was the chief *Smaartha* (knowing the Vedas and competent to conduct the trial of chastity as per the Namboothiri Community rules). Another one was the eldest Namboothiri from Desamangalam, the biggest landlord of 5 villages and having the right to try guilty persons of these 5 villages and punish them under the order of the Kochi Raja. The other two were prominent landlords of the area, one of them being the landlord of the area under which the *illum* of Savithri's husband was situated.

Savithri a.k.a. Tathri was accused of virtually running a brothel with herself as the prostitute without anybody knowing her identity with the use of veils. She had the unstinting support of her maid servant cum companion or thozhi, as per the custom of those days, a Nair girl. She was able to satisfy all who came to her so that her professionalism as a prostitute went far and wide and attracted the elite of the kingdom. When Savithri a.k.a. Tathri was caught on adultery, she was taken and accommodated in an isolation house known as Pacha olappura (house with green palm leaves) on the river bank at Chalakkudi. Such houses specially designated for this purpose were kept under guard so that the inmates do not escape, have opportunity to commit suicide or have contact with the outside world. She was provided with basic necessities for subsistence. It served as a remand home or a virtual jail till the inmate is declared innocent, which is very rare, or till punishment is awarded. Savithri a.k.a. Tathri was also not allowed to have contact with anybody till the case was resolved. Till then, as is the custom of the Namboothiris, she is considered as an inanimate subject and is known as the 'Sadhanam' or object.

Though this does not have my sanction and I have warned that this abominable practice must stop forever, I have nevertheless heard that accused women of the Namboothiri caste are subject to severe torture during this period. I am told of several inhuman methods followed. One such method is to roll the woman in a palm leaf mat, as one would pack a dead body and roll it down the slope of a slanting tiled roof. While the men would be absolved by any subsequent enquiry of torturing her due to the absence of any external or inflicted injury on her person, the shock with which she lands as she falls off the roof has left many girls incapacitated for life either physically or mentally. Sometimes other women whom she had offended will be given opportunity to torture the accused woman according to their fancy and capacity. Sometimes scores of highly poisonous snakes or boxes of ravenous and crazed rats will be let loose into the isolation place where the accused lady is kept with the obvious connivance of the guards. Her guilt is presumed even before the trial and she is generally labelled as a nymphomaniac or a cursed demon who has ruined the lives of successful men. A convenient method of destroying incriminating evidence and silencing the witness forever. The Namboothiri society was never really kind to their women and with so much restrictions, fetters and taboos, I was initially deeply concerned about the welfare of a 23-year-old whose guilt had yet to be proved.

It was about this time that I received information that, despite my warning, an attempt was made to physically torture Savithri a.k.a. Tathri by a group of about a dozen Namboothiris one late night, but that their efforts were thwarted by a young man named Sankaran, who wielding a Malabar chopper had threatened to behead anyone who disobeyed the king's orders. I lauded the young man's courage and immediately sent additional guards to support his efforts to protect the witness.

When the *Smaartha Vicharam* commences, and the questioning and answering is to be done, the accused lady will be required to remain unseen within the accommodation provided for her and the *Smaartha* and others outside, without each seeing the other, in case the beauty of the lady or her charms or even her pitiable condition influence the judgement of the *Smaartha*.

As an accused Savithri a.k.a. Tathri was also called to show cause. In her submission, which utterly shocked the tribunal, she admitted to far more than she was accused of. Naming very prominent persons as her clients, giving precise time and dates over many years, and recalling whether her encounter with the named preceded a festival or occurred post a landmark event, together with other specific and verifiable references such as whether the night was a full moon and revelations with regard to the clothes and mannerisms of her clients opened a Pandora's box of complex and immense repercussions. Her paramours included 30 Namboothiris, 10 Iyers, 13 Ambalavaasis and 11 Nairs. As a result, the *Smaartha Vicharam* trial took about 7 months to complete.

The sheer number of persons named and involved was amazingly high. Some of them were respectable high-class Namboothiris from aristocratic families. The accused were men of high caste, influential and reputed in the society. During the trial it was revealed that her *jarans* (men who have illicit relation with ladies) included 30 Namboothiris, 10 Iyers (Paradesi Brahmins, Tamil Brahmins or Pattars), 13 Ambalavaasis, (people in the services of temples like those who clean the altar in the sanctum sanctorum, those who play drums or perform *kathakali, koothu* etc. outside the sanctum sanctorum but inside the compound of the temple) and 11 well respected Nairs of royal and martial lineage.

In their initial submissions, all persons accused denied having had anything to do with the woman. But they could not refute the charges. Some of them engaged counsel and wanted to import the procedure of law courts. This I could not permit, as legal subtleties were out of place in the enquiry, which was a quasi-religious one and related only to questions of fact. Any violent breach from the past was bound to evoke strong opposition from the conservative Hindus whose sentiments had to be respected.

The final round of the seven-month long inquiry lasted for about a month from mid-June to mid-July, 1905. It turned out to be a sensational case for several reasons.

Savithri a.k.a. Tathri accused 65 men (*jarans*) and was asked to name them and substantiate it by describing their body marks. She could recite with utmost confidence, the names of the people involved and detailed description of the events, including identification marks on the body of the persons she named. The evidence includes some identification marks on the covered part of the body of the males and by identifying the persons in an identification parade. She even gave the details of the marks on or around the genitals of the persons so accurately that the persons had no escape. In many cases letters written by these people to her, years ago in a moment of weakness, now appeared as evidence.

Sixty-four persons were involved in the enquiry and all of them were excommunicated. This evoked strong resentment among the educated section of the people. I had anticipated this. But I was not for superimposing any drastic or violent changes on society when they were repugnant to the feelings of the majority of the people who were conservative.

When Savithri a.k.a. Tathri started naming her paramours one by one, she finally uttered the 64th name. Before she could name the 65th, prominent people were apprehensive that someone from their families might be arbitrarily named by her and started feeling the extreme heat of the situation. Their desperation and pleas finally forced me to stop the trial. It was attracting too much publicity even outside the kingdom, so much so that petitions filed in British courts were being used to pressurize me to transfer the entire matter to a British judge. Neither I nor the Namboothiri community wanted that to happen, which may lead to a complete retrial.

The verdict was pronounced on the night of July 13, 1905, indicting Savithri a.k.a. Tathri and the other 64 accused men. In the end only 64 men came under the category of guilty. Out of these persons two had died during the *Smaartha Vicharam* process and some others left the country to some foreign destination to escape the stigma and punishment. There were at least another three who escaped direct sentencing or community punishment by the tribunal. One of them by having given a false name and address to Tathri and who could not be traced, despite his having been her favourite and most frequented customer. Another was a Muslim. The Muslims do not have the Brashtu or excommunication system and did not come under the *Smaartha Vicharam*. One more escaped due to some other reason not known. Apart from these if there were any others, it was known only to the lady and her companion.

Savithri a.k.a. Tathri was given the punishment of *Brashtu*, which involved excommunication and social ostracism along with the available male members of the 64 tried by the tribunal. She was cast out of her society and thrown out into the street. After this, she being as good as dead for the family and community as well as to the other communities who depended on the Namboothiris, a final gesture ended her existence as far as her society was concerned. Her last rites were performed, as if she were dead.

Of the other 59 physically available and charged with the ultimate sin, barring two who had run away, 57 of the guilty left their homes humiliated, some I believe seen living on bare subsistence allowance and some begging on the highways for many years. Over the years many died or just faded away into oblivion. The fate of the 23-year-old Namboothiri girl since is unknown.

There ended the Raja of Kochi's account of the most sensational trial of chastity.

But what really happened to a beautiful 23-year-old girl from the day she was thrown out of the *illum*. Normally the worst awaits an unprotected girl, for she would be beaten, robbed of her clothes, molested, raped or simply carried away even before nightfall by devious elements whose ultimate aim would be to sell her as a slave. The only salvation that can be expected was if one of the co-accused or ostracized men offered to marry her. But their shame, anger and despair was more likely to cause her to die a horrible death in one of their hands.

Tathri had foreseen that perilous day, the day of her inevitable indictment. She had enough wealth stashed away to accomplish the impossible. Minutes before her sentence was pronounced a covered English carriage drew up conspicuously outside the premises where the *Smaartha Vicharam* was concluding, much to the confusion of the large crowd thronging outside.

Once her sentence was pronounced, she took permission and leave of the tribunal, covered her head with a veil so that her face could not be seen, and stepped out of her confinement for the first time in seven months. She was sentenced, but before she could be abused, mauled, spat at and brusquely hurled out into the streets of Kochi, she informed the tribunal that as one indicted, she was imposing exile on herself, never to come near the Namboothiri community again. With no further reason to hold her, she was allowed by the tribunal to leave. A stunned crowd watched in silence as she stepped out of the *Pacha olappura* in which she had been confined unseen by human eyes for so long. Now veiled in white she walked confidently to the carriage, unnerving everyone by her self-assured strides. Before even a word could be uttered by the onlookers, the two horses reared and set off in a gallop down the road she had breached for herself out of the impregnable Namboothiri fortress.

Sankaran and Madhvi had stopped serving the *illum* from the commencement of the *Smaartha Vicharam*. Madhvi was never blamed for any of Tathri's misdemeanours and she got married a few months following Tathri's dramatic departure from Kochi. Sankaran found gainful employment in the railways at Tirur and by 1920 rose to become an assistant Station Master at Podanur in the Madras Presidency. He was now 38 years old, happily married with two children studying at the Stanes School near the Coimbatore railway station.

Sankaran believed that his posting to Podanur was also an inextricable game played by destiny on him.

In 1921 a tragic movement referred to as the Malabar Rebellion broke out. Police attempted to arrest the principal rebel leader on a charge of having stolen a pistol but a crowd of 2000 Mappilas supporters from the neighbourhood somehow foiled the attempt. The following day, the police party hunting the rebels entered the famous Mambaram mosque at Tirurangadi. Some records were seized and a few rebels hiding there were arrested but rumour was spread that the mosque had been desecrated by the police. Hurt by the news, Moppilas peasants besieged the local police station at Tirurangadi. The police opened fire causing the mob to reacted in a mad fury. News of the incident spread and engulfed Eranad and Valluvanad for over two months. Then the situation took a new turn owing to rumours of Hindus having helped the police against the rebels and soon atrocities began to be perpetrated on Hindus. The relations between the two communities grew tense. To contain the situation British and Gurkha regiments were rushed to the area and martial law imposed. By November of that year, the rebellion was practically crushed.

On Nov 19th, 1921 a train started from Tirur with a wagon of about a hundred rioting Mappila prisoners headed for the Central Prison in Podanur. They were bundled into a freight wagon when the train started its journey. Sankaran was on duty when the train arrived. The crying and wailing from within the prisoners' wagon caused him to immediately order the guards to have it opened and checked. His eyes were met with the horrible sight of many dead men. They had died of exhaustion and thirst, having been given no water or any relief from their cramped condition through a long journey. 46 Mappilas were already dead and even as Sankaran along with porters and station staff carried out at least eight of the unconscious on to the platform, only two could be revived. Six of them died on the platform at Podanur station. Eighteen other prisoners in a semi-conscious condition were rushed to a local hospital of whom sixteen more would die in the hospital. Only 32 of the original 100 prisoners cramped into the wagon would survive.

The few prisoners left standing were chained and marched to an enclosure near the station where they were kept temporarily sheltered until arrangements could be made with the police and the prison guards to move them to the Central prison at Podanur.

It was at this juncture that Sankaran met Mr. Fred Meyers for the first time. Meyers had some medical experience in the army and was sent by the authorities to check and report on the condition of the remaining prisoners. Tethering his horse in the courtyard at the entrance of the station, he greeted Sankaran and introduced himself. "They look as if they have been to hell and back!" he sighed at the sight of them. "They're seriously dehydrated. Could you arrange for someone to immediately get as many tender coconuts as he can lay his hands on. Meanwhile could you be so kind as to also send a messenger to my wife to get some food in here as soon as possible. These thirty poor creatures look ravenous. She's at the St. Joseph's Church around the corner. They have coconut palms there too."

Sankaran immediately sent two porters to the local vendors outside the station for tender coconut water as Meyers had instructed. Just then the chief of the special guard for prisoners stepped on to the platform. Meyers walked towards him.

"What a human tragedy!" Meyers remarked sadly, leaning his tall frame against the station pillar. "What's the death toll?"

"52 of the hundred we loaded," replied the guard looking slightly flustered at Meyer's query. "18 are in hospital, and 30 have been held here till further orders."

Meyers shook his head. "Podanur will forever become known for this wagon tragedy, though more than half your prisoners died along the way. We don't know how many will make it back from hospital. For God's sake, isn't someone responsible for this, man?"

Curious onlooker had gathered at the entrance of the station and were being shooed away by the guards.

Meyers looked concerned. "We don't want the local muslim population getting motivated by the plight of their Malabar bretheren. What do you intend to do?" he addressed both Sankaran and the chief guard. But even as they spoke letters arrived on horseback addressed to the Chief Guard and the Assistant Station Master informing them that the jail was full and the prisoners were to be sent back to Tirur.

"What a waste!" exclaimed Meyers. "Can we now at least feed the living before they drop dead too? I'll see what I can pickup at the Bright Dawn Bakery ouside the station."

"If you can let me have your horse, I'll go meet Mrs. Meyers and get some food from the church." Sankaran stepped out behind him.

"Sure! Take him, but I hope the stirrups are to your length." Meyers pointed out.

"I'll manage," Sankaran replied as he untethered the horse and climbed on to the saddle. He then egged it forward and was soon riding out of the station gate and on to the road that lead to the church. The evening sun was still high and the temperature of the day had not dropped.

Tethering the horse outside, he entered the church compound. The evening mass was not due and most of the congregation had not yet arrived. An altar boy was wandering outside and Sankaran asked for Mrs. Meyers along with the message for food. The altar boy ran into the church and came out shortly to confirm that Mrs. Meyers was indeed there and some food could be arranged.

Sankaran looked up at few coconut trees in the church compound. "Could you climb up there and knock down half a dozen of those. We have some dehydrated prisoners in the station. Doctor's orders!" He smiled at the boy.

"I can get you a knife, but I don't know how to climb one of these," replied the boy as he foraged about the base of a neatly trimmed hedge. "Will this do?" he produced a machete from among some garden tools stored there.

"Oh no!" Sankaran sighed, then smiled at the boy. "Ever seen an Assistant Station Master climb a coconut tree? Well, it's been a while since I did this, but let's prove it is not impossible!"

It was with some effort that Sankaran slid up the first few feet. His age as well as his trousers would not allow him to move as freely as his *mundu* once did. Then a sense of familiarity came over him and he moved up with more ease. "Move aside, boy! The sky is about to rain cannon balls."

The boy moved away as Sankaran chopped down six coconuts, each thumping down noisily on to the church compound. Now he had to descend carefully.

"Jesus Christ! It has been a long time since I've spoken to someone perched on a tree!" the impeccable English accent of Mrs Meyers lilted in the evening breeze as she stepped out of the church building and stood below him. A shapely lady in an elegant skirt with a colonial coiffure hair syle covered by a pretty cloche hat. She wore a smart white blouse over a gored black skirt and riding boots of suede leather.

He descended carefully, feeling a sense of déjà vu. It wasn't a Malabar chopper but it had done its job. Was it the climbing of a coconut tree after so many years? Was that what triggered the déjà vu? No. Not until he stood and faced Mrs. Meyers did the waves of recollection hit him with all its force.

"Savithri?"

"Sorry! What's that you just said?" Mrs Meyers smiled, tilting her slender neck. "Are you Ok?" Sankaran was speechless.

She looked at him with magnetic eyes. "You look awful. Why are you so pale? I have food packed into two baskets. I hope Fred finds it enough," she smiled, a brilliant captivating smile baring a set of perfect white teeth and showing a hint of dimples.

"Tathri?" he tried again.

"I beg your pardon?" She frowned. For a moment a pained expression passed over her face. Momentarily. Then it seemed to have passed and she recovered. "Here, hitch these baskets on the saddle and be off, my good man! My kids are waiting inside. It is my youngest one's Holy Communion tomorrow, you know. I must be off." As she placed the baskets before him, her fragnance made his head spin.

He slowly hitched the baskets on to the saddle of the horse, stepped on the stirrup and urged the horse forward. He waved at Mrs. Meyers and the altar boy.

As he rode out of St. Joseph's church gate, he was not sure if he heard a soft feminine voice far behind him call out, "Thank you Sankara!" It must have been the breeze. He did not look back or stop. He had a wagon with the 68 dead bodies and 32 prisoners to send back to the waiting throngs at Tirur.

KISMAT AND KARMA

There is this condition of uncertainty that many have experienced in their lives as one passes the threshold into adulthood. Normally following a period of relief at having graduated from college, but not quite certain which career path to tread. A confusing period between being compelled to work for a living and waiting for the right kind of job to open up, if that luxury is affordable. It is a situation when one hangs in a limbo of ambiguity about one's future. This is often compounded by pressure, both intended and inadvertent, from friends, peers, parents and relatives.

"Hey Sankara! What do you really do up there?"

Below him stood Petty Officer Kutty of the Indian Navy, once his neighbor and friend, now transferred to the naval base at Kochi.

"Kutty!" exclaimed Sankaran in surprise. "Well, up here! You really want to know? I relax, I read, I listen to music. Sometimes I just gaze about. How is it that you're here today, Officer Kutty?"

"Wow! Kya Kismat! That must be some life! Could you please slide down here for a minute? I need to talk to you."

"Are you on some kind of furlough or something, Officer Kutty? Why are you in uniform?" enquired Sankaran, as he slithered down.

"Look at you! You are either high on the coconut tree or in deep waters," Officer Kutty laughed as he shook hands with Sankaran.

"Two places that keep me far from vices," Sankaran retorted. "I'm in no hurry to work."

"I don't know about that," remarked Office Kutty still laughing. "That palm of yours looks ripe for a nice swig of toddy."

"You don't look like you've come for toddy," noted Sankaran, observing the perfectly pressed white Naval uniform his friend had on.

"Definitely not. But we'll positively indulge ourselves one of these days when I'm off duty."

"So you're *on* duty today? Here? In Kannur?" Sankaran sounded surprised as they walked out of the grove on to the road.

"On an official errand," replied Kutty more seriously.

"Official errand? Are we building a naval base at Mappila Bay?" Sankaran tried to provoke some more laughter.

But Officer Kutty was not even smiling. "Sankara, you *are* the errand."

"What do you mean I am the errand?" Sankaran halted in confusion.

"Do you still do your deep water routine or have you decided to live on that coconut palm for the rest of your life?" Officer Kutty wanted to know.

"Well, I do occasionally take a dive to keep in practice," replied Sankaran. "The last time I defeated your Navy boys at the Open Championships, all they gave me was a trophy. But Lieutenant Commander Jacob was kind enough to present me a bottle of Glenfiddich single malt from the Gandhi Nagar CSD Depot at Kochi and five thousand rupees cash. That money came in handy to fix my roof during the monsoon."

"It's Commander Jacob who has sent me on this errand. He wishes to speak to you," explained Kutty.

"What is his number?" enquired Sankaran removing a mobile phone from a twist of his lungi tucked into his waist.

"That's not the way it's going to happen," explained Kutty. "He requires to speak to you, personally. That is, in person. At Kochi or wherever he is available when you are ready."

"I don't get it," complained Sankaran.

"Well, let me give you a brief," clarified Kutty. "Is there some place we can sit over a drink to talk this over?"

"This is Payyambalam Beach. What do you expect? Whisky? Let's check at the beach garden place. With some luck we'll get some coffee or tea."

Soon the two men found a bench they could straddle and sit upon, their contrasting appearances offering both a curious and delightful sight to others in the ramshackle cafeteria. Sankaran, in his mid-twenties, had no shirt on. His signature turban was on his head while his lungi was folded up to his knees. He had even forgotten his footwear at the base of the palm he had descended from. While Kutty, in his mid-thirties looked dapper in white naval uniform and extremely clean shoes.

"You have a challenger," announced Officer Kutty slowly, letting his words sink into the Sankaran's mind "A young Anglo-Indian lad who can almost duplicate everything you do in water. He's a young recruit in the navy and has been lately recommended for promotion for his swimming prowess."

"Great, we'll see about that at the next Open Championships," countered Sankaran.

"That's why I'm here today, Sankaran. Commander Jacob doesn't wish to wait until the championships," declared Kutty. "Even as we speak, he is conducting an extremely intensive training program for leading swimmers from various naval units, at the end of which he would be holding a series of subaquatic competitions for his boys. He naturally wonders how many of his boys would really stand up to a stiff challenge. The Anglo-Indian lad we have has so far proved quite a maestro, and has greatly impressed the commander."

"But I am a civilian," Sankaran pointed out. "What purpose do I serve in this naval training drill? Or shall I put it this way. Of what good is this business to me? How does it matter? It's not a recognized event."

"Well naturally, Commander Jacob is most curious to gauge this Anglo-Indian boy's talent when pitted against a civilian with your prowess," Kutty took pains to explain. "Just for a moment, forget the Open Championships, Sankara. For the moment, forget the Indian navy too. Just look at it this way. There is an individual out there who has suddenly emerged doing the very things you did at the sub aquatics last year, exhibiting similar skill and expertise, a quality which the Commander has greatly admired in you and appreciated to the extent of gifting you a bottle of Glenfiddich and a cash prize. Does it not matter to you to want to know how good this new challenge really is? Don't you feel a sense of curiosity? He's going to be your greatest adversary in the years to come. Won't the thought nag you now, after I'm gone, while you are aloft that tree of yours?"

"Believe me, nothing really matters when you're up there, Officer Kutty." Sankaran replied. "I was quite happy up on my palm tree, day-dreaming and living like a king on my perch." Sankaran smiled. "As for Commander Jacob. I quite understand his curiosity. He appears to be a man who's always striving and scouting for excellence. Though to what end, I've never understood. But somehow, to have to compete in this kind of thing, outside an accredited or recognized competition, is a little unsettling. I'm still trying to figure out its benefit for me. Apart from that, I do require a week or two of preparation too. These are not your Olympic-approved subaquatics. These are very dangerous games to play and need practice. Very few civilians participate in them."

"I agree with all that you say, Sankara," pleaded Kutty. "If you wish some kind of reward for undertaking this, I am prepared to try and work something out with the commander. In any case, it has already been decided that should you agree to come and participate, your entire expenses should be taken care of by the navy. But first, let me simply ask you to please consider this invitation. Come and meet Commander Jacob. At least for old-time sake. Hear him out thoroughly. Then you can decide for yourself whether you wish to compete with this Anglo-Indian lad from the navy. This is your destiny, your kismat."

Sankaran regarded the earnest face of Officer Kutty for a long time before replying. "Commander Jacob certainly has a lot of time on his hands to conduct these purposeless competitions. However, Officer Kutty, having been your long time neighbor and friend, and seeing that you've come a long way just for this, I shall certainly give this consideration. I am not so bothered by the outcome of this competition. In fact, I don't feel daunted by it at all. But I do think it should be fair. For which I am asking for time to shape-up."

"Okay, Sankaran. It's a deal," Petty Officer Kutty extended a hand. "Since you've agreed to compete, we'll skip this meeting with Commander Jacob altogether for now. I give you three weeks to prepare yourself. In three weeks I will be here to pick you up and escort you to Commander Jacob and to the competition that will follow immediately."

They shook hands over the decision that day on the Payyambalam Beach.

It was at the Indian Naval Academy at Ezhimala, thirty-five kilometers north of Kannur, and not Kochi, that Commander Jacob chose to meet Sankaran. Commander Jacob greeted him in Hindi and Urdu, which Sankaran didn't find surprising as this often happens among personnel of the armed forces even in cantonments in the South. Sankaran spoke Urdu well having picked it up from Muslim friends on the Mappila bay at Kannur.

"A little untimely, eh?" Commander Jacob admitted. "But I appreciate your willingness to come here and compete with our boys. Sankara, you have set standards that are hard to conquer. You have some inborn and natural affinity to deep water that no amount of training can help attain. We are the navy. I was keen that you should exhibit your skills. Our boys have a lot to learn from you. You really should have joined the Indian Navy. You do have the prerequisite educational requirements."

"Never saw myself as a soldier, sir," Sankaran admitted. "There's very little the navy engages in anyway. The army up north see plenty of action in Jammu and Kashmir. Even the air force is kept occupied by the necessities that arise from their strategic locations in the Western and Eastern sectors. But here, especially in the South, I perceive our navy in very placid waters."

Commander Jacob seemed pleased at what Sankaran said. "You're keen to see real action, are you?" the commander enquired. "So you do want to serve the country? That's why I keep asking, Sankara. Just join the armed forces. I'm only suggesting the navy because of your superior swimming and subaquatic skills."

More than twenty-five young officers were present at the sprawling indoor swimming-pool complex when Sankaran arrived at the entrance. Many knew him as the one civilian who had beaten them all. But the anticipation became palpable especially when a young trainee cadet, soon to become a commissioned lieutenant, made his appearance along with Petty Officer Kutty.

"Marvin," the young cadet introduced himself to Sankaran. "Marvin Cuthbert Coleman."

"Sankaran." They shook hands measuring at each other like a pair of combatants before an MMS bout. Both knew there were no other participants even remotely close to their level.

"We're conducting preliminary rounds as well as the finals of the first eight events here. The balance six events will be conducted a few miles out at sea on the INS Tir and INS Kochi. A submarine whose identity I cannot disclose will also surface with a new set of challenges we have never attempted before. That would be two more events. Sixteen in all and two days to wind it all up. Are we ready?"

Over the next two days, it was to become one of the most keenly fought swimming and subaquatic competitions that Lieutenant

Commander Jacob and Petty Officer Kutty were to witness in all their time in the navy. As expected, of the over two dozen participants, Marvin and Sankaran lead the field from the word go. From diving to conventional styles of swimming, to deep-sea diving and scuba. Each battle was fought between Marvin and Sankaran amidst loud cheering and breath-held suspense. Such was the competition from Marvin that, at the end of it all, though Sankaran emerged the overall winner, it was by an almost nonexistent margin. The navy had all but snatched the prize back from the civilian. Though the young naval cadet's performance was laudable, Sankaran was sure he himself had not under-performed. A realization that the navy was indeed grooming a champion for the years to come.

"Another trophy, maybe a bottle of Glenfiddich and if I'm lucky, some cash," thought Sankaran as he emerged from the showers, having dressed well enough for the usual prize distribution ceremony at the swimming pool complex. "Then it's back to Kannur and home."

His thoughts suddenly subsided when he noticed that there was nobody except Commander Jacob and Petty Officer Kutty waiting for him at the pool. The other young officers and cadets had been dismissed and were perhaps back in their rooms. The sudden lull after all the hullabaloo of the competition perplexed Sankaran. As he approached them it was Commander Jacob who spoke up. "Congratulations, Sankaran! You've proved beyond doubt that you are certainly some marine creature in the guise of a human!" He shook Sankaran's hand with a smile. But it was Kutty's solemn expression that Sankaran didn't miss. Both he and the commander appeared to be withholding something. Something that appeared to be more serious than the just concluded competitions. After a moment's pause Commander Jacob spoke again.

"Sankara, I understand from Kutty that it is really your family that will not be happy if you joined the services. The resistance is from your mother and father. I also do know that members of your family have served in the armed forces in the past in various capacities. So there is little doubt, you do belong to a lineage of veterans."

"Father feels I should be doing something more creative while mother is just plain scared at the thought of me in the services," explained Sankaran. "She firmly believes the Pakistanis are waiting for me to join the army before declaring war on us."

"But it's your call in the end, Sankara," the commander tried to induce him. "You'll be amazed at the opportunities you have for being creative. We don't live in a country that makes it compulsory for our youth to do active duty in the armed services. I can only advice you. However, it's as good a career as any other. There's also a short service commission you could consider joining. Besides, you've already made friends here in the navy. At least promise me you'll give it one last thought."

Sankaran would certainly think about it. Over the bottle of Glenfiddich he was handed by Petty Officer Kutty outside, along with an envelope containing ten thousand rupees and a hand-written citation from Commander Jacob. A vehicle for his return to Kannur awaited him outside.

"Coming from the commander, that's VIP treatment, Sankara. He must really like you. It was your kismat to have won this competition and Marvin's karma that he lost despite being a hair-breath of you in each event. I will come by in a couple of weeks," promised Kutty as the driver started the engine to drive him out of the magnificent facility of the Indian Naval Academy at Ezhimala, back to Kannur.

Sankaran had time to think. He certainly did not like the navy. In fact he was not enamored by the lifestyle or the uniforms of any of the armed services. Perched on his favorite palm, facing the beach, he pondered over the stories he had heard of the many in his family who had served in the armed forces, especially during the two world wars. And he wondered over the definition of kismat and karma.

A particularly poignant one related to his great grand uncle Govindan Nair and the legacy of a little tin box he used to call his

"Rani Petti". The story was told and retold many times among the family. Govindan has been a troublesome youth in the village, often involved in brawls and petty fights. Complaints poured in especially during the season when mangoes were due for ripening. Challenged and goaded by his companions, he would foray stealthly into some rich landlord's orchard just to prove he could befuddle the Nair guards and dogs in the compound and deliver the choicest of fruits to his ecstatic admirers. These adventures often went so out of hand that on occasions, the guards giving chase had fallen into open wells in the darkness of night and the frenzied dogs on the chase had bitten everyone but the intruder. His aficionados got him as well as the family into so much trouble that finally, when a "spot-recruitment" for soldiers was announced in the village, Govindan gladly volunteered to join and make a respectable career for himself just to buy peace with his relatives. While there was great relief in the village, the landlords hoped Govindan would one day pay for his karma.

The story goes that during World War I (1914-1918), Her Royal Highness, The Princess Victoria Alexandra Alice Mary, Princess Royal and Countess of Harewood visited hospitals and welfare organizations with her mother; assisting with projects to give comfort to British servicemen and assistance to their families. One of her best remembered projects was the Princess Mary's Christmas Gift Fund, through which a decorative brass tin was sent by her to all members of the British, Colonial and Indian armed forces for Christmas 1914.

Over 426,000 of these identical tins were distributed to soldiers serving on Christmas Day 1914. The tins were filled with various items including tobacco, confectionary, spices, pencils, a Christmas card and a picture of the princess. Today, across the Commonwealth, maybe in more parts of the world than one can really know, this little tin may have become a prized possession of families whose great grand or grandparent has served in the first Great War. Many tins were lost, destroyed or buried in the graves along with the dead soldiers as the war picked up momentum in the following four years. Today, more than100 years on, Sankaran wondered how many such tins remained in existence despite its mass production and distribution a century ago.

For, Sankaran too possessed such a tin box which he inherited from his incorrigible great grand uncle. Until recently, he did not know what its purpose was or that it was called the "Princess Mary Christmas Gift Box."

The family legend began when in 1918, a bearded and emaciated Sepoy named Govindan Nair disembarked from a Parsi merchant ship that had returned from the Middle-East to anchor in Bombay harbour and made his journey overland back to his hometown in Malabar (Kerala). Apart from his worn and weathered clothes which consisted of two shirts and a trouser, he also carried with him a brass metal box. The box contained a piece of soap and a pencil. Weak as he was when he arrived home, it took him several months to regain his strength. He spoke very little, as many in the village in those days didn't quite understand the man's narration or context of the events and his experiences in the theatre of war in the Middle East of which he was one of the few survivors. All they knew was that he had served the British in a horrific war in some foreign country. A few even wondered whether he was ill or mentally unstable. However, fragments of the stories he told his family were passed down the generations.

Govindan Nair was Sankaran's great-grandfather's youngest brother on his mother's side of the family. Following the "spot-recruitment", he had joined as a young sepoy of the Madras Regiment, a unit of which had been amalgamated into the 6th Poona Division following the Kitchener Reforms and formed part of the Indian Expeditionary Force D. The Expeditionary Force saw action during the Mesopotamian Campaign and Govindan was initially stationed in the port-town called Basra in 1914. A passing British supply vessel that delivered military ordinance and medical supplies also contained chests of Christmas gifts for the British soldiers stationed at Basra.

Sepoy Govindan, among others, also received the Princess Mary's Christmas Gift Box or "Rani's Petti" as he called it.

Besides uttering a few sentences in Persian and Kurdish, on his return home Govindan spoke of one "Nickson Saheb", a "Toinshend Saheb" and a "Dr. Carter of a hospital ship at Basra". It was "Toinshend Saheb" who led him and the 6th Poona through several small skirmishes with the German and Ottoman forces quite successfully. But following a major defeat, the British had to retreat to a place called Kut-al-Amara. In the siege of Kut-al-Amara, where Govindan along with the Indian Expeditionary Force D of the British army were trapped, severe rationing of food as well as death and disease among the soldiers ensued. Several battles over many months were fought in the siege of Kut-al-Amara before the British finally surrendered, and the 6th Poona was all but wiped out. Everything from battle injuries, starvation and diarrhoea to torture and ill-treatment of prisoners by the Ottoman Turks saw the demise of many of his comrades. Along with a few other Indian soldiers he escaped while en route to a prisoner-of-war camp near Aleppo, trekked through hostile regions along the Mediterranean for months before reaching the Suez, where a Bombay-bound Parsi merchant vessel finally brought him home. The shock from the battles fought, won and lost as well as his close shave with death on many occasions left him a silent and brooding individual. He was bitter and very critical of "Toinshend Saheb".

Govindan, for the rest of his short life in the village had also occasionally been the object of ridicule and the butt of jokes. His prized "Christmas Gift Box" or Rani-Petti which was rechristened by the locals as "murkam petti" (betel-leaf and nut container) was the prime target and cause. He was taunted with – "Is that all you have received for your services to the King?" and "there are better *murkam pettis* at home. Did you need to go to Arabia and fight for one?"

Though fed and supported by his ancestral manor or *tharavad*, Govindan lived a few more years in penury and without a pension. He never married and died many years before Sankaran's Great-Grand father in 1926, with only the Princess Mary Christmas Gift Box and some mention in family property documents of his ever having been in existence. That was the story of one of the men of Sankaran's family who had served as a combatant during the First World War. Someone, who many in the village believed, had paid for his karma.

Sankaran was often saddened at the sight of the little tin box displayed amongst other family memorabilia in the living room of his home. When he discovered the significance of the little box he requested *Bangalore Mirror* to publish an article about it. Which they did.

Later during the Second World War, in a battlefield closer home, another member of his family would participate in one of the fiercest battles of modern day warfare, the Battle of Kohima. The story of this man is even more remarkable as he was never recruited as a soldier nor did he ever intend to become a combatant. Least prepared, he was however destined to become part of a horrific clash of two armies.

It is one of the forgotten events from among Britain's greatest war victories. Later, in retrospect, the Battle of Kohima fought between 4th April and 22nd June, 1944, would be christened the *Stalingrad of the East*. The story of how a severely outnumbered 1500 combatants and 1000 noncombatants stopped a marauding division of highly motivated Japanese invaders from Burma.

Up until 1944, the Japanese war machine had swept through Asia destroying every army that stood in its path. Having taken Sarawak, British Borneo, Thailand, Malaya, Indochina, the Philippine Islands and even bombed Pearl Harbor in the United States, they took the Aleutian Islands, Alaska and virtually ruled over the Indian Ocean. They invaded the Andaman Islands, Celebes, Ambon and Timor, Java and the Netherlands East Indies. Pitched battles were being fought in Guadalcanal, Solomon Islands, Sumatra, Midway Island, Rabaul, New Britain and Kavieng, New Ireland. The Japanese were a disciplined, well-equipped but brutal force, who violated all rules and conduct of war, destroying towns and cities, killing war prisoners and civilian population with impunity, enslaving, raping torturing and spreading dread at every front.

In 1943, from Burma, their attention turned towards India, then under British rule. Their strategy was to enter the British colony with a two-pronged thrust through the Naga and Manipur regions, to neutralize the Indian garrisons at Kohima and Imphal and invade the Brahmaputra plain into India.

After many deliberations and meticulous planning, in April 1944, the Japanese 31st Division crossed the border into India and arrived a few miles outside Kohima. They were initially stalled en route by ambush and sniper-bullets, but they relentlessly marched onto Kohima in the fashion that they were used to throughout Asia, hoping to easily mop up any small resistance that they would encounter.

In the previous year, twenty-eight-year-old Padmanabhan, a cousin of Sankaran's grandfather, left his home in Malabar to work as an accountant in a British army depot at Fort St. George, Madras. As the war progressed he was transferred to Calcutta, and later to a garrison at Dum Dum where supplies and ordinance were being loaded on to flights to the north eastern region, where American and British soldiers were stationed.

Calcutta was on high alert when a reluctant Padmanabhan first arrived to report at the Fort William cantonment, as Rangoon had already fallen into Japanese hands and they were now targeting Chittagong and Calcutta with occasional air raids. Under orders of some senior English officers, suddenly noncombatants in the army stationed at Calcutta were also required to train in the use of light firearms in case of a Japanese invasion. During this training which was initially voluntary, but which later became mandatory, the use of a simple hand-held rifle was taught to civilians serving in the army establishments as cooks, cleaners, store-keepers, clerks and accountants.

At the firing range Padmanabhan excelled in the use of small firearms. He would sit cross-legged in an unconventional manner, looking more like a basket weaver or a priest and shoot at any given mark at any distance with ease. He could do this repeatedly at still and moving targets with both a rifle and a hand-gun much to the amusement of the army personnel deputed to train civilians. He would aim patiently and never missed the bullseye. Seeing this, the commandant even considered Padmanabhan for a larger responsibility: that of recruiting and organizing a civil defense unit in the Khidirpur dock area. Perhaps it was his commanding officer's note praising his firing skills to be one of "unfailing and deadly accuracy" that changed his life completely from that of an accountant.

Bored with trying to rally some youths to create a civil-defense unit and with little military experience at motivating them, poor in the local Bengali language as well as wanting some growth in his career, he resigned from the army administration and took up a job with a private tea company headquartered at Calcutta and owning considerable estates in Assam. The kind of work he had to now do was at least more predictable and above all better paid. From a noncombatant in the army establishment he had become a full-fledged civilian accountant. This good news, conveyed home in an inland letter posted from Alipore, would be among the last traces of his existence that Padmanabhan's family in Malabar would see.

Destiny had already assigned an inevitable role for him the day he left his home in Malabar and he would be left with no choice but to fulfill it.

Around mid-February, as the Japanese 31st Division was gathering west of the Chindwin river in Burma which gave them proximity to the roads into British territory, Padmanabhan was suddenly required to travel to Assam along with two senior accountants to conduct an audit on the company's plantations scattered mostly on the south bank of the Brahmaputra. The audit team left Calcutta towards the end of the third week, making it by train, road and steamer to the Assam Valley.

It took quite a few days to complete audits at each plantation, spread over the Brahmaputra valley. Thus the three men's stay in the Assam valley extended to over three weeks by the time the audit was thoroughly completed covering each estate at a time. Soon, the time to return arrived. But a trivial matter kept Padmanabhan and his two seniors from leaving for Calcutta. On the last estate they were in, the auditors were informed that a sizeable inventory including food, equipment and manpower had been requested by the army, who were building a road between Dimapur and Kohima, and that the estate, like many others in the vicinity, had to contribute to the war effort. Against which a formal receipt had to be procured from the commandant at Kohima to present before the tea company directors at Calcutta.

Padmanabhan being the youngest of the three offered to make a quick trip to Dimapur, then over the hills to Kohima to obtain the receipt while the two senior auditors awaited him on the tea estate in Assam.

"I'll just hitch a ride on one of the many army supply vehicles on this route. I should be back in three to four days," the two senior auditors heard him cheerfully shout out at them as the estate's jeep left the tea garden with Padmanabhan, to try and catch an army vehicle on the modest highway into the Naga hills. It was April Fools day, 1944. That was the last that they ever saw of the young accountant.

However, on the highway, while he awaited an army truck that was willing to take him to Dimapur, he had time to write one last letter home, sent back through the jeep driver to be mailed at Calcutta and which would arrive at Malabar about a month later. About the time when the Battle of Kohima was at its most intense pitch. His fellow accountants would call it his *kismat*.

Following the war, all that Sankaran's family would learn from the survivors of the dreadful battle was that a noncombatant from a tea estate in Assam who had arrived at the garrison the day before, was handed over a rifle on his personal request when the first Japanese attack took place on April 4th. He appears to have survived over a month. He was last seen alive on the 12th of May,1944 at 8.20 pm. His last known position was at one end of the commissioner's tennis court on a ridge that effectively repelled the Japanese from getting past a curve in the road below. A week later, during a lull in the battle, his decomposing and unidentifiable body, among many others that had been mutilated by grenade shrapnel, was found and hurriedly buried. Nobody knew or remembered his name. Neither was he on the official rolls of the garrison. His grave would be of the "unknown soldier." Many survivors would later wonder who he was, why and where he appeared from. Whether he was a soldier or a noncombatant didn't seem to matter. They would only remember him sitting cross-legged behind a small heap of sand bags patiently and effectively, locating and shooting down Japanese snipers by the dozen, with "unfailing and deadly accuracy."

The enemy had been vanquished. In the weeks to come, the Japanese would have to retreat from the rest of South-East Asia leading to their final defeat and surrender. Kohima had rung their death-knell. Today, on the commissioner's tennis court in Kohima an epitaph commemorates the great battle, a modern day Thermopylae.

> When you go home
> Tell them of us, and say
> For your tomorrow
> We gave our today

"Sankara! Are you coming down or do I need to climb up there to speak to you?"

The voice startled Sankaran and woke him up. It was Petty Officer Kutty and Cadet Marvin C Coleman. The young cadet had a guitar strung over his shoulder as he gazed up at his civilian rival.

"Amazes me how you don't just fall off!" exclaimed Kutty in genuine surprise.

"Watch me," Sankaran leaned back from his perch and hung upside down. Then sliding down almost the whole length of the tree, he stopped just short of striking his head against the ground. He then straightened himself up once again to unlock his legs and hop off the trunk.

"Oh bloody hell, man!" Marvin too exclaimed.

"You know, Officer Kutty, I think our *mallakhamba* should be included in the Olympics. It's a unique form of gymnastics. Hello Cole! Nice of you to come here." He greeted the young man who had been labelled his greatest adversary.

"It's Coleman!" Marvin corrected him.

"That's what I said, man!" Sankaran exclaimed.

"It's not Cole, man. It's Coleman, matcha!" Marvin tried again.

"Oh, ok. I get it, now. Coleman!" Sankaran smiled.

"What's this about gymnastics, da?" Marvin was curious. "You do that too? I've seen these buggers, oiled up and all, doing what you just did at a circus my nana used to take us to when we were *batchas*, man."

"Even the great Indian circuses originated here, Sankara," Kutty recounted. "Thalassery was a training hub for trapeze artists, tight-rope walkers and contortionists. Jugglers and animal trainers did roaring business in the days when the circuses were the pinnacle of entertainment. We do not need the Olympics for everything we do here. I'm sure every part of the world has its own regional sports and skills."

"Whatever happened to this place lately," pondered Sankaran aloud. "Does it still hold any mysteries, I wonder?"

"It always will," Kutty replied in a knowing tone. "It's not without reason that it has earned the name of God's Own Country."

"Man, but these snakeboat races are definitely unique and have really survived with vigor for so many years. Real traditional stuff, da. I was just telling everyone at the academy that we should participate as a naval team."

"Idea!" responded Kutty. "If at all, the boat race has only become more popular. These foreign tourists love it. We can suggest it to Commander Jacob."

The trio left Sankaran's grove and strolled up the road towards the beach.

"You get any grog around here, man?" Marvin enquired.

"This is Payyambalam beach. What do you expect? Champaign? Try some coffee?"

"Na-mind! I have a hip-flask," Marvin replied resourcefully.

"So what's new Officer Kutty? Does Commander Jacob have any new plans for me up his sleeve?"

"Strange you should ask," Kutty responded with raised eyebrows. "I thought you'd have made up your mind, one way or another."

"I have been giving it a lot of thought," Sankaran declared. "You see Officer Kutty, I've been thinking about a couple of my family members who had participated in the two great wars. It seems to me that it is not what we do or what decisions we make. It is what befalls us despite our decision, even those taken in good faith. I don't need a career, Kutty. I just wish to walk through doors that life opens for me."

Petty Officer Kutty looked confused and a little disappointed.

"Hey Marvin, do you play the guitar often?" Sankaran switched the topic in earnest. "Sure would like to hear you play something."

"Let's first find a place to park our asses, man," Marvin spoke in a complaining tone. "You know, I once had a band. Bloody, we played all the rock-n-roll and country music, man. But you know, everyone split after college. One guy left for Australia. The other found a dame and got married. The band just wound up like that."

"Do you compose music, Marvin?" Sankaran wanted to know. "I mean tunes. Say, can you put some of my lyrics to music. I've written some poetry, funny songs and stuff."

"Sure man, you Mallu buggers have brain, man," Marvin looked excited. "Writing lyrics and all. Let's put a band together, man. If it works out, bloody, I'll resign from the navy man! Hey, let's park our asses somewhere and discuss this, man."

Petty Officer Kutty looked alarmed as they entered Sankaran's regular beach garden place, where there were only wooden benches to park anything on. "Cool, man. Will do," Marvin declared as he unsheathed his guitar.

"Have you heard - *It's Hard To Kiss The Lips At Night That Chew Your Ass Out All Day Long?* It's great, man!" Marvin began to tune his guitar. "I should have known before that you like music, man. I would have come by more often."

"Aha, that song you just named reminds me of something I composed the other day sitting on my perch," Sankaran announced. "Come, Officer Kutty. Don't look so lost! I'm going to sing and both of you can sing with me. Marvin will play the guitar. Sing as you would sing any limerick. When the Irish reach these shores, they'll find I've been composing limericks. Sankaran's limericks!" he laughed. "Here goes…"

I loved a shy girl from Kochi
Dark hair and skin so peachy
But as she grew older
She became much bolder
And then turned *zimbly* bitchy

So one day I escaped to Saudi
Lived without arrack or toddy
I'm short like a Gurkha
So I hid in a burqa
And hoped that she wouldn't find me

But this Arab who knew no better
Sent me this long *lao* letter
I found out for myself

I couldn't hide in the *Gelf*
I was running like an Irish setter

I ran from the *Gelf* to Germany
To my *ungle* who was so handy
He gave me some brandy
Which angered my *aandy*
Who wanted me to go *yearn meney*

So, I said *sowrry* to my girl in Kochi
I shouldn't have lived like a gypsy
pope music and drum
nethila fry and rum
Now keeps me very, very *bissi*

My name is *zimbly* Sankaran
Been everywhere, seen everyone
But at the end of the day
I'm still at Mappila Bay
Jembing up back to square one.

Kutty sat in silence, tapping his feet, pretending he was enjoying listening to the two *greatest adversaries* singing together. He also realized there was little he could do to help Commander Jacob.

1969

1 969 was the height of the Cold War, with the US as well as the USSR vying for superiority in space technology. The Russians outdid the Americans by putting the first man, Yuri Gagarin, into outer space, as early as 1961. Not to be left behind, the Americans undertook the Apollo missions. Apollo 1 was the first manned mission of the United States Apollo program, which had as its ultimate goal a manned lunar landing. But a cabin fire during a launch rehearsal test on January 27 at Cape Kennedy Air Force Station Launch Complex killed all three crew members of that mission much to the American's dismay and embarrassment.

The space race between the two superpowers peaked with the July 20, 1969 US landing of the American astronauts on the Moon with Apollo 11. The USSR on the other hand tried but failed manned lunar missions, and eventually cancelled them and concentrated on Earth orbital space stations. The Americans emerged champions over the USSR, thanks to the three astronauts Commander Neil A. Armstrong, Command module pilot Michael Collins and Lunar module pilot, Edwin E. Aldrin, Jr. who finally landed on the moon.

Neil A. Armstrong stepped on the moon with his famous words, "That's one small step for a man, one giant leap for mankind."

Conspiracy theories abound on whether this landing and subsequent Apollo moon walks were really true events or if they had been faked in a studio set just to befuddle the Soviets or for the sole purpose of appearing the technological leaders of the world. On the other hand, there is another theory that there was an encounter with an alien and that the Apollo astronauts had other items of interest that they picked up on the moon apart from the moon rock.

If one was to listen to the declassified transcription, as the moment for landing on the moon arrived, serious anomalies can be heard in the tape. One of them is a hiss as if some text had been erased. Then there are the mysterious "USS" or unidentified space sounds like strange music from outer space. Even today it is hard to conclude what the astronauts discovered and why the tapes were kept classified.

APOLLO 11 AIR-TO-GROUND VOICE TRANSCRIPTION

TAPE 8 (Declassified)

00 00 00 04 ARMSTRONG	Roger. Clock.
00 00 00 13 ARMSTRONG	Roger. We got a roll program.
00 00 00 15 COLLINS	Roger. Roll.
00 00 00 34 ARMSTRONG	Roll's complete and the pitch is programed.
00 00 00 44 ARMSTRONG	One Bravo.
00 00 01 02 CC	Apollo 11, Houston. You're good at 1 minute.
00 00 01 06 ARMSTRONG	Roger.
00 00 01 54 CC	Stand by for mode 1 Charlie.
00 00 01 57 CC	MARK.
00 00 01 58 CC	Mode 1 Charlie.
00 00 01 59 ARMSTRONG	One Charlie.
00 00 02 03 CC	Apollo 11, this is Houston. You are GO for staging.
00 00 02 17 ARMSTRONG	Inboard cut-off.

00 00 02 19 CC	We confirm inboard cut-off.
00 00 02 44 ARMSTRONG	Staging.
00 00 02 46 ARMSTRONG	And ignition.
00 00 02 55 CC	11, Houston. Thrust is GO, all engines. You're looking good.
00 00 02 59 ARMSTRONG	Roger. You're loud and clear, Houston.
00 00 05 21 CC	Stand by the S-IVB to COI capability.
00 00 05 25 ARMSTRONG	Okay.
00 00 05 27 CC	MARK.
00 00 05 28 CC	S-IVB to COI capability.
00 00 05 30 ARMSTRONG	Roger.
00 00 05 35 ARMSTRONG	You sure sound clear down there, Bruce. Sounds like you're sitting in your living room.
00 00 05 39 CC	Oh, thank you. You all are coming through beautifully, too.
00 00 06 00 ARMSTRONG	We're doing 6 minutes. Starting the gimbal motors.
00 00 06 03 CC	Roger, 11. You're GO from the ground at 6 minutes.
00 00 06 08 USS	Perattin karayil vechu perenthennu chodichappol – pair-ekka! Ah- pair-ekka, ennu paranchoode!
00 00 06 16 ARMSTRONG	Houston, some garbled USS. Sounds sing-song. Over.
00 00 06 20 CC	Apollo 11, this is Houston. Level sense arm at 8 plus 17; outboard cut-off at 9 plus 11.
00 00 07 01 ARMSTRONG	Apollo 11's GO at 7 minutes.
00 00 07 04 CC	11, this is Houston. Roger. You're GO from the ground at 7 minutes. Level sense arm at 8 plus 17; outboard cut-off at 9 plus 11.
00 00 07 09 ARMSTRONG	Roger.

GRAND BAHAMA ISLANDS (REV 1)

00 00 08 52 CC	11, this is Houston. You are GO for staging. Over.

00 00 08 56 ARMSTRONG	Understand, GO for staging. And - -
00 00 08 57 CC	Stand by for mode IV capability.
00 00 08 59 ARMSTRONG	Okay. Mode IV.

VANGUARD (REV 1)

00 00 13 27 CC	Apollo 11, this is Houston. The booster has been configured for orbital coast. Both spacecraft are looking good. Over.
00 00 13 35 ARMSTRONG	Roger.
00 00 14 33 CC	Apollo 11, this is Houston. Vanguard LOS at 15 35; AOS Canaries at 16 30. Over.
00 00 14 43 ARMSTRONG	Okay. Thank you.

CANARY (REV 1)

00 00 17 38 CT	Houston COMM TECH. Canary COMM TECH.
00 00 18 18 CC	Apollo 11, this is Houston through Canary. Over.
00 00 18 23 ARMSTRONG	Roger. Reading you loud and clear. Our insertion checklist is complete, and we have no abnormalities.
00 00 18 30 CC	Roger. And I'd like to pass up your Delta azimuth correction at this time if you're ready to copy.
00 00 18 36 ARMSTRONG	Stand by.
00 00 18 40 ARMSTRONG	Roger. Go ahead. Ready to copy.
00 00 23 08 CC	Apollo 11, this is Houston. Coming up on LOS Canary; AOS Tananarive at 37 04, Simplex Alfa. Houston. Out.
00 00 23 23 ARMSTRONG	Apollo. Roger.

CARNARVON (REV 1)

00 00 53 03 CC	Apollo 11, this is Houston through Carnarvon. Over.
00 00 53 08 ALDRIN	Houston, Apollo 11. Loud and clear. Over.

00 00 53 11 CC	Roger, 11. We're reading you the same. Both the booster and the spacecraft are looking good to us. Over.
00 00 53 26 ALDRIN	Houston, Apollo 11. Would you like to copy the alignment results?
00 00 53 31 CC	That's affirmative.
00 00 57 27 CC	Apollo 11, this is Houston. One minute to LOS Carnarvon; AOS at Honeysuckle 59 33. Over.
00 00 57 37 ARMSTRONG	Apollo 11. Roger.
00 00 57 40 CC	Roger. And we request you turn up S-band volume for the Honeysuckle pass.

HONEYSUCKLE (REV 1)

00 01 02 48 CC	Apollo 11, Apollo 11, this is Houston on S-band. Radio check. Over.
00 01 02 55 ARMSTRONG	Roger, Houston. Apollo 11 reads you loud and clear.
00 01 02 58 CC	This is Houston. Roger. Reading you the same. Out.
00 01 03 05 USS	Perattin karayil vechu, perenthennu chodichappol – pair-ekka! Ah- pair-ekka, ennu paranchoode! Verikarayugil-nennu mailanji kaikondu – vazhaika! Ah-vazhaika, varthedu tanoode!
00 01 03 35 ARMSTRONG	Houston, we're experiencing some prolonged USS. Someone is singing. Do you roger that? Over.
00 01 04 24 CC	Apollo 11, this is Houston. A little over 1 minute to LOS at Honeysuckle. You'll be AOS at Goldstone at 1 29 02; LOS at Goldstone 1 33 55. Over.
00 01 29 09 CC	Apollo 11, this is Houston through Guaymas. Over.
00 01 29 14 ARMSTRONG	Roger, Houston. Reading you loud and clear.
00 01 29 17 CC	Roger. Reading you the same. Coming up on AOS Goldstone.

00 01 29 20 ARMSTRONG	Roger.

GUAYMAS (REV 1)

00 01 29 27 ALDRIN	Cecil B. deAldrin is standing by for instructions.
00 01 29 32 CC	Houston. Roger.
00 01 31 15 CC	Apollo 11, this is Houston. We are not receiving your FM downlink yet. We are standing by.
00 01 31 56 CC	Apollo 11, this is Houston. We are receiving your FM downlink now. We are standing by for TV modulations on the signal.
00 01 32 23 CC	Apollo 11, Apollo 11, this is Houston. Radio check. Over.

GOLDSTONE (REV 1)

00 01 32 27 ARMSTRONG	Roger. Loud and clear. We think we are transmitting to you.
00 01 32 31 CC	Okay. We are not receiving it yet, 11, although we have confirmed presence of your FM downlink carrier.
00 01 32 39 ARMSTRONG	Which switches do you want us to confirm?
00 01 32 42 CC	Stand by.

TEXAS (REV 1)

00 01 33 11 CC	Apollo 11, this is Houston. You were just on the fringes of coverage from Goldstone. We have just had LOS at Goldstone, and we'd like to push on and get the PAD messages read up to you here shortly.
00 01 33 26 ARMSTRONG	Roger. We are ready to copy.
00 01 33 36 USS	Perattin karayil vechu, perenthennu chodichappol – pair-ekka! Ah- pair-ekka, ennu paranchoode!
00 01 33 44 ARMSTRONG	Receiving garbled USS again. Sounds like that song again! You copy?
00 01 34 00 USS	Verikarayugil - nennu, mailanji kaikondu – vazhaika! Ah-vazhaika, varthedu tanoode!

00 01 34 44 ARMSTRONG	Texas, you copy that?
00 01 34 33 CC	Apollo 11, this is Houston. I am ready with your TLI-plus-90-minute abort PAD.
00 01 41 48 ARMSTRONG	Roger. Here's the pitch.
00 01 41 56 CC	Apollo 11, this is Houston. We are seeing the pitch hot firing and it looks good.
00 01 42 02 USS	Perattin karayil vechu, perenthennu chodichappol – pair-ekka! Ah- pair-ekka, ennu paranchoode! Verikarayugil-nennu, mailanji kaikondu – vazhaika! Ah-vazhaika, varthedu tanoode!
00 01 42 30 CC	11, we've traced the source. Could be the Soviets. We've set up a jam. Hear any more USS?
00 01 42 18 ARMSTRONG	Roger. Be advised that we are able to hear them intermittently.
00 01 42 22 CC	Roger. We copy.
00 01 42 24 ARMSTRONG	Have you seen all three axes fire?
00 01 42 31 CC	We've seen pitch and yaw; we've not seen roll to date.
00 01 42 36 ARMSTRONG	Okay. I'll put in a couple more rolls.
00 01 42 42 CC	Okay. We've got the roll impulses, and you're looking good here.

GRAND BAHAMA ISLANDS (REV 2)

00 01 43 36 CC	Apollo 11, this Houston. You are GO for RYRO ARM.
00 01 43 40 ARMSTRONG	Roger. Thank you.
00 01 43 57 CC	Apollo 11, this is Houston. If you will give us P00 in ACC
EPT,	we have a state vector update for you.
00 01 44 04 ARMSTRONG	Roger.

VANGUARD (REV2)

00 01 45 23 COLLINS	Roger. TLI PAD: 23514 179 071 001 547 104356 35575 357 107 041 301 287 319. TLI 1O-minute abort pitch, 223. Over.

00 01 46 03 CC	Apollo 11, this is Houston. Roger. Would you read back DELTA-VC prime again? You were cut out by some noise.
00 01 46 09 COLLINS	Okay. Roger. I'm picking up the squeal here, also. DELTA-VC 104356. Over.
00 01 46 12 USS	Perattin karayil vechu, perenthennu chodichappol – pair-ekka! Ah- pair-ekka, ennu paranchoode! Verikarayugil-nennu, mailanji kaikondu – vazhaika! Ah-vazhaika, varthedu tanoode!
00 01 46 25 CC	Apollo 11, this is Houston. Readback correct. Out.
00 01 47 06 CC	Apollo 11, this is Houston. We've completed the uplink; the computer is yours. You can go back to BLOCK. Would you verify that you have extended the probe? Over.
00 01 47 16 ARMSTRONG	Roger. That's verified; the probe is extended.
00 01 47 19 CC	Roger. About 2 minutes to LOS on this stateside pass. AOS Canaries at 1 50 13. Over.
00 01 47 28 ARMSTRONG	Roger. 1 50.

CANARY (REV 2)

00 01 50 42 CC	Apollo 11, this is Houston. Over.
00 01 50 45 ARMSTRONG	Roger. Houston, Apollo 11. Loud and clear.

CARNARVON (REV 2)

00 02 25 44 CC	Apollo 11, this is Houston through Carnarvon. Radio check. Over.
00 02 25 49 ARMSTRONG	Roger, Houston through Carnarvon. Apollo 11. Loud and clear.
00 02 25 53 CC	Roger. You're coming in very loud and very clear, here. Out.
00 02 30 42 ARMSTRONG	Very good.

ARIA (REV 2)

00 02 32 20 CC	Apollo 11, Apollo 11, this is Houston through ARIA 4. Radio check. Over.
00 02 32 28 ALDRIN	Houston, we read you strength 4 and a little scratchy.
00 02 32 34 CC	Roger. We're reading you strength 5, readability about 3. Should be quite adequate.
00 02 32 42 CC	Apollo 11, Apollo 11, this is Houston. We're reading you readability about 3, strength 5. Sounds pretty good. Over.
00 02 32 54 ARMSTRONG	Roger. We've got a little static in the background now.
00 02 33 09 USS	kadalinakkare ponore, kaana ponninu ponore, kadalinakkare ponore, kaana ponninu ponore.
00 02 33 22 ARMSTRONG	Here we go again CC. It's clearly a human voice. A song! You copy?
00 02 33 50 CC	Apollo 11. Setting up jam again. Over.
00 02 37 21 CC	Apollo 11, this is Houston through ARIA 3. Radio check. Over.
00 02 37 26 ARMSTRONG	Roger, Houston, Apollo 11. You are much clearer and adequately loud. Over.
00 02 37 32 CC	Roger, 11, You are coming in five-by-five here. Beautiful signal.
00 02 37 38 ARMSTRONG	This is a lot better than this static we had previously.
00 02 37 41 CC	Okay.
00 02 37 48 COLLINS	And we got the time base fix indication on time.
00 02 55 28 ARMSTRONG	Roger.
00 03 05 28 CC	Apollo 11, this is Houston. Our preliminary data indicates a good cut-off on the S-IVB. We'll have some more trajectory data for you in about half an hour. Over.
00 03 05 44 USS	kadalinakkare ponore, kaana ponninu ponore, kadalinakkare ponore, kaana ponninu ponore, poyi varumbol enthu kondu varum kai niraye, poyi varumbol enthu kondu varum
00 03 09 01 CC	Apollo 11, Apollo 11, this is Houston. Over.

00 03 09 16 CC	Apollo 11, Apollo 11, this is Houston. Over.
00 03 09 31 ARMSTRONG	Hello, Houston. Hello, Houston. This is Apollo 11. Sorry. Was a little distracted. I'm reading you loud and clear. That Russian song's beginning to sound good. Go ahead. Over.
00 03 09 37 CC	Roger, 11. This is Houston. We are tracing the source to destination surface. Not a song. Could be a gamma burst. We had to shift stations. We weren't reading you through Goldstone. We show PYR0 bus A armed and PYRO bus B not armed at the present time. Over.
00 03 09 50 ARMSTRONG	That's affirmative, Houston. That's affirmative.
00 03 09 54 CC	Roger.
00 03 14 08 CC	Apollo 11, this is Houston. You're GO for separation. Our systems recommendation is arm both PYRO buses. Over.
00 03 14 19 ARMSTRONG	Okay. PYRO B coming armed. My intent is to use bottle primary 1, as per the checklist; therefore, I just turned A on.
00 03 14 26 CC	Roger. We concur with the logic.
00 03 16 59 ARMSTRONG	Houston, we're about to SEP.
00 03 17 02 CC	This is Houston. We copy.
00 03 17 09 ARMSTRONG	SEP is complete.
00 03 17 12 CC	Roger.
00 03 17 32 ARMSTRONG	... and primary and secondary propellant B went... SEP.
00 03 17 40 CC	That was secondary propellant on quad Bravo?
00 03 17 45 ARMSTRONG	Quad Bravo, yes. Both the primary and secondary...
00 03 17 52 CC	Roger. We copy.
00 03 22 07 CC	Apollo 11, this is Houston. Radio check. Over.
00 03 22 12 USS	Oh ho ho ho ho ho ho ho.. Chandana thoniyeri ponore ningal poyi poyi poyi varumbol,....Chandana thoniyeri ponore ningal poyi poyi poyi varumbol

00 03 23 56 CC	Apollo 11, Apollo 11, this is Houston broadcasting in the blind. Request OMNI Bravo if you read us. Request OMNI Bravo. Out.
00 03 24 13 CC	Apollo 11, this is Houston. How do you read?
00 03 25 49 CC	Apollo 11, this is Houston. How do you read? Over.
00 03 26 47 CC	Apollo 11, Apollo 11, this is Houston. Do you read? Over.
00 03 27 54 CC	Apollo 11, this is Houston. Radio check. Over.
00 03 28 11 CC	Apollo 11, Apollo 11, this is Houston. Radio check. Over.
00 03 29 20 CC	Apollo 11, this is Houston. Radio check. Over.
00 03 29 24 ARMSTRONG	Roger.... poye, poye, poye...
00 03 29 26 CC	Roger. We're copying you about five-by-two, very weak. Can you give us a status report, please?
00 03 29 35 ALDRIN	Roger. We are docked. We do have acquisition with the high gain at this time, I think.
00 03 29 44 CC	Understand you are using the high gain. Over.
00 03 29 48 ARMSTRONG	Poi, poi, poi, verum-bowl...
00 03 29 49 ALDRIN	That's affirmative?
00 03 29 51 CC	Roger. I read you very loud and clear, Buzz. Neil is pretty weak. His speech is garbled.
00 03 30 00 ALDRIN	Roger. We've got the high gain locked on, now, I believe; AUTO tracking now.
00 03 30 05 CC	Okay. You're coming in loud and clear, but Mike is just barely readable.
00 03 30 12 COLLINS	That was Neil. How are you reading?
00 03 30 15 CC	Loud and clear now, Mike. And we understand that you are docked.
00 03 30 19 COLLINS	That's affirmative.
00 03 30 24 ARMSTRONG	Houston,... How do you read...?
00 03 30 28 CC	11, CDR, neither loud nor clear, Neil.
00 03 30 30 ARMSTRONG	Okay............. Boy, Boy, Boy, verum-bowl....
00 03 32 40 CC	11, this is Houston. Over.

00 03 32 44 ARMSTRONG	Houston, Apollo 11. Go ahead. Boy, boy, boy, way-room-bowl....
00 03 32 46 CC	Roger. When you commented on that quad Bravo problem at separation, you were a little weak. Could you go through what you did after you noticed the talkbacks barber pole again, please?
00 03 33 20 CC	We copied the - the primary and secondary propellant talkbacks on SM RCS quad Bravo 1 to barber pole on separation.
00 03 33 30 ARMSTRONG	Roger. Roger. That is affirmative, and we moved that switch to the OPEN position, and they went back to gray. Over. Boy, boy, boy, way-room bowl.....Talk about a catchy tune!
00 03 33 39 CC	Roger.
00 03 37 51 CC	Apollo 11, this is Houston. Over.
00 03 37 56 COLLINS	Roger, Houston. Apollo 11. Go ahead.
00 03 37 58 CC	Roger. Could you give us comments on how the transposition and docking went? Over.
04 03 24 13 ALDRIN	Houston, Eagle. The RCS hot fire is complete. How did you observe it? Over.
04 03 24 18 CC	Stand by. Eagle, Houston. The RCS hot fire looks super to us. We're all GO.
04 03 24 32 ALDRIN	Roger. Mike, would you confirm that thrusters B3 and C4 are off? Over. And your radar transponder off.
04 03 24 42 COLLINS	C4 is off; B3 is off. Transponder is to HEATER which is the same as being off, and I've got my roll jets back on now.
04 03 24 50 ARMSTRONG	And you're manoeuvring. Right?
04 03 24 53 COLLINS	Will be shortly, Neil.
04 03 25 00 CC	Apollo 11, Houston. We're GO for undocking. Over.
04 03 25 08 ALDRIN	Roger. Understand.
04 03 26 39 COLLINS	Starting a trim manoeuvre to AGS CAL attitude.

04 03 26 44 USS	Kaayalarikathu valayerinjappol vala kilukkiya sundaree, pennu kettinu kuriyedukkumbol oru narukkinu cherkkane....
04 03 28 05 COLLINS	Houston, Columbia. Switching frequencies or USS. Neil was right, I hear some kinda song, over
04 03 28 07 CC	Go ahead, Columbia. Is it Russian? Can you initiate a probe at your end? Over.
04 03 28 12 COLLINS	Roger. There will be no television of the undocking. I have all available windows either full of heads or cameras, and I'm busy with other things.
04 03 28 19 CC	We concur. Over.
04 03 28 23 COLLINS	Okay.
04 03 28 24 CC	And, Eagle, Houston. We'd like you to select aft OMNI now. It will be good for both LOS and AOS. Over.
04 03 28 33 ALDRIN	Roger. Going to aft OMNI.
04 03 29 07 CC	Apollo 11, Houston. One minute to LOS.
04 03 29 13 COLLINS	Columbia. Roger.
04 03 29 18 ARMSTRONG	... Columbia. Systems looking good.

04 03 51 -- BEGIN LUNAR REV 13

04 04 17 06 CC	Hello, Eagle. Houston. We're standing by. Over.
04 04 17 51 CC	Eagle, Houston. We see you on the steerable. Over.
04 04 18 01 ARMSTRONG (EAGLE)	Roger. Eagle is undocked.
04 04 18 03 CC	Roger. How does it look, Neil?
04 04 18 04 ARMSTRONG (EAGLE)	The Eagle has wings.
04 04 18 06 CC	Roger.
04 04 18 08 ARMSTRONG (EAGLE)	Looking good.
04 04 29 02 COLLINS (COLUMBIA)	Neil, I'm maneuvering in roll.

04 04 29 04 ARMSTRONG (EAGLE)	Roger. I see you.
04 04 29 10 ALDRIN (EAGLE)	Houston, Eagle. Are you copying the very large numbers for range and range rate in VERB 83? And did you just give us a state vector that changed one of the two vehicles? Over.
04 04 29 28 CC	Roger, Eagle. We gave you a LM state vector. We have not changed the CSM state vector, however. Over.
04 04 29 40 ALDRIN (EAGLE)	Okay. That explains it. Over.
04 04 34 38 COLLINS (COLUMBIA)	We're really stabilized, Neil. I haven't burned a thruster in 5 minutes.
04 04 35 26 COLLINS (COLUMBIA)	I'll make a small trim maneuver.
04 04 36 21 ARMSTRONG (EAGLE)	Mike, what's going to be your pitch angle at SEP?
04 04 36 27 COLLINS (COLUMBIA)	007 degrees.
04 04 36 28 ARMSTRONG (EAGLE)	Okay.
04 04 36 44 COLLINS (COLUMBIA)	Is that close enough for you or do you want it to a couple of decimal places?
04 04 36 46 ARMSTRONG (EAGLE)	No. That's good.
04 04 36 52 USS	Kaayalarikathu valayerinjappol vala kilukkiya sundaree, pennu kettinu kuriyedukkumbol oru narukkinu cherkkane! Kanninaalente karalin uruliyil enna kaachiya nombaram, kalbilarinjappol innu njammalu kayaru pottiya pambaram!
04 04 37 20 ARMSTRONG (EAGLE)	CC, Still no fix on the source of that interference. Your last communication sited destination surface. Can we still jam it? Over.
04 04 37 31 COLLINS (COLUMBIA)	Checking the possibility. Ignore it. I think you've got a fine looking flying machine there, Eagle, despite the fact you're upside down.

04 04 37 36 ARMSTRONG (EAGLE)	Somebody's upside-down. But this sound is more disorienting. Over.
04 04 38 53 COLLINS (COLUMBIA)	Okay, Eagle. One minute until TIG. You guys take care. I'll bet the Soviets are playing up.
04 04 38 56 ARMSTRONG (EAGLE)	See you later.
04 04 40 19 COLLINS (COLUMBIA)	Houston, Columbia. My DSKY is reading 4.9, in X, 5.0..., make it and EMS 105.4. Over.
04 04 47 35 USS	cheril ninnu balarnnu ponthiya hoori ninnude kayyinaal – ney choru vachathu thinnuvaan kothiyere unden nenchilaay.
04 04 47 58 COLLINS (COLUMBIA)	Eagle, Columbia. I am reading you loud and scratchy. Neil is not coming through too well on his VOX. It's another song, damn it. Could you be quiet for 15 seconds while I get this locked on. Where's this other guy who sang – Boy, Boy, Boy, we're in a bowl. That was more tolerable.
04 04 48 13 ALDRIN (EAGLE)	Okay.
04 04 48 33 COLLINS (COLUMBIA)	I've got a solid lock on. I have you at 0.27 miles.
04 04 49 07 CC	Eagle, Houston. We've got a state vector for you. We'd like P00 and DATA. Over.
04 04 49 15 ALDRIN (EAGLE)	You have it.
04 04 49 16 CC	Thank you, sir.
04 11 07 33 CC	Okay. And I got LOS amd AOS times for you.
04 11 07 40 COLLINS (COLUMBIA)	Go ahead.
04 11 07 48 COLLINS (COLUMBIA)	Go ahead, Houston.
04 11 07 50 CC	Roger. Your LOS at 107 plus 23 plus 03. AOS at 108 plus 09 plus 06. The next pass for...
04 11 07 50 COAS	tracking: your time of closest approach is 108 35 28. That's 3 miles south of track. Over.

04 11 07 53 USS	(static) oh ho ho ho ho ho ho pushpaka thoniyeri ponore ningal
	poyi poyi poyi varumbol......... pushpaka thoniyeri ponore ningal poyi poyi poyi varumbol.........
04 11 08 10 ARMSTRONG	I see the UFO on the screen.....looks like Soviet space debris. Evasion maneuver executed. We'll...
04 11 08 16 ARMSTRONG	The blighters. How did this go undetected so long by LCC?
04 11 08 26 CC	Correction. It's not quite round. A small protrusion at the end...like a ...like a coconut. Over.
04 11 08 35 COLLIN	An oval? A football shape?
04 11 08 39 CC	A de-husked coconut, the shell with a husky tail.
04 11 08 42 USS	(Static) pushpaka thoniyeri ponore ningal poyi poyi poyi varumbol.........
04 11 08 49 ARMSTRONG	It's that song again. The better one. The one with the catchy tune.
04 11 08 53 CC	CDR, you've gone faint......you're 3 min 45 sec to debris. Over.
04 11 08 59 ARMSTRONG	Roger. Could be more than debris. It's got lights. I see three coloured lights.
04 11 09 05 CC	Any identifiable markers?
04 11 09 10 ARMSTRONG	Not clear yet.
04 11 09 13 CC	Look for Russian alphabets. CCCP. Over.
04 11 09 16 ARMSTRONG	Roger. I see a K, and an A and an I...
04 11 09 19 ARMSTRONG	Followed by R-A-L-I! KAIRALI? What's Kairali?
04 11 09 24 CC	Appears to have left our destination. From the surface of Sea of Tranquillity. Over.
04 11 09 32 LCC	We'll keep this from Broadcast. The Soviets couldn't have landed on destination.
04 11 09 37 ARMSTRONG	Run the encyclopaedia. Ask LCC to pass it through CIA. Decipher KAIRALI. Over.

04 11 09 41 LCC	Roger. Will do. But maintain policy regulations.
04 11 09 45 CC	We are maintaining media silence. No comments on UFO

END OF TAPE

TAPE 9 (De-classified)

04 11 08 28 COLLINS (COLUMBIA)	I understand all that, but with this new information would you like me to try P22 and look for him in a different spot?
04 11 08 40 CC	Stand by a minute, please.
04 11 08 44 COLLINS (COLUMBIA)	Okay. Because I was looking in the wrong place last time. AUTO optics was not pointing me at the coordinates you gave me.
04 11 08 53 CC	Roger.
04 11 10 06 CC	Columbia, this is Houston. Over.
04 11 10 13 COLLINS (COLUMBIA)	Go ahead.
04 12 25 15 ARMSTRONG (TRANQ)	Okay. There it is. ECS MASTER ALARM, water separator.
04 12 25 20 ALDRIN (TRANQ)	Okay.
04 12 25 25 ARMSTRONG (TRANQ)	both suit isolation valves to SUIT DISCONNECT.
04 12 25 26 ALDRIN (TRANQ)	I'll get them.
04 12 25 28 ALDRIN (TRANQ)	Got it.
04 12 25 30 ARMSTRONG (TRANQ)	Okay. Disconnect LM hoses.
04 12 25 46 ALDRIN (TRANQ)	Okay.
04 12 25 50 ARMSTRONG (TRANQ)	Connect OPS O2 hose to right hand PGA blue connector and lock.

04 12 25 54 ALDRIN (TRANQ)	Let me do that for you.
04 12 27 58 ARMSTRONG (TRANQ)	Hold this... in your purge valve.
04 12 28 22 ALDRIN (TRANQ)	Locked and double locked.
04 12 28 25 ARMSTRONG (TRANQ)	Okay.
04 12 28 42 ARMSTRONG (TRANQ)	Position mike.
04 12 29 00 ALDRIN (TRANQ)	Sure wished I had shaved last night.
04 12 29 31 ALDRIN (TRANQ)	Got your mikes where you want them?
04 12 29 42 ARMSTRONG (TRANQ)	Roger.
04 12 30 07 ARMSTRONG (TRANQ)	Verify PLSS mode select in AR.
04 12 30 11 ALDRIN (TRANQ)	Verified.
04 12 30 19 COLLINS (COLUMBIA)	I don't know if you guys can read me on VHF, but you sure sound good down there.
04 12 30 46 ALDRIN (TRANQ)	And locked.
04 12 30 48 ARMSTRONG (TRANQ)	Okay.
04 12 30 53 ALDRIN (TRANQ)	All right. The vent window is clear. And remove LEVA from the engine cover. Verify EV visor is attached.
04 12 31 13 ALDRIN (TRANQ)	How's the COMM now, Houston? Over.
04 12 31 16 CC	Buzz, this is Houston. The COMM is very good. You are coming in loud and clear, and Mike passes on the word that he is receiving you and following your progress with interest.

04 12 31 27 ALDRIN (TRANQ)	Very well, thank you.
04 12 31 58 ARMSTRONG (TRANQ)	Got all the material up in the back?
04 12 32 40 ALDRIN (TRANQ)	Complete.
04 12 33 43 ARMSTRONG (TRANQ)	Helmet locked?
04 12 35 38 ALDRIN (TRANQ)	Wonder if we're triggering all the time.
04 12 35 42 ARMSTRONG (TRANQ)	I don't think so.
04 12 35 45 ARMSTRONG (TRANQ)	Houston, Neil. How do you read?
04 12 36 01 ARMSTRONG (TRANQ)	Okay. We're hearing a little bit of background noise, and I just wanted to make sure that we weren't continually keyed.
04 12 36 07 CC	Don't sound like it.
04 12 36 26 ARMSTRONG (TRANQ)	Want to put the light back up?
04 13 20 58 ARMSTRONG (TRANQ)	Okay. Can you pull the door open a little more?
04 13 21 00 ALDRIN (TRANQ)	All right.
04 12 21 03 ARMSTRONG (TRANQ)	Okay.
04 13 21 07 ALDRIN (TRANQ)	Did you get the MESA out?
04 13 21 09 ARMSTRONG (TRANQ)	I'm going to pull it now.
04 13 21 18 ARMSTRONG (TRANQ)	Houston, the MESA came down all right.
04 13 23 10 CC	Roger. We copy.
04 13 23 11 ARMSTRONG (TRANQ)	It takes a pretty good little jump.

Oh 13 23 25 CC	Buzz, this is Houston. F/2 - 1/160th second for shadow photography on the sequence camera.
04 13 23 35 ALDRIN (TRANQ)	Okay.
04 13 23 38 ARMSTRONG (TRANQ)	I'm at the foot of the ladder. The LM footpads are only depressed in the surface about 1 or 2 inches, although the surface appears to be very, very fine grained, as you get close to it. It's almost like a powder. Down there, it's very fine.
04 13 23 43 ARMSTRONG (TRANQ)	I'm going to step off the LM now.
04 13 24 48 ARMSTRONG (TRANQ)	THAT'S ONE SMALL STEP FOR (A) MAN, ONE GIANT LEAP FOR MANKIND.
04 13 24 48 ARMSTRONG (TRANQ)	And the - the surface is fine and powdery. I can - I can pick it up loosely with my toe. It does adhere in fine layers like powdered charcoal to the sole and sides of my boots. I only go in a small fraction of an inch, maybe an eighth of an inch, but I can see the footprints of my boots and the treads in the fine, sandy particles.
04 13 25 30 CC	Neil, this is Houston. We're copying.
04 13 25 45 ARMSTRONG (EVA)	There seems to be no difficulty in moving around as we suspected. It's even perhaps easier than the simulations at one sixth g that we performed in the various simulations on the ground. It's actually no trouble to walk around. Okay. The descent engine did not leave a crater of any size. It has about 1foot clearance on the ground. We're essentially on a very level place here. I can see some evidence of rays emanating from the descent engine, but a very insignificant amount.
04 13 26 54 ARMSTRONG (EVA)	Okay, Buzz, we ready to bring down the camera?
04 13 26 59 ALDRIN (EVA)	I'm all ready. I think it's been all squared away and in good shape.

04 13 27 03 ARMSTRONG (EVA)	Okay.
04 13 30 53 ARMSTRONG (EVA)	I'll step out and take some of my first pictures here.
04 13 31 05 CC	Roger. Neil, we're reading you loud and clear. We see you getting some pictures and the contingency sample.
04 13 32 19 CC	Neil, this is Houston. Did you copy about the contingency sample? Over.
04 13 34 56 ARMSTRONG (EVA)	It has a stark beauty all its own. It's like much of the high desert of the United States. It's different but it's very pretty out here. Be advised that a lot of the rock samples out here, the hard rock samples, have what appear to be vesicles in the surface. Also, I am looking at one now that appears to have some sort of phenocryst.
04 13 35 30 CC	Houston. Roger. Out.
04 13 43 24 ALDRIN (EVA)	Magnificent desolation.
04 13 43 47 ALDRIN (EVA)	Looks like the secondary strut...little thermal effects on it right here, Neil.
04 13 43 54 ARMSTRONG (EVA)	Yes. I noticed that. That seems to be the worst, although similar effects are on - all around.
04 13 44 -- BEGIN LUNAR REV 18	
04 13 44 07 MS	... powder, isn't it?
04 13 44 09 ARMSTRONG (EVA)	Isn't it fine?
04 13 51 46 ALDRIN (EVA)	We appreciate that. Thank you.
04 13 52 19 ALDRIN (EVA)	Neil is now unveiling the plaque gear.
04 13 52 27 CC	Roger. We got you foresighted, but back under one track.
04 13 52 40 ARMSTRONG (EVA)	For those who haven't read the plaque, we'll read the plaque that's on the front landing gear of this LM. First there's two hemispheres, one showing each of the two hemispheres of the Earth.

Underneath it says "Here Man from the planet Earth first set foot upon the Moon, July 1969 A.D. We came in peace for all mankind." It has the crew members' signatures and the signature of the President of the United States.

04 13 53 35 ARMSTRONG (EVA)	Ready for the camera?
04 13 53 38 ALDRIN (EVA)	No. I'll get it. No, you take this TV on out.
04 13 53 45 ARMSTRONG (EVA)	Watch the LEC, there.
04 13 53 53 ALDRIN (EVA)	Now I'm afraid these... materials are going to get dusty
04 13 55 57 ALDRIN (EVA)	And, we'll probably need a little distance. Back location television camera.
04 13 55 57 ARMSTRONG	Roger. Shadow at edge of crater with a small glimmering light. Is it caused by some of our light reflected from the LM?
04 13 56 02 ALDRIN (EVA)	Doubt it. It's too far.
04 13 56 07 ARMSTRONG	Worth an examination. We can carry back material evidence of Soviet debris.
04 13 56 12 ARMSTRONG	Commence motion towards mysterious light.
04 13 56 16 USS	Maanasa poykayile maayaa dweepile maada praavine konda tharaamo.... Aathiraa panthalil panchami thalikayil deva kanyakamaarude omal poo thaali tharamo.....
04 13 56 30 ARMSTRONG	The singing grows louder as I approach
04 13 56 34 ALDRIN (EVA)	Confirm distance to object
04 13 56 38 ARMSTRONG	Approx. 50 meters. Maximum I can go on safety cord.
04 13 56 40 ARMSTRONG	Camera on
04 13 56 44 ALDRIN (EVA)	See if you can avoid a flash.
04 13 56 49 ALDRIN (EVA)	Are you armed?
04 13 56 53 ARMSTRONG	Only regulation. I don't perceive any such danger.
04 13 56 57 ALDRIN (EVA)	Avoid confrontation, Avoid conflict.
04 13 56 59 ARMSTRONG	Looks like a campsite, pitched tent and all.

04 13 57 06 ARMSTRONG	The singing grows louder as probe is extended. It's plain radio-waves. I'm sure no sound is audible outside this helmet. Probably transmitted from the coconut UFO. How does he latch on to our frequency?
04 13 57 14 ARMSTRONG	Need to take a close look. I'll need more cable.
04 13 57 14 ALDRIN (EVA)	Neil, look at the minus Y-strut, the direction of travel there travel from right to left.
04 13 57 24 ARMSTRONG (EVA)	Right.
04 13 56 25 ALDRIN (EVA)	This one over here underneath the ascent engine where the probe first hit - the minus-Y probe first hit.
04 13 56 35 ARMSTRONG (EVA)	Got it. Great. I got plenty of cable?
04 13 56 38 ALDRIN (EVA)	You've got plenty. Plenty more.
04 13 56 48 ALDRIN (EVA)	Okay. I think I've got the end of it.
04 13 56 51 ARMSTRONG (EVA)	Something interesting: in the bottom of this little crater here - It may be -
04 14 00 41 CC	Roger. We have a large angular rock in the foreground, and it looks like a much smaller rock a couple of inches to the left of it. Over.
04 14 00 52 ARMSTRONG (EVA)	All right. And then on beyond it about 10 feet is an even larger rock that's very rounded. That rock is about - The closest one to you is about sticking out of the sand about 1 foot. And it's about a foot and one half long, and it's about 6 inches thick, but it's standing on edge.
04 14 01 16 CC	Roger.
04 14 01 26 ALDRIN (EVA)	Okay, Neil. I've got the table out and the bag deployed.
04 14 01 33 CC	We've got this view, Neil.
04 14 01 42 ARMSTRONG (EVA)	This is straight south.
04 14 01 45 CC	Roger. And we see the shadow of the LM.

04 14 01 48 ARMSTRONG (EVA)	Roger. The little hill just beyond the shadow of the LM is a pair of elongate craters about - probably the pair together is about 40 feet long and 20 feet across, and they're probably 6 feet deep. We'll probably get some more work in there later.
04 14 02 20 CC	Roger. We see Buzz going about his work.
04 14 02 22 ARMSTRONG (EVA)	How's that for a final?
04 14 02 26 CC	For a final orientation, we'd like it to come left about 5 degrees. Over.
04 14 02 36 CC	Now back to the right about half as much.
04 14 02 42 ARMSTRONG	Okay?
04 14 02 53 CC	Okay. That looks good there, Neil.
04 14 03 00 ARMSTRONG (EVA)	Okay.
04 14 03 20 ARMSTRONG (EVA)	Okay. You can make a Mark, Houston. Deployed.
04 14 03 24 CC	Roger. Solar wind.
04 14 03 36 ALDRIN (EVA)	And, incidentally, you can use the shadow that the staff makes to getting it perpendicular.
04 14 03 50 CC	Roger.
04 14 04 05 ALDRIN (EVA)	Some of these small depressions that tend to sink - oh, maybe 2 or 3 inches. Suggest exactly what the Surveyor pictures showed when they pushed away a little bit. You get a force transmitted through the upper surface of the soil and about 5 or 6 inches of bay breaks loose and moves as if it were caked on the surface, when in fact it really isn't.
04 14 04 43 ARMSTRONG (EVA)	I noticed in the soft spots where we had footprints nearly an inch deep that the soil is very cohesive and it will retain a - will retain a slope of probably 70 degrees alongside of the footprints.
04 14 06 29 ARMSTRONG (EVA)	Okay?
04 14 06 30 ALDRIN (EVA)	Yes. I think that's excellent.

04 14 06 39 ALDRIN (EVA)	They didn't come off?
04 14 06 46 ALDRIN (EVA)	get the...
04 14 07 01 ARMSTRONG (EVA)	that part? A rock here.
04 14 07 38 ALDRIN (EVA)	You'll have to extend that one.
04 14 07 58 CC	Columbia, Columbia, this is Houston. Over.
04 14 08 26 ALDRIN (EVA)	Reading you.
04 14 08 53 COLLINS (COLUMBIA)	Houston, Columbia on the high gain. Over.
04 14 08 55 CC	Columbia, this is Houston. Reading you loud and clear. Over.
04 14 09 00 COLLINS (COLUMBIA)	Yes. Reading you loud and clear. How's it going?
04 14 09 01 ARMSTRONG	We see some inscriptions here on a sheet of cardboard. Not hieroglyphics. Sort of rounded alphabets. Run it through an all language translator. These Soviets are on to something.
04 14 09 05 CC	Roger. The EVA is progressing beautifully. I believe they are setting up the flag now.
04 14 09 14 COLLINS (COLUMBIA)	Great.
04 14 09 18 CC	I guess you're about the only person around that doesn't have TV coverage of the scene.
04 14 09 25 COLLINS (COLUMBIA)	That's all right. I don't mind a bit.
04 14 09 33 COLLINS (COLUMBIA)	How is the quality of the TV?
04 14 09 35 CC	Oh, it's beautiful, Mike. It really is.
04 14 09 39 COLLINS (COLUMBIA)	Oh, gee, that's great! Is the lighting half way decent?
04 14 09 43 CC	Yes, indeed. They've got the flag up now and you can see the stars and stripes on the lunar surface.
04 14 09 50 COLLINS (COLUMBIA)	Beautiful. Just beautiful.

04 14 10 16 ALDRIN (EVA)	That's good. See if you can pull that end off a little bit. Take that end up a little.
04 14 10 33 ARMSTRONG (EVA)	It won't pull out.
04 14 10 39 ARMSTRONG (EVA)	Okay.
04 14 12 21 CC	Neil, this is Houston. Radio check. Over.
04 14 12 27 ARMSTRONG (EVA)	Roger, Houston. Loud and clear.
04 14 12 29 CC	Roger. Out.
04 14 12 30 ALDRIN (EVA)	Loud and clear, Houston.
04 14 12 32 CC	Roger, Buzz.
04 14 13 15 ALDRIN (EVA)	I'd like to evaluate the various paces that a person can be traveling on the lunar surface. I believe I'm out of your field of view. Is that right, now, Houston?
04 14 13 30 CC	That's affirmative, Buzz.
04 14 13 37 CC	You are in our field of view now.
04 14 13 42 ALDRIN (EVA)	Okay. You do have to be rather careful to keep track of where your center of mass is. Sometimes, it takes about two or three paces to make sure you've got your feet underneath you.
04 14 14 05 ALDRIN (EVA)	About two to three or maybe four easy paces can bring you to a nearly smooth stop. Here change directions, like a football player, you just have to to have foot out to the side and cut a little bit.
04 14 14 38 ALDRIN (EVA)	So called kangaroo hop does work, but it seems that your forward mobility is not quite as good as - it is in the conventional - more conventional one foot after another.
04 14 15 06 ALDRIN (EVA)	It's hard saying what a sane pace might be. I think it's the one that I'm using now. It's the pace of that song. Boy, boy, boy, were-in-bowl - would get rather tiring after several hundred, but this may be a function of this suit, as well as lack of gravity forces.

04 14 15 18 ARMSTRONG	Watch me go… Boy, boy, boy, that's it….Boy, boy, boy… here's the best rhythm for moon walking. Boy, boy, boy…..boy, boy, boy….
04 14 15 32 ALDRIN (EVA)	I thought the lyrics sounded like Poye, poye, poye, verin-bowl.
04 14 15 47 CC	Tranquillity Base, this is Houston. Could we get both of you on the camera for a minute, please?
04 14 16 00 ARMSTRONG (EVA)	Say again, Houston.
04 14 16 02 CC	Roger. We'd like to get both of you in the field of view of the camera for a minute.
04 14 16 09 CC	Neil and Buzz, the President of the United States is in his office now and would like to say a few words to you. Over.
04 14 16 23 ARMSTRONG (EVA)	That would be an honour.
04 14 16 25 CC	Go ahead, Mr. President. This is Houston. Out.

THE FOLLOWING IS A MESSAGE FROM RICHARD M. NIXON, PRESIDENT OF THE UNITED STATES; THE MESSAGE ORIGINATED FROM THE OVAL ROOM OF THE WHITE HOUSE, WASHINGTON, DISTRICT OF COLUMBIA

| 04 14 16 30 PRESIDENT NIXON | Neil and Buzz, I am talking to you by telephone from the Oval Room at the White House, and this certainly has to be the most historic telephone call ever made. I just can't tell you how proud we all are of what you've achieved for every American. This has to be the proudest day of our lives. And for people all over the world, I am sure they, too, join with Americans in recognizing what an immense feat this is. Because of what you have done, the heavens have become a part of man's world. And as you talk to us from the Sea of Tranquillity, it inspires us to redouble our efforts to bring peace and tranquillity to Earth. For one priceless moment in the whole history of man, all the people on this Earth are truly one; |

one in their pride in what you have done, and one in our prayers that you will return safely to Earth.

04 14 17 44 ARMSTRONG (EVA)	Thank you, Mr. President. It's a great honour and privilege for us to be here representing not only the United States but men of peace of all nations, and with interest and a curiosity and a vision for the future. It's an honour for us to be able to participate here today.
04 14 18 12 PRESIDENT NIX0N	And thank you very much and I look forward - All of us look forward to seeing you on the Hornet on Thursday.
04 14 18 21 ALDRIN (EVA)	I look forward to that very much, sir.
04 14 18 31 CC	Columbia, Columbia, this is Houston. Over.
04 14 18 37 COLLINS (COLUMBIA)	Loud and clear, Houston.
04 18 18 31 CC	Roger, Tranquillity. We observed your equipment jettison on the TV, and the passive seismic experiment recorded shocks when each PLSS hit the surface. Over.
04 18 18 47 ARMSTRONG (TRANQ)	You can't get away with anything anymore, can you?
04 18 18 51 CC	No, indeed. By the way, we received a translation of the inscription, from the CIA, on the card-board sheet you saw at the campsite near the crater. By the look of it, the Soviets are attempting to throw us off track.
04 18 18 59 ARMSTRONG	Why? What does the translation say?
04 18 19 04 CC	Something quite incomprehensible at the moment. We'll be investigating that later.
04 18 19 09 ARMSTRONG	I copy. But what was the message in the translation?
04 18 19 18 CC	Hardly a message. Looks more like a menu of some kind. It reads..... it reads..... Sankaran's Military Hotel: Appam, Fish-curry, Kerala-Porota, Vegetable stew and Beef fry.

04 18 19 30 ARMSTRONG	What do the Soviets want us to believe? That they've been here before us? Jeez! Here goes another of their songs...
04 18 20 00 USS	Appozhum paranjille poranda porandannu, poranda porandannu........... Appozhum paranjille poranda porandannu, poranda porandannu..........

END OF TAPE

BACK TO SQUARE ONE

(A word from Sankaran)

Dear Reader,
      Every single one of us is immortal. I know, because I am one.

We are spiritual beings having a human experience. The stories narrated in this book are proof of mine. And we will come back again and again until we are able to grasp the enormity of our existence.

Be wary of the living not the dead. For it is the living who will put you through challenges and trials. The stories narrated in this book are proof of mine.

But while you are here, be happy and try climbing that coconut tree. Climb with a purpose. Go for the fruit. For that is the nature of our short visit to earth.

There is only one satisfactory direction - Up. A direction neither a compass or the latest Google map will be able to guide you by. They are still living in flat-earth mode.

And remember, like that coconut tree, we are remembered only by what we produce. This holds true for every single human being that has ever lived. Our identities are forged on the anvil of history only by our contribution and not by our mere existence. Nobody remembers a burp.

He succeeds who can see things from the top. So happy climbing and enjoy the fruits of your labour.

And if you have to again start from square one, remember, it's a great place to start afresh.

Sankaran

ABOUT THE AUTHOR

Born in Cannanore, Kerala, educated at St. Edmund's school and college, Shillong, Jo Nambiar was an athlete, an equestrian and also holds a Master's Degree in Kung Fu. In the 1980s as a Physical Educationist at the International Youth Centre, New Delhi, his students of unarmed combat included members of the Delhi Police, Indo-Tibetan Border Police, the Assam Rifles and the President's Body Guard. He worked as a Tea Planter with the Assam Company for over a decade. He has acted in Shakespearean as well as contemporary theatre. As a numismatist, Nambiar has one of the largest collections of ancient coins and rare currencies in the country which has global recognition. Nambiar has the distinction of being the Convener of the largest Children's Carnival in the world, the BALA MELA for underprivileged children every year at Bangalore. He is also a painter and a sculptor.

Printed in the United States
By Bookmasters